TO SAVE A VISCOUNT

JESSIE CLEVER

SOMEDAY LADY PUBLISHING, LLC.

For Lady Barks-a-lot and Captain Licky

CHAPTER 1

$\mathcal{L}$*ondon*
    August 1815

HE HAD GROWN SO accustomed to the sound of gunfire that he did not hear the shot that was meant to kill him.

This would have worried Richard Black, the Duke of Lofton, if he had had time to think on it. But as the situation inherently required immediate action, prolonged and abstract thinking on the subject was neither prudent nor wise. So he refrained. Instead, he wondered whom it was that smashed into him at incredible speed, sending him tumbling backwards off the walk along the Thames and into the bitter, black water below.

He had been meeting his contact there along the water at an unholy hour, and darkness had lain all about him. The exchange had gone as planned, and he now held the knowledge that he knew would prove key to his current assignment with the War Office. But as the inky water of the

Thames closed over his head, he wondered if he would ever get that information to the necessary people.

And then as the last of the light disappeared, he thought of Jane, his wife. His Jane. He did not think of her in specific instances or certain memories that lay in his mind. He thought of her in pieces. Her smell. Her laugh. The sound her hair made as she brushed it at night. The way she always laid her hand on top of his whenever they should find themselves sitting next to one another. Her amazing talents with chestnut roasters.

He would have laughed if such an action would not speed up the inevitable drowning that suddenly became all too real, flushing thoughts of Jane from his mind. His arms began to push against the water as his feet began to pulse, driving him toward the surface. Only he did not move. Whoever it was that had slammed into him still held him about the waist, dragging him deeper into the water. He began to struggle, the need for air and life and Jane surging through his veins in a way he had never felt before.

And then a hand brushed against his cheek, and slender fingers came to rest across his mouth. He wanted to open his eyes, but he knew it would do no good in the black water. But he let the feeling of his attacker's hand brush against his skin, the shape of it press into his face, the narrowness of limb and the delicate arch of bone.

It was a woman who held him beneath the water.

And he stopped struggling.

He hung suspended in the water of the Thames, the thoughts in his mind the only thing still carrying velocity.

What was happening? Who was this that held him so carefully beneath the surface?

And then he remembered, or perhaps recalled for the first time, the gunshot he had heard before suddenly catapulting into the river. She had saved his life, and she continued to save his life by holding him beneath the water and out of sight. He remained perfectly still, and eventually her hand drifted away and her arm left the circle of his waist. He felt the water pull about him, and then a tug at his shoulder.

She was going up.

His arms reacted before his brain could keep up, and he pushed, surging toward the surface above. He did not rocket through the water as he wanted, as his burning lungs pleaded. Such a motion would have attracted too much attention had his planned assassin still been in the vicinity. He surfaced quietly, his eyes springing open, sweeping the surface about him.

But all he saw were the algae-riddled planks of a wooden skiff.

And then someone grabbed the collar of his jacket and wrenched him from the water. He spilled into the boat, water sloshing along the floorboards with the rest of him. He didn't have time to sit up as a canvas tarp was thrown across his body. Once more plunged into darkness, he lay there, his other senses reaching out to replace his lack of sight. A small body came to rest against him under the canvas tarp, and he knew it was the woman from the river. Her frame was small and thin, and she smelled deplorable. But he was certain he did as well. People did not voluntarily bath in the Thames for numerous reasons, lack of perfume being just one.

And then that slender hand came to rest against his arm, not quite squeezing it but applying enough pressure that he stilled his breathing and willed his racing heart to calm.

His ears scanned the space around him, and they picked up the shuffled gait of the person who likely pulled him from the water. He heard raspy breathing, heavy puffing, and the sound of wood striking wood. The breathing he could understand would come from a man with a rather generous beard, but the sound of striking wood lay just beyond his grasp. He had heard the noise before, but it remained just unfamiliar enough to go without name.

The boat began to move beneath them, the conveyance jerking with the motions of oars cutting through water in great swallowing strides. The minutes passed, and a chill began to spread along his wet skin despite the relentless heat that had gripped London these last few days. But even before the chill could start his teeth chattering, the boat stopped, and the sound of wood striking wood resumed. And just as the canvas was pulled from before his face, and he could see the man who had yanked him from the river, the sound finally met its match in his mind.

And when his eyes adjusted to the darkness now before him, Richard whispered, "Reginald Davis."

"Oh, aye, your grace. Now get your pansy arse out of my boat," the man whispered back, his eyes glinting in what little moonlight reached the surface of the water from between the buildings rising up on both sides of the river. The man stepped back, his peg leg sounding against the boards of the vessel.

Richard sat up, realizing the woman beside him had already exited the boat. He blinked, pushed water from his eyes, and saw they had pulled up to a dock. The woman who had rescued him stood there, reaching down a hand to pull him from the conveyance.

His breath seized in his lungs as his eyes fixated on the woman, wreathed in moonlight and sopping wet. It had been more than twenty years, but he knew those freckles. He knew that set of impossibly straight white teeth.

"Lady Margaret Folton," he whispered again.

"Quite," she said. "Now if you don't mind, I'd like to finish saving your life."

CHAPTER 2

$\mathcal{T}$he knock came at exactly quarter past the hour, three days after someone tried to kill him.

He ran a finger along his collar, feeling the sweat pool and spill over onto his skin, his clothes so soaked, they would absorb nothing more.

"Who is it?" he said.

"The Duke of Wellington," came the feminine reply.

He moved closer to the door.

"Fine weather we're having, eh?" he said.

"Finer than the fields of Waterloo," came the reply.

Richard pushed the dresser away from the door of his safe room, undid the three bolts, and opened the latch to admit Lady Margaret Folton. He immediately shut the door and redid the bolts, shoving the dresser back into place in front of the door. He turned to find Lady Folton placing a bundle on the broken down writing desk in the corner of his small quarters. When she straightened, he caught sight of her face for the first time, the meager sunlight poking in from the shaded window throwing shadows over her features.

She looked exactly as she had over twenty years ago when

she had sat across from him at the War Office, explaining the intricate workings of a body-snatching ring. She had been only a child then, and he still could see that child inside of her, hiding behind a cold exterior she had erected after watching her parents be tortured and killed. Only now she was taller.

"It's rather hot, isn't it, my lady?" he said by way of greeting.

Lady Folton only smiled her straight white smile at him.

"I hadn't noticed," she said, and looking about her person, he saw neither a crumpled handkerchief nor sweated brow. It was as if the absurd heat wave gripping London had no effect on her.

Her hair was pulled tightly back in a plain chignon, fringe perfectly straight across her brow, a small cap perched on her head. Her gown was simple as well, falling straight to the floor in a cascade of muted tones, her gloved hands demurely clasped in front of her. Her only display of color was the spray of freckles across her nose. She was rather slight, almost what Richard would have called skinny and what Jane would surely have suggested needed a pie, but he thought that if Lady Folton held any loyalty to her character, she likely found no pleasure in food.

"We've informed your family of your death," she said, and he arrested his casual perusal of her person, his heart missing a beat in his chest.

So Jane thought him dead.

His fingers found the back of the only chair in the room, his hand sliding along its wooden and warped surface as his body sank into it, the energy releasing from his muscles at the thought of what Jane was feeling at that very moment. He looked back at Lady Folton, noting the crease that had appeared between her eyes, marring her otherwise unflustered exterior.

"It had to be done, your grace," Lady Folton said, and he nodded mechanically.

The sound of traffic came through the meager crack in the window he had been afforded. The sound of horses and carts felt oddly removed and somewhat out of place, although they shouldn't have. He pulled at his already sweat soaked collar, sucking air into his lungs that never seemed to be adequate.

"We have another problem to discuss, your grace. That is why I'm here."

Richard had never moved his eyes from the woman, but he noticed he had to blink several times until she came into focus.

"What is it?"

"It's about the person who tried to kill you."

Richard sat up straighter, pushing away thoughts of Jane. He had to remain objective. They were all in danger as agents for the War Office, and only he knew of it. He couldn't fail her. He couldn't fail Jane.

"What about him?"

Lady Folton folded her hands in front of her. "The intelligence we have gathered so far suggests that it is in fact someone working from inside the War Office. The assassin has intimate knowledge of the movements of our agents. He is two steps ahead of us wherever we may go."

"Who has access to such privileged information?"

Lady Folton frowned. "That is what I'm here to ask you, your grace. Is there anyone who would have such knowledge of your whereabouts?"

His mind flashed to his family, to Jane, and that night he had left to meet his contact. And just as the thought flashed in his mind, he blinked it away, shaking his head.

"Not that I am aware of," Richard said, "Surely, we don't keep a complete list somewhere of agent assignments."

If it had been anyone else, Richard would not have noticed the change that overcame Lady Folton at his words, but as she was so precise in not displaying emotion, he noticed right away.

"We do?" he asked, his voice softer than he had meant it, the incredulity of such a fact pressing down on him.

Lady Folton did not respond.

"Why on Earth would we keep such a list?"

"It's not really a list," Lady Folton finally said.

Richard stood, the need to pace pushing his legs under him and propelling him to the single boarded up window with the small crack at its base.

"Then what is it?"

He stopped at the window, bending his head to see through a slit in the boards.

"It's a book."

Richard spun around. "Oh good, a book. I hope the assassin had a happy read."

"It's written in code."

Richard raised an eyebrow. "Code?"

"Yes," Lady Folton said, turning her body to face him without swishing a single petticoat. "No single agent at the War Office, no matter his rank, is privileged to know what assignment each agent is on. Such an arrangement prevents anyone from acquiring too much knowledge of the mechanics of England's spy network."

"Yes, I know that," Richard said.

"However, should anything catastrophic happen, it also means there is some knowledge that may be lost if certain agents are lost."

"So we wrote a book about it," Richard murmured, the enormity of the situation setting in. "And we believe the assassin has somehow acquired this book?"

Lady Folton nodded. "That is the current assumption. But

it's a bit more complex than that."

"How is that?"

"The book is written in code. Four codes actually."

Richard frowned. "Four codes?"

Lady Folton nodded again. "There are four series of agents in the War Office reporting to four senior agents."

Richard stepped away from the window, feeling the momentum of the story picking him up.

"Each series has its own code," he said it as a statement and not a question, but Lady Folton responded as if it were a question.

"Indeed. Each senior agent is instructed in a certain code to document the assignments of their agents. The documentation is then passed to a single agent that keeps the book. The original documentation is destroyed."

Richard shook his head. "The four senior agents each document their agents' assignments in a code. The parchment on which they document this is then passed to another agent. This agent copies the code into the book. Our assassin must be this central agent. He's the only one with access to the book with all four senior agents' notes."

Lady Folton was already shaking her head before he finished. "The central agent, who happens to be a woman," she said this last bit with a slight more tartness. "Doesn't know the codes. She only copies what's written on the parchment given to her."

Richard's shoulders slumped. "So she's not the assassin because she doesn't know what the book actually says."

Lady Folton shook her head.

"Perhaps she's been threatened or questioned or something," Richard realized he was beginning to rattle and stopped himself, drawing a deep breath of humid, putrid air.

"She's already been questioned. As well as any of the staff in her location."

"Location?"

"The book is not housed at the War Office."

"Where is it housed then?" Richard asked.

"The location is privileged."

Richard scratched at the stubble that was forming along his chin after three days of festering in his hiding hole.

"So what do we do now?"

"That's why I'm here. We have a problem with the action plan we put into place to ferret out the assassin."

Richard exhaled, the air stinging as it left his lungs. He shuffled back to the warped wooden chair and sat.

"Proceed," he said, crossing one leg onto the opposite knee.

"In an effort to ferret out the assassin we created a fake agent."

Richard raised both eyebrows. "A fake agent?"

"Yes, an entirely false identity and planted his fake assignments in the book."

"And?"

"We gave this fake agent a title, so the assassin would think he was operating on more sensitive information."

"Brilliant. But where's the problem?"

"The Prince Regent just awarded our fake title to a returned decorated officer."

Richard barked out a laugh before he could stop himself. "Terribly sorry, but that was not what I was expecting you to say was the problem."

"Indeed," Lady Folton said, and Richard suspected he almost saw a hint of a smile on her face.

"Any idea how this happened?"

Lady Folton shrugged. "Somehow our request to file the title was mistaken for the title they planned to award this military officer."

"And now the poor bloke has a target on his back." Richard rubbed his hands on his thighs.

"Yes, and the title now fits too nicely with the background we gave our fake agent."

"How's that?"

"The decorated officer was titled for his work in the Mediterranean. He commanded the fleet there around Italy, reinforcing Austria and keeping Murat at bay."

"Sounds like a perfect cover for some espionage."

"Precisely," Lady Folton said, pursing her lips. "And we must now devise a way to keep him from getting killed."

Richard looked up at her. "What plan might that be?"

Lady Folton adjusted her gloves as if preparing to take her leave. "I must get close to him, gain his confidence. We're not certain if the assassin has even seen the pages we added to the book regarding this fake agent, and we cannot be sure how he will react. But the bait has been planted, and we must protect our unknowing target."

"Who will be doing the protecting?" Richard asked.

"I'm afraid it is to be me," Lady Folton said, finishing with her gloves. "We've moved most of our titled agents back. They seem to be the ones the assassin is targeting. There is only a skeleton crew left in town."

Richard shook his head dismally. "What a terrible fate. You serve your country, and they make you a mark. God save the king," Richard murmured, dropping his head to his chest, but he picked it up again in only a moment. "What is your infiltration plan? How will you get close enough to him for protection's sake?"

Lady Folton smiled her eerily unfeeling smile. "There seems to have been an issue with his writ of summons granting him the title. He was expected to receive a parcel of land, but as the titles were mixed up, the one the War Office created obviously had no land attached to it."

"So you will be assisting him to straighten out this matter?"

She cocked her head, a gleeful glint coming to her eye. "I make a rather convincing government clerk, do I not? I will surely be able to clear things up about this mishap."

Richard shook his head. "Agents of the War Office being reduced to government clerks. What's next?"

He had expected Lady Folton to laugh, but then he remembered to whom he was speaking, so he just let his gaze drift out the window.

"Is there anything you need, your grace?" Lady Folton asked some moments later.

Richard looked over at her words, the thought of Jane pressing once more on him. He turned, angling himself over the bureau shoved against the door. Ripping a scrap of paper from the copy of the Bible some former tenant had left there, Richard used a stubby pencil he had found in one of the bureau's drawers to scratch a note.

"Could I ask you to have something delivered for me?"

He handed the note to Lady Folton. If his note was perplexing, she made no outward sign of it.

"Of course, your grace."

She tucked the note into her reticule and turned toward the door. "Agent Crawley will be along tonight with more refreshments for you."

"Crawley? Isn't he dead by now?"

Lady Folton finally smiled that severe straight smile. "It's his son," she said.

"Ah, indeed," Richard nodded, bending to move the bureau from the door so Lady Folton could exit.

He paused with his hands on the wood.

Turning back to her, he said, "Just out of curiosity, what is this poor chap's name that inherited a quite volatile title?"

"Commodore John Lynwood," Lady Folton said.

CHAPTER 3

"*H*ow do you find the situation, Captain?" Commodore John Lynwood asked his first mate.

He had to look down a good five feet to see his first mate where he had taken up residence in an old flower pot, curled about himself with his head hanging over the side, his long ears flopping over his face. The captain didn't look at all comfortable, but the dog had not moved in some time, so he supposed he enjoyed his current position.

"I will translate that to mean you find the situation admirable," Jack concluded and clipped the last of the roses to fill the basket at his side.

He paused in his scan of the garden about him, stopping when his eyes fell on the newly finished bed still dark with overturned soil. He had pulled up the previous owner's attempts at a tropical garden complete with a palm tree that had been there. What on Earth the gentleman owner in question thought would happen to a palm tree in the terribly unwelcoming climate of London, he did not know nor wanted to understand.

Pulling the dead tree from the ground had been more work than he had cared for. But the exertion was a welcomed respite from the thoughts in his head that ran in a loop one after the other. A viscount. Viscount Pemberly. What in God's name had he done to deserve it?

But that was the point, wasn't it?

Nothing.

He hadn't done anything to deserve it.

He was a third son. Choices were limited, and he had selected the military. It wasn't as if he had had much say in the matter. It was just what was done. He had watched countless men die in battle, but by some twist of fate, here he was in Mayfair pulling up the roots of a dead palm tree. What made him so bloody lucky?

He looked at the captain, but the dog continued his uncomfortable looking nap.

Bloody Viscount Pemberly.

"Perhaps I should have gone with an assortment of cone flowers," he said then, his tone casual and flat as was usual in his conversations with the captain.

Captain gave no sign that he'd heard him. Captain gave no sign that he was alive really.

Jack looked over at the new bed once more, perusing the assortment of salvia and peonies that clashed in vibrant colors and textures. It would do for now. Perhaps later he would try the coneflowers.

He placed his pruning shears inside the basket with the blooms he had selected that morning, carefully tucking them under the stems of the flowers that nestled inside. He set the basket down at his feet as he sat on one of the crumbling benches in the garden. He would have to get around to fixing that as well someday, but dead palm trees took priority. He looked at the garden about him, assessing the progress he'd made since his return from the front mere weeks before. It wasn't bad, but it wasn't terrific. He was a military officer. He should have the entire thing finished by now.

But for whatever reason the drive wasn't in him.

Bloody viscount.

He was the third son. By all accounts of probability, he should not have a title at all. And now he was the bloody Viscount Pemberly.

"I'll trade you your flower pot for a bag full of luck," he said to the captain.

Captain did not reply.

And not for the first time, Jack sat in silence and wondered how it was that luck had become so firmly affixed to his backside and refused to budge no matter how hard he tried to leave it off.

"Bloody viscount."

He hadn't realized he had spoken aloud until his newly acquired butler cleared his throat nervously behind him. Jack turned his head in the direction of the doors that led back into the house. Reynolds was a small man, and Jack had rather liked how precisely he did up his waistcoat to match the line of his cravat. After so many years in the navy, Jack liked a man of precision.

"What is it, Reynolds?" Jack finally asked after the small man hesitated for too long on the threshold.

"You have a caller, my lord," Reynolds said, and Jack automatically opened his mouth to correct him as he had done so often in recent days.

But then Jack realized he should be addressed as my lord.

Bloody viscount.

"A caller?" Jack asked.

He was tired of all of the callers. He was tired of the cards, of the invitations, of the inexplicable number of bouquets. First, it disturbed him that so many matrons would send him bouquets in the first order, and why on Earth they should do that. Secondly, they were all terribly ugly. He could arrange a far more exquisite ensemble with just what he had here in this half makeover atrocity of his newly acquired townhouse garden. Were these society matrons really trying to welcome him to their brethren with terrible bouquets? What an outrageously stupid idea. If this is what it meant to be a viscount, he was happy to go back to being just a commodore.

"Yes, sir, a lady caller."

Jack wanted to roll his eyes. There had been a number of lady callers in the past few weeks that he had been in town, and he had been conveniently unavailable at each of their unexpected visits. Why Reynolds would think his status would be any different for this one, he could not say.

"You must make my excuses, Reynolds. I am unavailable," he said and returned his gaze to his garden in progress.

"But, my lord--" Reynolds started to say when the captain suddenly sat up from his napping spot in the flowerpot.

The entire set up of dog plus crockery tipped over, sending the hound flying in a mass of moving fur, over-large feet, and dangling ears in the direction of the bricked path that led to the house. The crockery rolled harmlessly on its side as the dog took off in the direction of the door Reynolds had left open behind him.

The dog had not let out a sound, choosing instead to let his nose communicate for him.

The captain smelled something, and the chase was on.

Jack found it unusual that Captain should catch a scent from the air, as it was usually the ground that carried the tracks his intricately calibrated nose sought. But perhaps whatever it was, was intriguing enough to have the sleeping hound off his perch and into tracking mode.

And then Jack remembered his caller.

His lady caller.

"Captain!" Jack called, surging to his feet.

He nearly toppled little Reynolds as he ran past the man and into the darkness of the house beyond. The temperature plummeted as he wove his way through the maze of furniture that had come with the house, all carefully shrouded in dust cloths he had not bothered to remove. Although he was out of the sun, he could still feel the heat of the unusually warm weather press in on him even as he moved deeper into the house.

He followed the sound of the captain's paws on the floorboards, the nails striking like staccato at a pianoforte. Captain let out not a single bay, muted or otherwise, to let him know where it was that Reynolds had left their guest waiting, but at least the sounds of stampeding hound feet gave him some indication. He rounded the bend into the corridor that led into the front of the house, the sound of the captain's footfalls seeming closer.

He had almost made it to the front drawing room when the crash reverberated through the corridor.

* * *

MARGARET HELD her breath and squeezed her eyes shut, praying to a god she had long forgotten that the assault would be over in due haste.

She had heard the oddest sound right before the attack, but she had not expected such a noise to be coming from a dog. Let alone such a strange looking one. He was squat, longer than he was tall, and his ears sailed out behind him like beacon flags. She had had only a moment to glimpse him before his front paws came up and connected with her hip, sending her backwards into one of the dust cloth-shrouded mounds of furniture that littered the room where she had been told to wait for Viscount Pemberly.

She wasn't certain what was under the unidentifiable

mound, but whatever it was, it was breakable as evidenced by the resounding splintering of glass when her body connected with it and thus it with the floor. And then the dog was on her, and she had seen nothing else. Nothing, of course, except for the snatches she glimpsed of his long, granular tongue swiping at her face as he licked his way back and forth from one cheek to the other as if trying to clean her face from her morning meal. She was quite certain she had left nothing behind, but the dog must have thought otherwise if his perseverance was anything to go by.

"Captain!" she heard a man yell, and then blessedly, the dog disappeared from her lap, and air rushed into her lungs as she opened her mouth.

She blinked, taking in her surroundings as she came to the realization that she was covered in what must have been the dog's drool. She could feel it as the air moved across her face, and for the first time in days, she felt a bit cooler. Which she found revolting when she realized it was because the drool was drying on her face. It took her a few moments more to realize she held her hands in front of her as if the dog would attack her again, her fingers splayed wide at absolutely nothing. She snapped her hands to her lap, hoping no one had seen her ridiculous gesture.

Somewhere behind her she heard shuffling, and a man muttering something about manners before a door shut with a click. She looked about her just as said man knelt in front of her.

And then she forgot everything entirely.

Including, most likely, her name.

It was Margaret something, wasn't it?

He was gorgeous.

And he was unclothed.

The air she had so recently coveted rushed from her lungs, leaving them burning once more as she stared at the man in front of her. No one had informed her that Viscount Pemberly was...

She wasn't even sure what the word was for it, having never felt the like of it before. Having felt nothing at all before. Not since then. Not since her parents had died.

She swallowed and blinked at the same time, hoping the movement would somehow restore her senses to their usual, objective self. But instead, it only brought his hands to her shoulders, obviously in a moment of concern for her person, which did, in fact, do nothing for her sudden lack of calm.

So she did what she had so often done in the years since her parents' death. She turned it all off. With the mental flick of her mind, she tuned out the world about her and focused on her breathing. This did nothing to assuage the obvious guilt of the man kneeling in front of her, shaking her shoulders as he tried to find out if she were all right. But in that moment, she just needed to breathe. So she did.

And then she said, "You're naked."

The man stopped asking after her welfare and simply stared at her, which was fine as she could only stare back at him in that moment.

"I beg your pardon?" he finally said and then looked down at his person as if to determine the validity of her statement.

She followed his gaze, taking in the lack of collar, his opened shirt, and the sleeves rolled to his elbows. She had never seen the forearms of a man, and his held her fascination longer than she thought possible. The muscles were clearly defined and covered with a sheen of light colored hair, a contrast to the thick mane of straight, nearly black hair that fell at an angle across his brow. Perhaps the sun did that to the hair on his forearms, made just the touch lighter. She wanted to reach out her fingers and feel it, which scared her. She had never had such an attraction to a man, and most certainly, not to a specific part of his body.

"I've never seen a man in such a state of undress," she finally said, and he looked up at her.

For the first time, she was able to take in the soft color of his eyes, a rich brown that reminded her of puppies and hot chocolate by a warm fire. Such an association was absurd by any standards, and from her, it was downright ludicrous. Perhaps she had hit her head in the fall.

Which reminded her-- "I may have broken something of yours, and I do apologize most sincerely. Of course, I shall pay for the item in question," she said, realizing she had just stated two completely different things in a breath so short he had not had a chance to answer the first statement. If a statement truly required answering, although by definition a statement did not require such a thing but--

The fall had definitely rattled her brains. She had to stand up and get away from this man with his hairy forearms. She pushed against the floor and started to rise, but at the same moment, he reached forward to take her arms as if to haul her up. The movement brought his face perilously close to hers, and for a moment, she wanted to kiss him.

She froze.

Every particle in her body coming to a full stop, all motion ceasing from the air in her lungs to the blood running through her veins to the moisture covering her eyes. Everything ceased except for this man who, until a moment ago, had not even existed in her life, but who for some unknown reason had created in her something she had never thought to ever experience again.

Something she had once called desire.

SHE WANTED TO KISS HIM, this mysterious lady caller who had

stood so innocently in his drawing room not expecting to be pummeled at any moment by a long-eared hound dog.

She was overly thin for his taste, her eyes wide, her chin coming to a point, and had the most incredible set of straight white teeth. But the part that captivated him was the fringe that hung in a curtain across her forehead. There was something about it that made him want to push it off her face or, at the very least, mess it up to see what she would do about it. He wondered if she would get upset. She had said he was naked, when in fact he was just rather unkempt, and something about her statement goaded him into wanting to see what other kind of reaction he could get out of her.

But when he went to help her up and his face came close to hers, he knew that she wanted to kiss him. And that she didn't like that feeling. So for just a moment, he tilted his head closer, bringing his lips almost to hers. And when he was that close, he saw with great detail the splash of faded freckles across her nose and the unusual pale blue hue of her eyes.

And then he wanted to kiss her.

So he drew away, helping her to gain her feet.

"I apologize for Captain Edwards' behavior. We're still working on the niceties of things," he said. "And so I cannot accept any recompense for anything that may have been broken."

He surveyed the room, largely shrouded in dust cloths like all the other rooms in the house and simply shrugged.

"And I couldn't tell you what it is that you may have broken as I've only just purchased this house."

She looked at him, her head moving to the side in a question. "You've purchased this house?" she asked.

He nodded. "Yes, you see, I've newly acquired a title that I don't rightly deserve, and I was told a house in town was appropriate as my duties at the House of Lords will demand such a necessity. I didn't have a house in town, so I purchased this one. What do you think of it?"

She looked about them much as he had done just moments before, but he couldn't tell what she was thinking. Her expressions were rather plain, and if he had not felt to his very bones that she had in fact wanted to kiss him only moments before, he would be tempted to say that she lacked feeling entirely.

He stepped back for a moment, noticing for once her plain gown and equally plain small hat and quiet features. Overall, she was rather a lot of nothing dressed up for a call on a person she'd never met. Which should have seemed odd.

"I beg your pardon, but I never received your name," he said.

Suddenly he felt a measure of unease, and he chided himself for not realizing that she was an unchaperoned young woman in the home of a bachelor.

"I'm Lady Margaret Folton," she said and extended a hand to him when he had expected her to curtsy. "I'm from the government actually. I was sent to sort out a certain misallocation of land. Are you aware of the land grant that comes with this title?"

His mind flashed for a moment to Reynolds standing hesitantly in the threshold whilst trying to tell him something about their caller when the captain had unexpectedly awoken. It was likely Reynolds was trying to say that this was not a social call.

"Indeed," he said, and gently squeezed her hand, only to find her handshake surprisingly firm. "I believe something was mentioned about land. I've never been a bl--" he cut himself off before using his favorite adjective for his new title. "Uh, a viscount before, so I'm not sure what must be done in that situation."

He pushed at the hair that fell across his brow, scratching

his forehead as he looked about the room. And that was when he smelled it.

He had turned just enough that the air in the room shifted, bringing her scent to him.

"Lilacs," he said, before he knew he was going to say anything.

She looked at him, startled. "Yes, lilacs," she said, but her voice did not match the firmness of her handshake.

It had gone soft like the petals of a budding tulip.

"An unusual scent for a woman, is it not?" he asked, not sure why the question seemed pertinent.

She shrugged and hesitated. She wanted to say something, but she held it back, and he wondered briefly if Lady Folton was telling him the truth about being from the government. As a commodore in the navy, he felt that he should likely know just about every chap in the place, but he had never met Lady Folton before. Of that he was certain.

"Your fragrance must have been what alerted the dog. Although, how he smelled it from out in the garden, I cannot be sure. We've only been acquainted these last few weeks since my return, and we're still getting to know each other."

Her forehead had folded into a look of confusion, and it was his turn to tilt his head in question.

"The dog," he clarified as if that were the point of confusion. "I've only had the dog for the last few weeks. He lived with my uncle before that, and my brother before that. He's a bit confused about...well, everything."

She still watched him with that wrinkled look about her face.

"You see, dogs like routine, and poor Captain Edwards keeps shifting homes, so he's not sure about a routine for anything. He's just happy when there's a bowl of food for him now and then. My uncle said my brother was training him with his pack, but the captain could never quite keep up. I'm not sure exactly what all the dog was taught, and now that Roger is gone, I can't ask him. The dog's largely all I have left of my family. Well, besides Uncle Willy, but I don't think he really counts. He's too often in his cups for counting anything."

Her look had not changed.

"You've never had a dog, have you?" he finally settled on.

Her face immediately relaxed. "No, I'm afraid I never did. I don't really understand the creatures."

He wouldn't have said that her face relaxed into a smile, but it was a good deal more jovial than it had been moments before, either when she wanted to kiss him or when he was spouting nonsense about his drunken Uncle Willy or his dead brother. So he counted that as improvement.

He motioned with his hand to her cheek.

"The captain left a bit of a present on your face. Likely something he picked up in his drool and kept on his jowls to share with someone special later."

He made an aborted motion again with his hand when she didn't move to wipe it from her cheek. When she still didn't make a motion to wipe it away, he finally reached for his own shirt. Filthy as it was, he didn't carry a handkerchief when he was in the garden, and it was his dog that had left the smudge on this poor woman's face.

"Here," he said and pulled his shirt loose from his pants.

He took a piece in his hand and stepped forward, gently wiping the dirt from her cheek with the linen. He backed away to admire his work when he noticed she had gone completely devoid of color.

"I'm sorry," he said immediately, making a half attempt to tuck his shirt back in. "I think I've made you uncomfortable."

She opened her mouth, but no sound came forth. He took a concerned step forward.

"Lady Folton?" he said. "Do you need a glass of water or something?"

But instead of answering his question, she said, "I will be in touch when we've learned something about your land situation, my lord. Good day, Lord Pemberly," turned about, and left.

When he heard the sound of the front door closing, he heard a responding whine from the closed door to the adjoining sitting room where he had momentarily imprisoned the hound. He walked to it and opened it, finding Captain Edwards sitting majestically behind it, the girth of his strong neck on full display, tail thumping dust clouds from the carpet.

Jack looked at the dog and said, "You're not going to believe what just happened."

CHAPTER 4

*J*ane sat in the chair before the dormant fireplace of the drawing room wondering when it last was that she had changed the draperies in that room. She looked at the careful cascade of the shimmering pale blue fabric as it pooled precisely to the floor, perfectly framing the smoldering scene of London beyond the window. The pale blue carefully complimented the mint green walls of the library, creating a space that was fresh and inviting, bright and yet subdued in its tranquility.

Sod it all to hell, Jane thought.

It was half past ten o'clock in the morning, and she reached for the nearly empty snifter of brandy at her elbow. It was the third glass of the stuff she had drunk that morning. The children had not said anything when she had started in with the drink exactly thirty four seconds after she had been told the news of her husband's death. And now, three days later, they still said nothing. Although she knew bloody well what they were doing. They were taking shifts watching her. They didn't say it, but she knew it nonetheless. She wasn't sure what they expected her to do. Her husband was dead.

Was she going to spontaneously run off to the continent and become a gypsy? Bloody unlikely. And it wasn't as if she couldn't hold herself in strict decorum around the servants. It was only brandy for God's sake.

She looked over at the current selection of child guard. It was her newest daughter-in-law, fat with child, sitting quietly in the chair opposite, needlepoint in hand, the perfect image of domesticity except for the fact that she glistened as much as Jane could feel herself glistening. Bloody heat.

"Have you eaten?" Jane suddenly asked, watching Nora finish the row of stitches she worked into the fabric of her needlepoint.

Nora looked up, her wide brown eyes landing delicately on her, so unassuming in their gaze, so unlike the gazes of her husband and his brother.

"Have you?" she said, and Jane wanted to smile at her boldness.

No one had questioned the Duchess of Lofton like that in a very long time.

Jane swallowed. She was no longer the Duchess of Lofton. It was hard for her to remember that. The title had moved on already to Richard's son and heir and his wife, Alec and Sarah Black. Sarah was now the Duchess of Lofton. Jane did smile then. Sarah would make a wonderful duchess. She had been worried at first, as any mother would, when the War Office had made those two wed in order to better serve crown and country, but it had worked out in the end. Jane needn't worry any longer.

Jane needn't worry any longer about many things. Like if Richard had enough collars for the coming week's social obligations, whether she had planned for several of Richard's favorite meals throughout the week, or whether he had cleaned the pistol he usually hid in his boot recently. None of those things really mattered anymore, did they?

"Jane?"

Jane started, realizing she had not responded to Nora's question.

"I have eaten, my dear," she finally said and watched Nora's face relax almost imperceptibly. "I just can't remember which day it was when I did so."

Nora frowned, her face becoming pinched once more. Jane waved a careless hand at her.

"Do not fret. I am in no danger of wasting away," she said and returned her gaze to the empty grate in front of her.

"It is not a fear that you should waste away that has me worried. It is the effect of the spirits you are consuming on an empty stomach."

Jane looked briefly at the now empty glass of brandy at her elbow and frowned. "What does the contents of my stomach have to do with anything?"

Nora did not answer but instead set her needlepoint aside, pushing herself from the chair with great awkwardness. Jane reached out her hands as if to help the poor girl, but it wasn't as if Jane was going to be terribly useful if Nora suddenly tipped forward under the weight of the babe growing in her belly. When Nora gained her feet, steadying the girth of her belly between her two hands, Jane frowned at the tableau the other woman struck.

"Aren't you rather large for being in your fifth month?" Jane asked.

There was one thing about the former Miss Eleanora Quinton that Jane had always admired, and it was her ability to never react to anything any member of the ton could throw at her. But now, if Jane had not been family, she was certain Nora would have killed her.

"Haven't you had too much to drink today?" Nora responded, and Jane sat back in her chair, silent as the room about them.

"Well played," she finally murmured.

Nora said nothing more but shuffled her way over to the bell pull in the corner. When the footman appeared, Jane heard her order a teacart with only toast and a pot of mild tea. Jane couldn't hear what kind, but if Nora expected her to drink the stuff, it must be laced with brandy first.

Nora resumed her seat across from Jane and picked up the needlepoint as if the exchange between them had never occurred. Jane looked at the woman once more and noted the soft wrinkles at the corners of her eyes, and the slight strain at her brow. She must be so tired. Jane felt an old twinge resound in her chest, but it was dull now and without power. Jane had long ago laid her sadness to rest in that area. She had never had children borne of her own flesh and blood, but she had two very healthy young men she had the honor to call her sons. And that was enough. But right then, her concern for Nora was greater than any old concern she may have once carried.

"Are you feeling all right?" Jane asked.

Nora did not look up when she answered, "Quite all right, thank you. It's just so hot. I haven't slept much lately."

Jane nodded, only able to imagine what it must be like trying to sleep in this heat in Nora's condition.

"Have you heard from Samuel recently?" Jane asked, referring to Nora's son.

Nora nodded, rethreading the needle in her hand with a brilliant teal thread.

"He is quite thoroughly enamored of a dog on Aunt Lydia's estate. He's asked Nathan if he can bring him home when he returns next month."

Jane raised her eyebrows.

"I think that's a marvelous idea," she said as Nora looked up, her brow furrowed in concern.

"Marvelous idea?" she asked.

Jane nodded. "When I wed Richard, the boys asked for a goat, so a dog is a marvelous idea in my opinion."

Nora set the needlepoint in her lap. "A goat?"

Jane nodded. "They named him Biscuit. He ate everything, including one of Richard's cravats. How he got the cravat, neither of the boys would admit."

Nora laughed, the sound soft and unusual in a room that had only been filled with the silence of grief for so many days. Jane liked the sound of it.

When the door to the library opened moments later, Jane didn't bother to see who it was. She was certain it was one of the maids bringing the tea tray. But when the butler, Fitzwilliam, arrived at her elbow, Jane jumped, startled.

"My lady, I beg your pardon," Fitzwilliam said.

Fitzwilliam had been a butler at Lofton House for a mere five years, ever since Richard had given Hathaway, his trusted and loyal butler of thirty years, an early retirement in honor of the man's steadfast service. It was rather an unusual post being butler to a house full of spies, and Richard had recognized Hathaway's resilience. Jane wondered for a moment where Hathaway was then. She hoped he was enjoying himself wherever he was. A brief moment in time sprang up in her mind, and like so many thoughts of the past few days, she squashed it away, the pain too great to recall any more.

"My lady," Fitzwilliam said, and Jane realized he still stood beside her chair.

Now her mind focused on Fitzwilliam, and the man's youth blared at her like it had never done before. He was rather young for a butler, but other than his age, there was nothing about him upon which to remark. His manners were refined, and his service with the staff was adequate. But the only thing he shared with Lofton House's former butler was his decidedly sparse head of hair. Jane frowned, wondering once more where Hathaway was.

And then she realized Fitzwilliam was holding a rather large parcel.

"What on earth is that?" Jane said, coming to her feet.

Fitzwilliam backed up a step to let her stand, but he held the large parcel fast to his chest.

"It was delivered just this morning, my lady. Shall I open it for you?"

Jane shook her head and pointed at the rosewood desk in the corner of the room. "Put it on my desk. I'll open it."

She saw the slight hesitation as if Fitzwilliam would deny her request, but he did as she asked and quietly left the room. Jane watched the door as the man closed it behind him, her thoughts scattered until she returned her gaze to the parcel.

"What do you think it is?" Nora asked, and Jane realized the woman now stood beside her.

How was it that people so easily snuck up on her these days?

"How should I know?" Jane said, shrugging.

She made her way over to the desk and peered at the parcel. Who would be sending her a package on a day like this? Parcels were not her first priority.

"Would you like me to open it?" Nora asked, but Jane shooed her away with her hands.

"I'll do it, dear," Jane said and bent to retrieve a sharp letter opener from the desk.

With one strike, she split the string holding the wrapped parcel, and the brown paper fell away. Jane stood very still, looking at the object nestled in the folds of paper.

"Is that a chestnut roaster?" Nora asked, her voice riddled with confusion.

"Oh my God," Jane whispered, a hand going to her month.

She stared at the roaster, her mind shuttering from

complete emptiness to a chaotic whirlwind of too many thoughts, finding little or no space within her conscious to form a single coherent idea.

"Jane?" Nora asked. "Are you all right?"

No, she was not bloody all right. Nothing was bloody all right. It was damn well perfect is what it was. And instead of answering Nora, she seized the chestnut roaster and ran from the room.

* * *

"You sit in it."

Nathan raised a single eyebrow in his little brother's direction.

"You sit in it. You're the duke," he returned.

Alec raised his own eyebrow in defense. "But you were born first," Alec said.

Nathan raised his other eyebrow. "That is as irrelevant as it always has been," he replied.

"And perhaps later, we can go to the park to see which man can skip stones the farthest in the Serpentine."

They both turned to look at Sarah, Alec's wife, and now the Duchess of Lofton, standing with her hands on her hips in the middle of their father's library.

Or maybe it was Alec's study now.

The events of the past few days were jumbling together in his head, and all he wanted to do was lie down, close his eyes, and rest his head in Nora's lap. But instead he stood in his father's study, fighting with his brother over a chair that neither of them had believed one day would belong to someone other than their father.

"I don't see how that's relevant," Alec said, and Nathan watched Sarah roll her eyes. But her fisted hands relaxed, slipping from her hips, and Nathan knew that Sarah understood.

The past few days had been even more confusing for his little brother, Nathan was sure. He hadn't planned on becoming the duke this early in life if ever, if Nathan knew anything of it. He watched the man his brother had become and noted the dark circles casting shadows beneath his otherwise brilliant green eyes. And not for the first time, he worried how he would take care of them all now.

Alec might have been the duke, but he was right when he said Nathan was first born. Nathan was first in all ways that mattered to his family. It was only society that neglected to notice.

And it was this that kept Nathan up at night, lying restless beside his wife, watching the way the sheet rose and fell taut against her expanding stomach. He had a wife, a son, and a baby about to enter the world, and his father was gone.

Nathan had been counting on him to take care of everyone else while Nathan took care of his young family. But his father was gone. He swallowed and looked back at Sarah.

"Are we certain the solicitor said Father's journals were in here?"

Sarah nodded, the loosened tendrils of blonde hair framed her face in a gentle sway.

"Livingston said Richard always kept meticulous notes of everything in his desk drawers. I would assume he meant this desk," Sarah said but still took a moment to look about the room as if there may be another location for Richard's journals.

"I hate farming," Alec said suddenly, and Nathan looked at him sharply. "How many tenant farmers does the Duke of Lofton have?" Alec continued.

"It depends on which estate you are questioning," Sarah answered.

Nathan swiveled his gaze back to her and felt not unlike a dog being teased with a bone by an errant child.

"There's more than one estate?" Alec asked.

Sarah nodded. "Of course, there is."

"How do you know all of this?"

Sarah frowned, the lines around the overbite of her upper lip attaining greater definition as she did so.

"I asked Jane," she said. "I knew I would be the duchess one day whether or not I wanted it, and I wanted to be prepared."

It was exactly like Sarah to research all means of preparation for any endeavor she undertook, and somehow, knowing that Sarah had asked Jane about being the Duchess of Lofton, made him feel somewhat more settled for the first time in days. If the rest of them hadn't been prepared, at least Sarah was.

"I still don't want to sit in that chair," Alec said.

Nathan heard Sarah sigh as he bent to open one of the desk drawers, only to find it locked. He heard rustling and assumed Sarah had moved closer to Alec as soothing noises started coming from the area over his head. He ignored it and tried another drawer, only to find that one locked as well. Perhaps his father had left a key somewhere hidden underneath the desk, so he bent farther under the mammoth wooden piece to prod the darkness in the corners beneath its top. And that was why he walloped his head on the underside of his father's desk when someone came bursting through the study doors.

"Get away from that desk!"

Nathan hit his head a second time at the shouted words but managed to straighten in time to see Jane fly through the abandoned library doors, a glaring, metal object held triumphantly in her left hand. Nathan frowned, but not at the explosive intrusion or his throbbing head. He frowned at his very pregnant wife wobbling in behind Jane, clearly out of breath and struggling to keep pace. He went to her immediately, side stepping Jane and her triton of glory to find a seat for his wife.

"What on Earth is that?" Alec asked from the opposite end of the room.

Nathan stood beside his wife as she struggled to catch her breath from the seat he had found her on the nearest sofa.

"It's proof!" Jane cried, but Alec only frowned harder.

And Sarah said, "It looks like a chestnut roaster from here."

Nathan's head stopped throbbing, and his mind stopped racing with concern for his wife. His heart slowed to a placid trot, and his muscles uncoiled for the first time in days.

"Holy God, he's alive," he whispered.

"What?" Nora asked, looking up at him in confusion.

Only then did he realize he had spoken aloud, and Alec responded from across the room.

"Baby Jesus, he's alive."

"Yes!" Jane cried, her hand shaking with the chestnut roaster rattling in the air. "And I will forgive you the blaspheme, but yes, he's alive and trying to tell us something!"

"Who's alive?" Sarah asked.

"Richard's alive," Nora whispered the response, and Nathan looked to her now, watching her eyes as they traveled across Jane's elated face. "He's alive, and somehow this chestnut roaster is his way of telling you without putting you in danger."

Nora's natural intuitiveness never failed to amaze him. Her instincts had only sharpened since she had become pregnant with his child, and he wondered if somehow the babe were feeding her telepathic signals.

"With a chestnut roaster?"

This was from Sarah who stood patiently by a now pale Alec.

"That story was true?" Alec said, but his voice barely made it above a whisper.

Jane brought her arm down with a snap, her tone changing from one of triumph to accusation. "Alec Black, did you think I didn't have it in me?"

Alec swallowed. It was visible from where Nathan stood on the other side of the room.

"It wasn't that I thought you incapable of such an act. It's more that I thought my brother would make up such an outlandish tale to--" he struggled for words, and Nathan could imagine all of the things he selected and discarded based on how Jane may respond, but finally he finished with, "frighten me."

Nathan wanted to groan at his little brother's very poor choice of words, but it wouldn't have been wise at the moment.

"Do you find me frightening?" Jane asked.

"Yes," came the reply, but not from Alec.

The reply was a very much American tone of voice, and the whole lot of them turned in the direction of the doors.

"Matthew Thatcher, what nerve. Disappear for months and when you decide to show up again, you insult me," Jane said.

It was in fact Matthew Thatcher standing in the doorway of their father's study with his arm entwined with none other than Katharine Cavanaugh, the Countess of Stirling. Or rather, Mrs. Thatcher now, if Nathan had the latest corre-spondence from the War Office correct. The story went the pair had been wed on a ship in the middle of the Mediter-ranean after an assignment had gone wrong, and even more, it was rumored they were married by Reginald Davis himself, dressed to the nines in his pirate garb. Ridiculous to be sure, but that was the intelligence feeding back to the War Office. Nathan would have to remember to ask them about the truth later.

"It wasn't an insult, darling. It was a compliment," Thatcher said. "But I'm not sure that's relevant just now. Did you say the Duke of Lofton is alive?"

"The War Office sent us a missive. It said he had been killed," Mrs. Thatcher said, her head tilted just slightly enough to suggest her confusion.

Nathan noted how tall the woman was and how perfectly she matched Thatcher. He smiled even as he squeezed Nora's shoulder beneath his hand.

"It appears to be that way," he said and nodded in the direction of the flagging chestnut roaster. "Did you hear the one about the rookie spy taking a hot chestnut roaster to the face of an intruder?"

Mrs. Thatcher shook her head. "I had thought that a legend, a myth perhaps."

Jane let out a puff of air on a sigh. "I really must speak to whomever it is that is spreading these rumors about me to ensure they spread them correctly next time," she said and sank into the nearest chair, the chestnut roasting quietly banging against her legs. "And on the topic of accuracy, I was not a spy at the time."

"At the time of what?"

"The time when Jane saved Alec and me from an intruder, a hired man sent to hurt us by a woman committing treason," Nathan said, summing up the experience for those who had not been present.

He could still remember that day, but the memories became more blurred with age. Their father had said something about the house being secured. Nathan recalled only a few times when that had happened in his youth, and one of them had been with Jane in the house with them. She had roasted chestnuts with them to distract them from their fears. He had somehow known that at the time, but how, he could not say, for he had been just a boy. But the impression was there. Knowing that Jane would always be there to protect in whatever way she could.

"The man broke into the house while Father was at the War Office," Nathan said, retelling a story he had heard many times and knew more from the retelling than from the fading memories. "He came into this very study where Jane had hidden us under that desk"--here he pointed to his father's desk on which he had so recently hit his head--"And when he came in the door, Jane struck him in the face with a hot chestnut roaster."

The first gasp came from Sarah with the second closely followed by Mrs. Thatcher. Nora let out a soft, "Indeed."

"Richard always muttered about putting in a secret entrance to this library," Jane said then, her head turning as she scanned the room for an imagined secret door. "Some sort of moving panel or something. He was always going on about how there should have been another way out when it seems to me I performed adequately with the chestnut roaster."

It was then that Nora made the connection.

"And that is the reason for the chestnut roaster. He's telling you something with it. Perhaps, he's telling you to be strong?" Nora suggested.

Sarah stepped forward and took the chestnut roaster from Jane's limp hand. It seemed now that everyone understood the hidden message in the unexpected delivery, she could relax and let the rest of them figure it out. But Nathan knew better than that. He knew Jane was secretly sitting there pondering its meaning.

"Perhaps," Sarah said. "Or perhaps he's saying the culprit

is the woman who was committing treason so many years ago. Maybe she has come back with a new scheme?"

But Jane was shaking her head before she finished.

"Lady Straughton killed herself in prison," Jane said.

Sarah's face wrinkled into thought. "Or perhaps not," Sarah mumbled and walked away from the group towards the windows on the outer wall, the chestnut roaster twirling, forgotten, in her hands.

"Perhaps it's more general than that."

This came from Mrs. Thatcher as she stepped into the room and pulled off her gloves and hat. For the first time, Nathan noticed the sheen of sweat on her brow and the dampness at Thatcher's collar. But Nora was already ahead of him, standing before he could tell her to remain seated and reaching for the bell pull in the corner of the room.

"I'm terribly sorry," she said. "You're likely in need of refreshment. I cannot imagine when this heat will break, but I can imagine us all cooked to bits before it does."

Mrs. Thatcher smiled as she took a seat on the sofa closest to Jane.

"You're looking very fine, Mrs. Black," she said as she settled her skirts around her. "The last time I saw you, you were a good deal smaller. And dressed like a man if I remember."

Nora smiled brightly before resuming her seat. "Quite on both counts."

"But it appears we have a new assignment, even if the War Office hasn't officially given us one," Mrs. Thatcher said.

Jane stirred in her seat. "Alec, who was it that told you Richard had been killed?"

Alec now lounged against their father's desk, one hip resting on the wood as his body sank in on itself, a burden Nathan could not have imagined having been lifted from his shoulders with a single unexpected delivery.

"It was a woman. From the domestic unit. Long name like Matilda or Meredith or some such."

"Margaret?" Jane supplied.

Alec snapped his fingers in response. "Oh aye, that's the one. Margaret. Lady Margaret..." his voice trailed off.

"Lady Margaret Folton," Jane said, and Alec went to snap his fingers again, but Nathan knew the look on Jane's face stopped him. It stopped Nathan from breathing even as he stood there.

"Who is Lady Margaret Folton?" Nora asked.

Jane swallowed, a rare sign of weakness that Nathan had only witnessed from Jane on a number of occasions.

"She is..." And then she said nothing else.

She merely shook her head while her eyes traveled to the carpet.

"I cannot explain who she is, but I can say that she was the agent to give Richard the information he needed to connect Lady Straughton to the treasonous plot."

"You must have the wrong lady then," Alec said, "Because the woman I spoke to was only just my age. Perhaps a year or two older but not much. She certainly wasn't an agent when the great chestnut roaster incident occurred."

But Jane shook her head again. "She was an agent. She was just a child then."

Jane did not move her eyes from the carpet.

"She's been an agent since she was a child?" Sarah asked, turning towards them from her perch by the window.

Nathan saw Thatcher take his wife's hand.

"Something terrible happened to her. Something that has driven her for a very long time," Jane said, and her voice dropped to a near whisper. "A very long time."

Finally, Jane looked up, and her eyes were clear.

"Richard is alive, and he's telling us something with that chestnut roaster. We must figure out what it is."

She stood, her body elongating in fractions until she reached her full height. Jane may have been nearing her mid-sixties in age, but her posture and her presence gave no such evidence of maturity.

"We must secure the house," she said then, and Nathan felt his body straighten without his command, his senses taking on an edge they had not assumed since he heard the news of his father's death.

"Should I tell Fitzwilliam then?" Alec asked, straightening as well.

Jane's chin came up a little higher. "No, Fitzwilliam will not do," she said and turned to Nathan. "I need you to find Hathaway."

"Hathaway?" Nathan asked, recalling the name of his father's old butler. "Why Hathaway?"

"Because Richard is telling us we're in danger, and Hathaway will know what to do."

CHAPTER 5

*S*he wasn't sure what she had been expecting, but an invitation for a stroll in the park was not it.

Margaret stared at the missive in her hand, contemplating the age of the paper and the expertise of the handwriting. She surmised two things. The first of which was that Viscount Pemberly found the paper in his newly acquired home, likely a relic left behind by the previous owner, and the second of which was that he had extraordinarily fine handwriting for a gentleman. She assumed this was the result of years in the military and writing correspondence to the troops in the field. Or was it captains in the seas? She wasn't certain how that worked exactly.

She stood from the breakfast table, the missive still in hand, and moved in the direction of her study. She had taken a step into the corridor when she heard Timmons, her butler and one of only three servants employed in the house.

"My lady," Timmons said. "You haven't broken your fast."

She looked up, startled to realize Timmons had been there all along, and she had failed to notice him, and startled even more that she had sat down to partake of breakfast, then had removed herself from the table without having completed the task.

"Oh, quite right," she said, resuming her seat at the table.

She knew Timmons watched her, but she busied herself with setting the invitation from Pemberly on the table and picking up the copy of the Times, neatly ironed and placed at her elbow. But while she ignored Timmons and pretended to focus on the newspaper, her mind remained fully entranced by the unexpected invitation.

She had never received the like before in her life. Nor had she ever felt the need to receive such invitations. Since her parents' deaths, she had had only one objective in life, that objective did not require any emotion in one form or another. And honestly, she quite preferred it that way. But from the first moment she had opened her eyes and seen Viscount Pemberly, his warm dark eyes staring into hers with an intensity she had never known, the resulting impact on her person was terrifying.

She had wanted to kiss him. Had wanted to kiss a man. She had wanted something at all, which was never something she contemplated happening again. Since her parents' deaths...

She let the thought trail off. She couldn't think about how she had felt since her parents had died, because she had felt nothing at all. Nothing. It was like her parents' deaths had resulted in a void that left nothing in its wake. Nothing could come from nothing, and thus, she remained empty. She often wondered if people thought her cold or unfeeling when, in fact, it was simply that she had no feeling at all.

That was until now.

And what did that mean precisely?

Was she to act on this inexplicable occurrence?

She sat there, her eyes roaming the minuscule text of the Times and not really understanding anything she was seeing as her mind wandered through the past twenty odd years of her life. She had once thought she felt attraction for a young man at the War Office. He was the Duke of Lofton's son, Alec, and she had come to understand that he had that effect on all women. So she had dismissed it and never thought on the subject again until now.

Because until now she had never felt, well, anything.

Her eyes darted to the invitation on the table.

If she ignored it, perhaps it would go away. This sounded ridiculous to even her, but she really didn't know if she trusted herself to be in his presence.

This brought her back up as she was a trusted agent for the War Office, and it was her duty to protect this man who had served a country that had placed a target on his back. She must answer this missive, and she must go with him to the park. It was her duty for crown and country.

At least, that's what she told herself.

She rose immediately, snatching the invitation from the table and turning to the door, determined to go directly to her study and respond to his request. That was until Timmons stopped her.

"My lady," he said, "You failed once more to break your fast."

She looked at him. Oh, bugger.

* * *

"Do you know if I've even unpacked the cravats?" Jack asked, his head buried in the armoire in his dressing quarters.

It had been so much easier when one's attire consisted of whatever uniforms remained intact at the end of a long campaign. This having to deal with various pieces of varying color, texture, and finery was exhausting. And completely unnecessary in Jack's estimation. What was wrong with a good uniform? If the war were not such a recent memory or the fact that his uniform declared him quite decorated, he would have hauled the remaining uniform that was fit for company from its trunk and donned it in a moment. But he had no desire to fend off matrons and their debutantes today. He wanted all of his attention to be centered on one thing. Or, one person rather.

The extraordinary Lady Margaret Folton.

He was surprised she had responded so promptly to his invitation for a stroll in the park, and then he was surprised that he was surprised. He had spent too much time being surrounded by blokes in uniform and had forgotten the complexities of females. And this one was turning out to be rather complex.

He unearthed what he thought was a cravat and extracted himself from the armoire. He held up the material to Captain Edwards.

"How's this?"

The captain twitched a long ear at him, and Jack looked at the material in his hand. It was a fine, black sock, but it wouldn't do really. He returned to rummaging in the armoire.

Perhaps the uniform would be his only option in the end, but he regretted it even as he thought of it. Surely there must be a cravat in there somewhere. His hand came into contact with the smooth surface of a well-made wooden box, and he yanked it toward him. Pulling the box and himself from the armoire, he held the find aloft and declared to the captain, "I did unpack the cravats." He looked at the box in his hand. "Well, I mostly unpacked the cravats. At least they were out of the trunk."

Captain Edwards tilted his head, and Jack imagined he was questioning Jack's decision not to hire a valet. Jack had not had a valet in quite some years, including those spent in the navy. Although his position called for such an assistant, he had felt it superfluous and rejected any man the crown sent his way. Men were needed in action. Not ironing his waistcoats.

"But the cook is rather good, is she not?" Jack said in defense to the question the captain did not ask.

Jack imagined Captain Edwards nodded in agreement when the only thing the dog actually did was lie down, his head coming to rest between his over-large paws on the faded carpet of the dressing quarters. Jack nodded as if to complete the action for the dog and opened the box to select a cravat. The smell of must erupted from the box, and Jack turned his head, immediately changing his mind about the necessity of a valet. With little ceremony, Jack shoved the box back into the armoire. Turning, he looked back at the hound.

"I'll see to hiring a valet immediately," Jack said and walked past Captain Edwards to find the trunk with his last remaining uniform.

* * *

"Splendid day for a stroll, my lord. So glad you thought of it."

Margaret wanted to swallow her tongue. She sounded like one of those empty-headed debutantes. She was an agent for the country's most critical offices, and she sounded as if she should be selecting the color of ribbons she would wear for the season.

"I wasn't sure if government agents were allowed to partake in such niceties, but I'm glad you were able to join me," Viscount Pemberly said in return.

At the word 'agent,' she felt a shiver pass over her skin despite the absurd heat. She had hoped her cover of being sent from the government to ascertain the settlement of his title was believable. It was all the War Office had given her when they had sent her to protect Pemberly. She was doing the best she could with the deplorable cover. But when he had said the actual word 'agent,' her heart had skittered a little. There was no way he could know the facts of the matter, and she was not at liberty to tell him. The less anyone knew of the possible mole in the War Office the better. And the less the accidental target knew of the situation, the better for his peace of mind. And possibly, his life.

Margaret adjusted the parasol to keep most of the sun out of her face as she attempted polite conversation with the viscount.

"I trust you are settling in well. Your townhouse seems lovely," she said and once more felt the stupidity of her words.

"My townhouse is a macabre of dust cloths," Pemberly said in return, and she snorted a laugh.

The sound was so unexpected from her and so unladylike in general, she quickly pressed a gloved hand to her mouth as if to abort the sound even as it had already left her mouth.

"Oh, you're quite right to laugh. It's a bit of a mess," he went on. "But I didn't purchase it for the interior."

She let her hand fall from her mouth, his words having caught her attention.

"You didn't purchase the home for its interior? Then why purchase it at all?"

"For the gardens," he said without hesitation.

Margaret felt another laugh coming on and squelched it with all of the emptiness she had carried for the past twenty odd years. This man was rattling her carefully eradicated senses, and it would not do. She needed all of the emptiness she could muster to concentrate on keeping him safe. Now was not the time to suddenly have a feeling.

"Gardens?" she asked instead.

He nodded and for the first time, Margaret realized how odd he looked in his uniform. She scanned the walk around them, nearly empty for the lateness of the season and likely the extreme heat, but if they were to encounter anyone, surely his uniform would attract attention. It was resplendent with his various decorations declaring to all the world that he was quite the catch. Any passing mama with a girl to wed off was sure to inquire. What little she knew of the viscount, it didn't seem that such a situation would be enjoyable for him.

Except he was walking with her.

He had invited her for this stroll specifically with an invitation sent round to her house. She stumbled on the path and only a quick grab by the viscount kept her from spilling over.

"Are you all right?" he asked as he righted her, and she blinked up at him, finding those warm brown eyes that reminded her of puppies much too close to her.

"Quite," she said with a wobbly smile. "Just stumbled a bit. How clumsy of me."

She was about as clumsy as she was giggly, which were two attributes that had suddenly gotten away from her since she had met this man.

"You were telling me about your gardens," she said to deflect his attention.

He blinked at her, and she thought he was likely determining how all right she really was. She tried smiling harder, which felt terribly unnatural to her, but he looked away, so she felt it had worked, despite the uncomfortableness of the act.

"Yes, the gardens," he said. "They were quite large, and I could tell they had once been grand, but for a bit of tampering by the previous owner. With any luck, I'll find that he did not have enough time to tamper properly with them.

I've already righted several of the beds, and I have high hopes for the others."

"You've righted them?" she asked, and he nodded quickly.

"Yes, I've been carrying plans for my garden around in my head for the past three campaigns. It's nice to see them finally come to life in the soil."

If she had stumbled before, she would have fallen directly on her face when he turned his smile upon her just then. She had thought him gorgeous before, and now she had completely lost all grasp of English vocabulary because she couldn't have said what he looked like with his face lit up with a smile so genuine it caused actual pain to settle on her chest.

"Gardening plans?"

Was she to be cursed with inarticulate sentences around this man?

"Oh yes, loads of gardening plans. I grew up in Yorkshire on my Uncle Willy's estate, and his wife, Aunt Dottie, had the most splendid gardens. She let me follow her about. Taught me a thing or two about them. Ever since I left for Eton, I've been thinking about what my own garden would look like one day."

She found herself with nothing to say and only stared at him in silence. She had expected this assignment to be rather banal, but when a man she had an obvious attraction to suddenly begin speaking of some past that begged for questioning, she found this assignment was not simple at all. She would have to see about being reassigned.

But even as the thought came into her head she dismissed it. The War Office had already pushed back most of their agents because of the mole. She was one of a skeleton crew left in town. She straightened her shoulders. She would need to fend off this man with his ridiculous puppy eyes and gardening speak.

"You lived with your aunt and uncle then," she said.

Surely that was plain enough.

He nodded. "Yes, I went to live with them after my mother and oldest brother were killed in a carriage accident."

His words were said so carelessly Margaret almost tripped again. His mother and oldest brother were killed? In a carriage accident? None of this was in the file she had received on him. How was this unknown to the War Office? Obviously, the title the Office had conjured was never meant for a real person, but when it found itself a new home in the viscount at her elbow, surely someone at the War Office had done the due diligence to discover whom the poor man was. Well, at least more than just his name. But it appeared as if that weren't true.

"I'm terribly sorry," she said and realized quite abruptly how cold and casual her own words sounded.

Had she always sounded that way when speaking of death? She thought of her parents, and for the first time, she wondered how deeply her scars ran.

"It wasn't your fault, but thank you. I hardly remember her now, and my brother even less. I was quite young. They had gone into the next town to do some shopping. I was to go with them until I came down with a bit of the sniffles. My mum thought it best if I stayed home."

He didn't continue, but he didn't have to. Margaret finished his thoughts in her head. He was alive when his mother and brother were not. For a breath, she felt sympathy for him. She knew that feeling. That feeling of being left behind. She squeezed his arm where she held onto his elbow as they strolled, the action more of a reflex than anything she meant to do. He turned and smiled at her. Not the powerful smile of moments before when he had been speaking of his garden, but a smile of quiet reassurance that he was all right. He couldn't possibly know that her reaction had been one of understanding, and she would not tell him so.

"Ever since I've been cursed with an unusual amount of luck," he said and abruptly came to a stop.

She had been so focused on his story, she had not realized they had arrived at the Serpentine, the water rolling languidly along as it moved through the park. She questioned the pureness of the water in it, but the day was so hot she allowed herself a fantasy of throwing her entire body into it, letting the water close over her head.

Much as it had that night she had pushed the Duke of Lofton into the Thames.

The memory was enough to push her back into the present and the assignment at hand. She could not let herself get distracted by the viscount's sorrowful tale. She had enough sorrow to last her a lifetime. She needn't borrow from another.

"I don't think luck should be a curse," she said, following the roll of the Serpentine past them.

"It is when your aunt dies of the same fever you lived through," he murmured, and Margaret wasn't sure she was meant to hear it. But then he turned to her. "Aunt Dottie died just before I left for Eton. We were stricken with the same fever. I survived, and she didn't. Uncle Willy has been in his cups ever since. Can't say I blame him."

This last part was muttered as well, and Margaret felt the inexplicable urge to let her mouth fall open. Was he telling her tales of woe to earn her sympathy? When it came to earning one's sympathy, she was not the person with which to compete on the subject of woe. But again, he needn't have known that.

"I'm truly sorry," she said, no longer feeling the urge to sympathize with him, a finger of doubt creeping up her back.

He shrugged. "I was raised largely by boarding schools

and Uncle Willy at that point. My only other brother still living stayed with my father. Raised to acquire the title one day. Earl of Heresford. But every year there was a hunting trip, and it was the one time I saw my father and brother. They had nothing to say to me, and I nothing to say to them. Then one year they left for the trip, I was called to the front. They were both killed when other hunters mistook them as deer. I received the news just before I left port."

Now she knew he was making this up. No one could have such a tragic story.

"My six-year-old nephew became the Earl of Heresford, and I left, shipped off to fight Napoleon."

His voice changed, subtly, but enough that Margaret noticed. Just a slight inflection to his voice. And she realized he was no longer looking at her or the Serpentine. His gaze had moved off into the distance, seeing something from long ago that she could only imagine.

And then, "The next time I received news on board a ship, I found out I'd been given a bloody title. A title I hadn't even earned. The only reason I was in the Mediterranean was because they had literally run out of men. Everyone had died, and there was only Captain Lynwood left to promote to commodore. A bloody twist of fate, and I'm cursed with a title I didn't earn."

And it was then that Margaret realized he was telling the truth. The edge of real anger in his voice resonated inside of her, pinged against her own awful truth.

Now her mouth did fall open. "Oh God," she whispered before she could stop herself.

Pemberly turned suddenly to look at her. "I'm quite sorry, my lady. I think I'd forgotten you were there." He tried to smile, but the man who had so passionately spoken of gardening plans was gone. In his place was a terrible shell of a man. It was like looking in a mirror. "I've been speaking to

Captain Edwards too much of late. Shall we continue to walk?"

She only nodded as he resumed their stroll along the water, returning once more to the footpath leading to the other side of the park. Conversation was largely lost as she could think of nothing to say after hearing him speak of his past. It had struck too close to her own, and she didn't know what to say. She was supposed to be a government clerk, come to see about his titleship. How was she to speak of her real past?

"My lord," she began and stalled.

There was something in her that compelled her to speak. After more than twenty years of silence, it was as if she could no longer hold back the quiet. The words wanted to erupt from her in a torrent. The only thing she regretted was that it would be the poor belabored Viscount Pemberly to hear it.

"My parents--" she said, and then she said nothing else as a curricle came out of nowhere, racing toward them with a speed unwise on most cultivated roads, let alone a footpath. The horses pulling the vehicle seemed possessed as the driver on the seat sat hunched in a sea of dark cloak, his face hidden from them.

Reacting in the moment without a thought as to what it might look like, Margaret dropped her parasol, freeing both hands to latch onto the viscount.

"I do beg your pardon," she said.

And just as the runaway curricle would have struck them both, Margaret jumped backward, tumbling them both into the Serpentine.

* * *

"I CAME AS SOON as I received his lordship's missive, my lady," Hathaway said as he bowed over her hand.

Jane smiled at the nearly bald palette of Richard's most trusted servant.

"Hathaway," she said, a genuine smile in her voice that she had not felt in days. "So good of you to come."

Hathaway set down the heavy case he carried with him, but she noticed he did not move away from where it sat on the study floor.

Their group had not largely changed over the last several days it had taken Nathan and Alec to locate the retired servant in a humble cottage in Surrey. Nathan and Nora, Alec and Sarah, and even Thatcher and his new wife, Kate, had now made permanent residence in their townhouse. It seemed Alec and Nathan were determined to never allow her a single moment alone, and Thatcher and Kate felt it their duty to protect the Black family in general. The house was suddenly full to the brim, and Jane would not have wanted it any other way.

A crisis was underfoot. A crisis they knew very little about, but that carried great danger. Jane was not going to let her family out of her sight.

"It appears we have need of your expertise," she said to Hathaway, and her gaze traveled over the man's shoulder to where Fitzwilliam stood uncertainly in the doorway after having escorted Hathaway to the library.

"That will be all," she said to the man, and for a small moment, she thought she saw hesitation in his eyes.

But she blinked, and the moment was gone. Fitzwilliam bowed and backed out of the door, closing it behind him.

"Now, where were we?" Jane asked, looking to Hathaway. "Oh yes, your expertise."

From anyone else, Jane would have expected a silly, over confident smile, but from Hathaway she received nothing more than a "By your leave, your grace."

She smiled at his usual steadfastness and looked about at

the audience of the room. All of Lofton House's current, if temporary, residents were in attendance, scattered about Richard's study like an obscure puppet show gone horribly wrong. She gestured behind her to where the chestnut roaster now lay on Richard's desk.

"We received this after word of Richard's death was passed to us from an agent at the War Office."

Hathaway nodded in the direction of the chestnut roaster.

"That weapon of choice looks familiar," Hathaway stated, and now Jane did smile.

"Indeed," she said. "And this came shortly after the chestnut roaster."

Jane handed a slip of parchment to the man and, for the first time, she noticed how age had settled on him like an ill-fitting jacket. If she were nearing five and sixty, Hathaway was likely nearing his seventieth year, if he had not already surpassed it. And yet, his virility denied such an age even as the spots on his skin and the wrinkles of his face told differently. Hathaway unfolded the parchment as if to read the message within, but Jane summarized for him.

"It's a directive from the War Office advising us to leave town," she said, and Hathaway looked up sharply at her.

"There was no body recovered, Hathaway," she said plainly and knew that Hathaway understood her meaning.

"Something is afoot, your grace," he said.

And Jane nodded. "I leave this house in your hands. I know Richard would have wanted that."

Hathaway nodded. "I thank you for your trust, your grace. I will see the master's wishes fulfilled."

"How exactly do you plan to do that?" Alec asked from his perch on one of the sofas by his wife.

Without hesitation, Hathaway bent to retrieve the heavy case at his feet, placing it on a table at the side of the room with a heavy thunk. He reached for his waistcoat then, and Jane thought he would pull his pocket watch from its place to check the time. But when he pulled the chain loose, there was no pocket watch where there should have been one. Instead, there was a small key that fit precisely into the lock on the heavy case. The lock sprang loose at the turn of the instrument. Putting the key away with one hand, Hathaway unsnapped the remaining latches of the case until he could lift the lid.

"Dear Lord in heaven," Alec whispered when he and everyone else in the room could see into the case.

Hathaway promptly removed two pistols and a bag of shot from the case and began to arm himself.

"It's an arsenal," Sarah said.

Hathaway turned and said in his most dour butler's tone. "Not quite, my lady. But I do try. If you will excuse me, your grace," he said, turning to Jane. "I have my orders."

And with that he left the study.

Jane looked about the room and suddenly realized a part of her family was missing.

"Where's Thatcher?" she asked and was met by a suspicious wall of silence.

FOR THE SECOND time in a fortnight, Margaret surfaced through water that was better left untouched. The Serpentine relinquished her with a gulping suck as she sprang from its depths. The surface about her lay still until Viscount Pemberly broke through it in a loud swallow of air. He came up very much how she would imagine a dog would, water spraying in all directions as he shook his head about and wiped water from his eyes. For a second, she regretted the now total ruin of his resplendent uniform.

"Are you all right?" she asked when he finished shaking water from his person.

"Aren't I supposed to ask that of you? Me being the gentleman and you being the lady," he said.

She realized it was quite possibly true that that was the case, but in this instance, it was her assignment to ensure he was safe. So she averted his questioning.

"It was I who pulled you in here," she said, smiling a dubious smile in the hopes he would believe her ridiculous ploy.

He returned her smile with what she thought was an equal amount of wobbliness, but he nodded in assent.

"I suppose it was," he said and then took her arm, pulling her in the direction of the shore.

"I do hope you're all right," she said, looking about them as they neared the bank for the maniacal driver who had made an attempt on the viscount's life.

She was getting rather weary of these assassination attempts.

"Quite," he said as he helped her up on shore.

They both stood there, water dripping from every spot on their body and every fold of fabric on their person, and for a terrible moment, she remembered her wish to be submerged in the Serpentine if only for a moment's relief from the heat.

And so she laughed.

She wasn't certain which it was that disturbed her more. The fact that she was laughing so soon after an attempt on the viscount's life or that she had laughed so much already in this man's presence that the sound no longer seemed odd. It was likely both that disturbed her, but she kept laughing anyway.

"What is it?" Pemberly finally asked when he had let her go on for a few moments.

He smiled, too, as he wrung water from his sodden coat.

"I was just thinking how nice it would be to plunge into the water," she said, and the need to laugh struck her anew. Only now Pemberly joined her, the sound of his laugh equally vibrant in the heat of the day.

As the sound of their laughter died away, she reached for where her hat should have been only to find her sodden mess of hair tumbling about her shoulders. She began to wring the water from it as she surreptitiously took in their surroundings. There was no sign of the driver or the curricle. It was as if nothing had happened at all. And as the path had been unusually vacated, there were no witnesses about to question as to the whereabouts of the curricle or any direction it may have taken.

"What an odd thing that was," she said as cooly as she could manage. "The driver must have been inexperienced or the horses spooked. How dreadful," she finished and looked over at Pemberly to find him staring at her, his eyes wide, his mouth slightly parted as if he were ready to wet his lips.

"What is it?" she asked, but as it was her person at which he was staring, she took a moment to look down at herself.

Only to find the very clear outline of her small breasts and erect nipples staring back at her. She quickly crossed her arms over her chest, bending her back as if to obscure the silhouette of her body.

"Oh dear," she murmured, but before she could say more, Pemberly stood in front of her as his uniform jacket came to rest on her shoulders.

She took the lapels of the jacket in her hands, pulling the sides of the jacket closer together to shield her even more.

"I'm terribly sorry," she said, feeling as if she'd said the same thing too many times that afternoon.

Pemberly only shook his head.

"You apologize with alarming frequency, Lady Folton," he said.

He was very close again, his brown eyes focused and intense, and she had to run her tongue over her suddenly dry lips. She watched those same eyes register the betraying move and her resulting swallow. Only then did she realize Pemberly still had his hands on the coat as well, holding the lapels together just below the place where her hands stayed. If she moved just a little, let her hands slip just a little, she could touch him. She could feel the heat of his skin against hers. She could know what it felt like to run her fingers over the fine hairs of his wrists. If she just moved a little more.

"Are you two all right there?"

She jumped, nearly knocking both of them back into the Serpentine. Instinctually, she put her body between the viscount and whomever it was that had so rudely interrupted them. Even if it were an interruption of concern. Having lost her hat and her parasol, Margaret raised a hand to shield her eyes from the sun as she looked up at the intruder.

It was a rather nice looking gentleman with an all around unassuming air with the slightest touch of laziness about him, but that didn't seem quite right with the rest of him. It was his voice more so than his body that drew her attention.

"Are you an American?" she blurted out before she could stop herself.

She felt a hand on her shoulder as Pemberly made his way out from behind her. She caught the look he cast in her direction, and she wondered for a moment if she'd been too obvious in her attempt to protect him. Perhaps it was slightly odd for a lady to stand in front of a gentleman in this circumstance. Perhaps slightly too odd. But then he turned to address the man in the roadster in front of them.

"It seems we've had a mishap, sir. An errant driver and a team of runaway horses. Lady Folton's wise thinking saved us from imminent disaster it would seem," Pemberly said addressing her with a gesture of his hand.

"Is that so?" the gentleman said, and then he did the oddest thing with his hat, tipping it slightly forward as if in a bow to her. "Ma'am," he said. "I am an American, but I'd be much obliged if you'd let me assist you."

She looked at the small buggy he rode in. A vehicle mostly used by a single rider, her mind could not fathom how he expected to assist them with so inadequate a vehicle.

"My residence is not far from here," she heard Pemberly say beside her. "Would you be so kind as to convey us?"

Margaret looked at him. Perhaps he had hit his head on the way into the water. She should see about sending for a doctor if that were the case.

For the second time in a fortnight, Margaret surfaced through water that was better left untouched. The Serpentine relinquished her with a gulping suck as she sprang from its depths. The surface about her lay still until Viscount Pemberly broke through it in a loud swallow of air. He came up very much how she would imagine a dog would, water spraying in all directions as he shook his head about and wiped water from his eyes. For a second, she regretted the now total ruin of his resplendent uniform.

"Are you all right?" she asked when he finished shaking water from his person.

"Aren't I supposed to ask that of you? Me being the gentleman and you being the lady," he said.

She realized it was quite possibly true that that was the case, but in this instance, it was her assignment to ensure he was safe. So she averted his questioning.

"It was I who pulled you in here," she said, smiling a dubious smile in the hopes he would believe her ridiculous ploy.

He returned her smile with what she thought was an equal amount of wobbliness, but he nodded in assent.

"I suppose it was," he said and then took her arm, pulling her in the direction of the shore.

"I do hope you're all right," she said, looking about them as they neared the bank for the maniacal driver who had made an attempt on the viscount's life.

She was getting rather weary of these assassination attempts.

"Quite," he said as he helped her up on shore.

They both stood there, water dripping from every spot on their body and every fold of fabric on their person, and for a terrible moment, she remembered her wish to be submerged in the Serpentine if only for a moment's relief from the heat.

And so she laughed.

She wasn't certain which it was that disturbed her more. The fact that she was laughing so soon after an attempt on the viscount's life or that she had laughed so much already in this man's presence that the sound no longer seemed odd. It was likely both that disturbed her, but she kept laughing anyway.

"What is it?" Pemberly finally asked when he had let her go on for a few moments.

He smiled, too, as he wrung water from his sodden coat.

"I was just thinking how nice it would be to plunge into the water," she said, and the need to laugh struck her anew. Only now Pemberly joined her, the sound of his laugh equally vibrant in the heat of the day.

As the sound of their laughter died away, she reached for where her hat should have been only to find her sodden mess of hair tumbling about her shoulders. She began to wring the water from it as she surreptitiously took in their surroundings. There was no sign of the driver or the curricle. It was as if nothing had happened at all. And as the path had been unusually vacated, there were no witnesses about to question as to the whereabouts of the curricle or any direction it may have taken.

"What an odd thing that was," she said as coolly as she could manage. "The driver must have been inexperienced or the horses spooked. How dreadful," she finished and looked over at Pemberly to find him staring at her, his eyes wide, his mouth slightly parted as if he were ready to wet his lips.

"What is it?" she asked, but as it was her person at which he was staring, she took a moment to look down at herself.

Only to find the very clear outline of her small breasts and erect nipples staring back at her. She quickly crossed her arms over her chest, bending her back as if to obscure the silhouette of her body.

"Oh dear," she murmured, but before she could say more, Pemberly stood in front of her as his uniform jacket came to rest on her shoulders.

She took the lapels in her hands, pulling the sides of the jacket closer together to shield her even more.

"I'm terribly sorry," she said, feeling as if she'd said the same thing too many times that afternoon.

Pemberly only shook his head.

"You apologize with alarming frequency, Lady Folton," he said.

He was very close again, his brown eyes focused and intense, and she had to run her tongue over her suddenly dry lips. She watched those same eyes register the betraying move and her resulting swallow. Only then did she realize Pemberly still had his hands on the coat as well, holding the lapels together just below the place where her hands stayed. If she moved just a little, let her hands slip just a little, she could touch him. She could feel the heat of his skin against hers. She could know what it felt like to run her fingers over the fine hairs of his wrists. If she just moved a little more.

"Are you two all right there?"

She jumped, nearly knocking both of them back into the Serpentine. Instinctually, she put her body between the viscount and whomever it was that had so rudely interrupted them. Even if it were an interruption of concern. Having lost her hat and her parasol, Margaret raised a hand to shield her eyes from the sun as she looked up at the intruder.

It was a rather nice looking gentleman with an all-around unassuming air with the slightest touch of laziness about him, but that didn't seem quite right with the rest of him. It was his voice more so than his body that drew her attention.

"Are you an American?" she blurted out before she could stop herself.

She felt a hand on her shoulder as Pemberly made his way out from behind her. She caught the look he cast in her direction, and she wondered for a moment if she'd been too obvious in her attempt to protect him. Perhaps it was slightly odd for a lady to stand in front of a gentleman in this circumstance. Perhaps slightly too odd. But then he turned to address the man in the roadster in front of them.

"It seems we've had a mishap, sir. An errant driver and a team of runaway horses. Lady Folton's wise thinking saved us from imminent disaster it would seem," Pemberly said, addressing her with a gesture of his hand.

"Is that so?" the gentleman said, and then he did the oddest thing with his hat, tipping it slightly forward as if in a bow to her. "Ma'am," he said. "I am an American, but I'd be much obliged if you'd let me assist you."

She looked at the small buggy he rode in. A vehicle mostly used by a single rider, her mind could not fathom how he expected to assist them with so inadequate a vehicle.

"My residence is not far from here," she heard Pemberly say beside her. "Would you be so kind as to convey us?"

Margaret looked at him. Perhaps he had hit his head on

the way into the water. She should see about sending for a doctor if that were the case.

"My lord," she said in order to get his attention. "We cannot possibly all fit in this gentleman's carriage. It's merely a personal vehicle. Not one for touring."

Pemberly shook his head. "Then we'll just have to set you on my lap to make room."

His words were spoken at a level only she could hear, but if the American stranger in the roadster had only an adequate degree of vision, he would have seen the blush that rose to her cheeks and ascertained that the conversation was of a delicate nature.

"I see," she said and allowed Viscount Pemberly to take her elbow.

In a less than graceful experience, she found herself securely nestled on the lap of Commodore John Lynwood, lately the Viscount Pemberly, and in an equally less than graceful mood, she felt all of her dignity as an agent for the War Office seep from her body. Cocooned in his sodden jacket to keep her traitorous body from revealing any more of her feminine nature than it already had, she allowed herself to rest the entire length of her body against that of a man she hardly knew.

And it wasn't until the roadster began to move, and she could no longer bear the silence that allowed her to concentrate over much on the feel of Pemberly's arms about her, that she looked at the American on the seat beside them.

"I'm sorry," she said. "I don't believe I caught your name."

The American turned to her with a wide smile, his curly blond hair shaking beneath the rim of his hat as the roadster moved along.

"You can call me Thatcher, ma'am."

CHAPTER 6

$\mathcal{J}$ ack watched their American rescuer roll away in his roadster and disappear around the corner. He stood on the pavement in front of his town-house, the sun beating against his now largely dried uniform. Or rather, what parts of his uniform he still wore. He looked down at himself for a moment. Now he had exactly no uniforms left in wearable condition. He was surprised to feel a bit of regret at the thought. He had always been a military man by necessity and not really passion. But he supposed that, after a time, the experience had come to mean something to him, and now he suffered from the loss of an idea he had carried about with him.

He tilted his head back up at the sky and for the first time noticed clouds in the distance. God, he hoped it would rain. He turned to look up at the townhouse, its facade still unfamiliar to him. He thought of Uncle Willy alone in Yorkshire and, shaking his head, mounted the steps to the front door. Reynolds had appeared at the door before the roadster had come to a complete stop, stepping up to the conveyance to assist Lady Folton in the climb down. Jack had been surprised at how quickly the little man moved to assist the lady, and how quickly he disappeared inside with the woman, leaving his master to drip on the pavement.

He ran his fingers through his hair, pushing it off his forehead long enough to climb the stairs and go through the front door. Closing it softly behind him, he heard Reynolds in the first floor sitting room asking the lady if she would require tea or perhaps a towel. Jack made his way to the room.

"We'll require both, Reynolds," Jack said as he stood in the doorway and surveyed the lady in question, standing as still as a statue in the center of the room.

She looked oddly like a sculpture in progress, as if she had been left in the sculptor's studio, surrounded by shrouded works of creation. The shrouded works of creation were only old furniture, but in his mind, the scene was one of beauty and intrigue, and it cleared his thoughts of anything else until Reynolds said, "Very good, my lord," and exited the room.

The drapes had been pulled shut in this room, likely when the previous owner had vacated, and had not been opened since. The room lay in a gray darkness, not quite light and not quite dark. The air itself was thick like pudding, and he went to open a door on the other side of the room to help with the flow. It wasn't until he opened the door completely that he remembered it was the room that the captain had taken as his own.

The hound came bounding inside, likely having been awakened by the sound of voices and his master's footfalls. But Jack caught him neatly by the scruff of his neck before he could pounce once more on Lady Folton. From her rigid stance, Jack feared she would likely topple over again at the captain's advance, but this time it would likely be her to shatter into a thousand pieces instead of some long forgotten piece of pottery. And he would regret the loss.

"I would invite you to sit down, my lady, if you can find a place to do so." He gestured with one hand while he continued to hold the captain with the other. It was difficult to make out Lady Folton's expression in the dimness, but he thought he saw her relax just the littlest bit.

She was looking at the dog, and her mouth began to soften. "I think you can let him go. I'm ready," she said.

The words sounded like a challenge, and thinking of her actions in the park, Jack let go of Captain Edwards. The dog surged forward and just as he would have leapt to connect his front paws to Lady Folton's hip, she stepped backward. The captain flew across the room, catapulting face first into a covered sofa. He landed on the floor, tail wagging, ears flopping about his head.

Lady Folton laughed as she squatted, one hand going to scratch the space between the captain's long ears while the other held his uniform jacket closed across her chest. The movement reminded him that, although he might be nearly dry, Lady Folton carried with her many more layers of clothing than he and was likely still quite damp. And likely uncomfortable.

"My lady, you require a change of clothing. Perhaps I can send for something--"

"That's quite all right," she said and stood, leaving an infatuated Captain Edwards gazing up admiringly at her. "I'm really quite dry. And I must be going soon. I want to thank you for a lovely stroll in the park," she said, turning to smile at him.

Her perfectly straight white teeth dazzled him for a moment, and it took him a breath to realize what she'd said.

"I would hardly call it lovely," he returned and smiled as well.

She removed his coat, and he saw she was in fact rather dry. Her hair had dried to soft waves hanging about her shoulders and framing her pointed face in delicate folds. He wanted to run his fingers through it, feel the tresses fall between them.

He cleared his throat. "I shall have Reynolds hail you a hackney," he said.

She nodded but did not say anything more and neither did he. They stood in awkward silence in the gray light of the room, the only sound the captain's heavy breathing as he sat at his new love's feet, staring up at her with absolute adoration.

"Well then," he said, and he knew absolutely nothing to say next.

Should he invite her to dinner? Did bachelors do that? Was it allowed if the circumstances were that she was a government clerk and he a newly titled gentleman attempting to learn the intricacies of his title?

That sounded weak to his own ears.

"Will you be attending the Harrisons' gala next week?" Lady Folton said, relieving him of the need to find something to say.

"Harrisons?" he asked.

Lady Folton nodded. "It's a gala the Harrisons hold every summer. Usually in August. It's like a long end of season celebration. Although August is rather late, but tradition is tradition. And if there's one thing society goes on, it's tradition."

She held out his coat to him.

"Thank you, my lord, for use of your jacket. I'm sorry--" she stopped herself, a soft smile coming to her lips. "I was about to apologize again," she said.

He returned her smile, taking his jacket from her. "I believe you did, in fact, apologize," he said.

Once more the silence settled on them, but it was not awkward as he thought it would have been. It was just the two of them standing in a darkened drawing room, surrounded by furniture, unseen in weeks as it lay sleeping under layers of dust cloths while a Basset type hound mooned at the woman Jack feared he could fall in love with.

In some distant part of his brain, he heard the rattle of a teacart coming and knew Reynolds would arrive imminently with the towels and tea. And in that moment, there was something in him that made a decision before he realized he had. Dropping the coat at his feet, he reached up, cupping Lady Folton's small, pointed face between his hands, and he leaned down, sealing his lips to hers.

It was a chaste kiss by his standards, but when his fingers touched the warm skin of her face, his insides melted in a pool of unadulterated desire. Just the feel of her, the slightest bit of her under his fingertips was enough to engulf his entire body in a torrent of flaming passion, and all he had done was lay his lips against hers, hold her face in his hands. And just as quickly as he had done it, he stepped back, severing the connection.

Lady Folton did not so much as blink. If he had not been the one to actually do the kissing, he would have thought nothing at all had occurred to her or with her. She simply stood there much as she had been standing there before.

"Tea, my lord," Reynolds said as he wheeled the squeaking teacart, another relic of the previous owner, into the room, slowly dodging the shrouded furniture.

Jack gestured in the direction of the teacart to offer Lady Folton a fortifying cup, but his invitation never left his lips as Lady Folton said, "I'd best be going. Good day, my lord."

And once more, she turned about and left, the front door clicking softly closed behind her.

Jack blinked at the spot where she had stood moments before until he let his gaze drift to the equally confused dog sitting on the carpet in front of him. He held up his hands as if in surrender.

"What did I tell you?" he asked the captain.

Captain Edwards had no reply.

* * *

"You followed them?"

"Of course," Thatcher said, settling on the sofa beside his wife.

Jane watched the man get comfortable even as she fanned herself with a forgotten copy of the Times. Surely, this incessant heat wave must come to an end soon. They were all likely to melt into puddles of peerage before then. She looked about the room to survey the condition of her family. Nathan and Nora sat together at the chairs by the dormant fireplace, while Alec and Sarah sat across from them, their hands connected between the space of their chairs. Thatcher and Kate occupied the sofa facing the fireplace while Jane paced in front of it, the Times flapping in her hand.

"This Lady Margaret Folton is our only clue as to what happened to Lofton. I followed her to see if I could learn anything."

"And?" Sarah prompted, so Jane didn't have to.

"I think the situation is about what we've estimated it to be," Thatcher said.

"And that is?" Kate asked.

"Extremely dangerous."

"What gave you this indication?" Alec asked.

Thatcher selected a small sandwich from the remnants of

tea spread out on the low table before them, inspected it, and said, "Because someone tried to kill them."

Jane would have dropped the copy of the Times if she had not been expecting something along those lines to come from the rather calm American.

Nora sat up, pushing a hand against her back. For a moment, Jane wondered what it felt like to carry a child, but when she saw Nathan reach over and rub his wife's shoulder, the thought escaped her, and she smiled softly at her son.

"Tried to kill them?" Nora asked, as Nathan rubbed at her shoulders.

"A man in a curricle. Tried to run them over." He took a bite of sandwich, chewed, and swallowed. "Rather daring as he did it in the park, but Lady Folton is a quick thinker. She pulled them both into the Serpentine. Saved their lives."

Kate spoke up, saying, "It must be a mole. Someone is attempting to assassinate agents of the War Office. But who would commit such an act? And who would have the knowledge to carry it out?"

Jane gripped the newspaper tighter. "It's not possible," she said. "There's no one agent with such extensive knowledge of the Office. There's no single agent that knows where every other agent is working or even who the agents are. It's a failsafe in case this very thing happens."

"But someone knows," Alec said. "Or at least someone knows enough to go after the agents."

Nora spoke again, "Was Lady Folton alone?"

Everyone looked at Thatcher.

"You said them earlier. She must've been with someone. Did you recognize him or her?"

Thatcher shook his head. "It was a gentleman, nice dress and all, but I didn't recognize him. Looked to be military. Navy, specifically."

Kate turned toward her husband. "How do you know it was navy?"

Thatcher selected another sandwich, having successfully finished off his first.

"It looked like one of those men who met us in Palermo," he said, and Jane figured he was speaking about his rescue earlier that year from Naples. He had been picked up by a naval ship and taken to Palermo.

"Any one of the men in particular?"

Thatcher was shaking his head before Kate finished the sentence.

"He had a much nicer uniform. I'm thinking probably general, or whatever it is for a navy."

"Commodore," Kate said, but it was only a whisper, the kind of tone that had the hair on the back of Jane's neck standing up.

"Kate?" she said, but everyone in the room was already leaning forward.

Her husband had stopped chewing his sandwich.

"There was a commodore in Palermo. He had left for the front before I returned with Thatcher. I had heard he was recently returned and given a title in honor of his service."

"And then someone tries to kill him?" Alec asked.

"If that's the commodore that was with Lady Folton, then perhaps," Kate said. She looked up at Jane. "Should I pay him a social visit? He's an old friend of the family. It wouldn't look out of the ordinary."

Nathan shook his head before she could answer.

"I don't think it's wise for anyone with a direct connection to the War Office to leave the house alone. We would need to orchestrate some sort of network with many pairs of eyes on you before you step a single foot out of this house."

Jane smiled at how much Nathan sounded like his father.

"I agree. We'll need a plan. Thatcher, if you saw this commodore again, would you recognize him?"

Thatcher nodded. "Of course, it's hard to miss a man who has sat two inches from your face. A roadster is not a large vehicle, and it's not like I was expecting guests."

Kate frowned at him.

"They were soaked to the core. It wasn't as if I could leave them there. I gave them a ride back to his townhouse."

"You gave them a ride together to his residence?" Sarah asked and looked to Nora quickly before turning back. "Do you remember the address?"

"Actually, I do, because I thought what an unlucky number the house number was. Number 13 Claremont Street."

Sarah again looked at Nora, but Nora shook her head.

"It was sold only recently, and the staff decamped. Apparently, the previous owners were rather eccentric, and the lot of them wanted to try their luck elsewhere. I don't know anyone still on staff there."

Jane frowned, realizing Sarah was hoping to make a connection between the staff in the house and Nora's history as a housekeeper.

"Then a social visit must do. Are you ready to make your first social call, Mr. Thatcher?" Kate asked.

"I reckon," Thatcher said and finished off another sandwich.

Jane rose and walked toward the door of the library. "Will you be needing--"

The question was cut short when Jane opened the door to find Fitzwilliam standing just beyond, his head bent in just such a way as to betray his actions. Jane frowned. It appeared her erstwhile butler had been listening at the door.

"Fitzwilliam," she said, her tone going cold. "Is there something amiss?"

The tepid man shook his head, his weak jaw slagging back and forth with the effort.

"No, your grace," he said. "Just passing through the corridor. Is there anything you require?"

Jane felt the hairs at the back of her neck twitch.

"No, Fitzwilliam," she said. "And I would advise you to be more careful when passing through corridors."

At these words, she felt Nathan step up behind her, his large presence filling the doorway behind her and adding muscle to her speech.

"Very good, your grace," Fitzwilliam said before bowing and departing down the corridor.

"I don't think I trust him," Nathan said from behind her when the butler was out of earshot.

"I don't either," Jane said.

* * *

SHE HAD FORGOTTEN to button the uppermost button of her frock.

Richard sat in the rickety chair in his voluntary prison and watched Lady Margaret Folton pace back and forth in the small space in front of him. He wasn't sure which required more of his surprise, the fact that she had left a button unbuttoned or the fact that she was pacing. Her agitation was clear in the way her very skin seemed to vibrate in the thick heat of the room. Something was bothering the impenetrable Lady Margaret Folton, and he wondered very much what it was.

"Have you encountered the unlucky chap with the falsified title?" he asked, and he watched as Lady Folton collided with the bureau blocking the door, her steps clearly misjudged in their length.

He hid a smile behind his hand.

"Yes, I have made contact with the mark," she said. "There has already been an attempt on his life."

Richard raised an eyebrow. "What sort of attempt?"

She stopped pacing, thank God, but now she turned her attention on him, her hands attempting to shred the very gloves from her fingers.

"A curricle nearly ran us over in the park two days ago," she said, and although he could tell she was trying to remain aloof, he noted the carefully strained use of the word us.

Again, he wanted to smile at her, but he thought urging on her agitation at this moment may prove explosive.

So he kept his reaction in check as he said, "Evidence?"

She shook her head. "None at the scene," she said. "In order to avoid his imminent assassination, I pulled us both into the Serpentine. By the time we resurfaced, the driver and runaway conveyance had long left the area."

Richard coughed to cover a laugh.

"You seem to have a talent for water submersion," he said and coughed again as the laugh in his throat refused to cease.

Lady Margaret Folton cocked her head.

"I would hardly call it a talent," she said. "I would rather hope to be known for something other than pulling people into polluted bodies of water."

Richard scratched the beard that had now filled in on his unshaven cheeks.

"Is it really polluted?" he asked. "It's been years since I've had the time for a stroll in the park, but I had rather hoped the Serpentine would remain in all its aquatic beauty."

Lady Margaret Folton stared at him, clearly annoyed that they were having this conversation at all.

"Your grace," she said. "The War Office has asked your family to leave town."

Richard stopped scratching his beard.

"And?" he prompted when she did not continue.

"They have not fulfilled that request."

Richard frowned dramatically.

"Is that so?" He shook his head. "I wouldn't think they would fulfill that request."

Lady Folton stopped attempting the complete destruction of her gloves in order to fist her hands on her hips. The position was one of both annoyance and dominance and neither suited the slight stature and otherwise markedly calm exterior of Lady Folton. But he did not comment on this as she was clearly directing her anger at him.

"Would there be any reason for your family to suspect the truth of the matter?"

He thought of a chestnut roaster but shook his head instead.

"For all I know, they think I'm dead. My son, Alec, is probably already swimming in the ducal coffers. Likely deciding how best to spend my money on his glamorous wife."

Lady Folton continued to stare at him, and Richard wondered for a second how much Lady Folton knew of his family. By unwritten rule, War Office agents did not frequent the same circles. One never knew when a connection would be made or a slip up would occur. It was best to practice avoidance at all costs. But Lady Folton had been particularly resourceful on more than one occasion, and Richard would not doubt she was capable of obtaining more knowledge about his family than the War Office had already provided to her.

"Quite," was all Lady Folton finally said. "Is there anything you're in need of?"

Richard looked about him at the stacks of books the young Lord Crawley had brought him. Not that he had read a single page in any of them. His mind kept drifting to Jane and the boys, his ineffectiveness as a prisoner of his own Office eating at him. If only there was a way he could leave this place unnoticed. If only there was a way to get to them. To protect them. But he knew even as he thought it that he could not leave this prison. If the assassin thought for a moment that he had not been successful, Richard would be the one to have put his family in so much greater danger. No, he had to stay. A prisoner not only of this physical space but of the rampant thoughts in his mind. Only the thought of once more holding Jane in his arms, of watching his coming grandchild grow kept him from going entirely crazy in his confines.

"No, there is nothing," he said to Lady Folton.

She watched more carefully than he would have liked, but eventually, her fisted hands slid from her hips, and if he had not known her better, he would have thought he saw a sheen of sympathy on her face.

"Very good."

She moved toward the door.

"Lady Folton," he said, stopping her. "This attempt on the commodore's life."

She turned and nodded as she listened to him.

"Was the commodore at all suspicious of the encounter?"

Lady Folton shook her head. "He seemed quite distracted after the matter when an American showed up to give us a ride back to the viscount's townhouse."

Richard worked hard to frown instead of letting the smile that begged to spread across his face surface.

"An American?" he asked, hoping his tone sounded as incredulous as he wanted it to.

Lady Folton nodded. "Most absurd thing. An American in Hyde Park driving a roadster."

Now Richard did smile.

"Yes, quite absurd," he said.

* * *

"Do you think perhaps my choice of house number is working after all?" Jack asked the captain as he pulled a dead cluster of marigolds from a pot he had found hidden under one of the benches in the garden.

Captain Edwards currently had his head buried under an arrangement of honey perfume roses tucked into a corner of the house, and Jack could only think of thorns going into the animal's flesh. But the hound seemed hardly to notice his whereabouts as he moved deeper into the patch. Jack only saw the dog's hindquarters, and he hoped the sound of snorting was coming from a vigorously engaged nose.

"I still think it was rather brilliant of me to choose a house with such an unlucky number for an address. Even if people thought me absurd. But I was nearly killed yesterday. Surely that should mean something."

He tossed the last dead head of marigold into the refuse as he reached to upend the pot of its used and lifeless soil into another bucket. Once the pot was empty, he reached for his trowel in the container of fresh soil he had procured that morning from the market. It was fragrant with the aroma of manure, and at the moment, he could not think of a smell he liked better.

Except for perhaps lilacs.

His mind drifted to that moment when he had first caught the unusual scent of Lady Folton's fragrance that morning in the sitting room. Lilacs, while not terribly obscure, were not as popular as the ever-present rose water. Jack knew from his colleagues at the Gardening Society that quite a few gentlemen of the peerage used the proceeds of their sale of various species of roses to toilet water manufacturers to replenish the coffers of their once resplendent titles. The entire transaction was kept most discreet, as a member of the peerage would never admit to dabbling in such trade. But Jack had heard the talk at several of the society's meetings. Some members were even going so far as to produce their own hybrid versions of roses to attract a higher price.

Jack looked down at the mysteriously vibrating bundle of honey perfume roses in front of him and wondered what types of roses would work best in a crossbreed scenario such as that. He had heard one gent had crossed the plum variety with a heritage plant. The combination rioted in Jack's mind, but he had had the opportunity to smell the end result. And he would be the first to admit it was top rate. Both variety of roses were quite ardent on their own, and together the scent was unmistakable. Only one man had successfully crossed the two plants, and he had become quite a legend of the society.

Captain Edwards let out a terrific snort just then and exploded from the bushel of roses in front of him, his nose covered in the dirt and mulch of the rose patch.

"Find anything good?" Jack asked, but the captain only shook his head, tendrils of drool flying in opposite directions with a dollop landing on his snout. "I guess not then," Jack said and reached for the packet of basil he planned to put in the now ready pot.

Herbs were the one thing he missed during his days on deck. There was nothing so robust as a bite of fresh basil or a sprig of parsley, a hint of oregano, or even a fresh cup of mint leaves steeped in boiling water. He had dreamed of the day he could plant his own herbs and reap their bounty, but as he had yet to uncover all of the garden, he wasn't quite sure where he wanted his herb bed to go. For now, he would coax these seedlings out in a potted garden along the terrace leading from the house and hope something came of them. Herbs tended to be more forgiving, but Jack didn't trust the heat that had decided to so assiduously grip London. He looked about at the rest of his parched garden and hoped it would hang on just a little longer. Surely, the rain for which London was noted would come soon enough.

He had just patted the first of the basil plants into place when Reynolds appeared much as he had the day Lady Folton had first arrived, standing timidly just in the threshold of the doors leading into the house.

"My lord," he said. "You have a caller."

Jack felt a sense of deja vu and wondered if Reynolds was attempting some strange sort of amusement. Jack had plainly told him he would not accept visitors and here it was that, twice in one week, Reynolds was asking of his availability of callers.

"A young woman and her husband, my lord. She says you used to chase her sister with frogs."

Reynolds' face pinched at this last bit, but Jack could only smile, feeling genuine amusement for the first time since his life had been upended with the writ of summons declaring him a titled man.

"Kate," he said, dropping his trowel on his workbench.

In the time it took him to wipe his hands on his trousers and take a step toward the door, doubt fell on him like a marriage-seeking mama on a pack of eligible bachelors at a ball.

Katharine Hadley was here?

Although, the last time he had seen her, she was called something else. And Reynolds had just said she was here with her husband, so perhaps her name was different again. But the last time he had seen her, she was making a mad rescue of a gentleman from some trading baron's home in

Naples. He had left Palermo before learning of her success, but her sudden appearance in his home had him pausing.

Why would Katharine Hadley suddenly be here? It was true they had been acquaintances as youths. Her family had had an estate next to his father's estate in Heresford. But he had not associated with Kate's family since his mother and brother were killed, and he had been sent to live with Uncle Willy and Aunt Dottie. And to have her appear in his life again, not once but twice, in the span of months after so much time apart, unsettled him.

Jack watched Reynolds standing in the same place he had been, his face a mask of uncertainty much as it had been when Lady Folton had arrived.

A government clerk, she had said that first day. Did the government truly have female clerks that handled such matters involving a writ of summons? And then there was the way she had saved him yesterday, pulling him into the water with her. She was a slight woman, but she had had the strength to topple them both off the bank. In pieces, everything seemed quite normal, but when he stopped to think on it, the entire situation rang oddly to him. He looked again at Reynolds and then turned back to the captain.

"Captain Edwards, you'll come with me. I have need of your nose," he said and walked into the house.

* * *

"Perhaps he hasn't quite settled in yet," Kate said, as she kept her hands clasped firmly in front of her, afraid to touch any of the moving crates and haphazard array of shrouded furniture in front of her.

It was an odd room in which to have one's visitors wait, but if Jack had only just returned, Kate could forgive him the oddity. And to have a shiny new title set on one's shoulders didn't help the matter in the least.

"I reckon it's a lot to unpack at once," Thatcher said from beside her, and she looked up at him.

The faraway look that used to come with alarming regularity was in his eyes then, but with it came a degree of understanding. Kate reached out and squeezed her husband's hand. At her touch, the look vanished from his face, and he turned to her, smiling the smile that had made her fall for him.

"Yes, it is quite a lot to unpack," she said, and gave an inward sigh to their own unpacking that had not occurred.

They, too, had only returned from the Mediterranean to receive the missive from the War Office about the Duke of Lofton's death. Only it looked as if he hadn't died. Thatcher had a past with the Duke of Lofton that he did not often speak of, but Kate knew it ran deep. And as soon as they had understood the meaning of the missive, he had insisted they go to Lofton House, and that is where they had stayed these past weeks, waiting for whatever was to happen next.

And that was why standing there in the clutter of a house in transition was the best feeling Kate had had in days. They were finally doing something, and perhaps today, they would learn of something that would bring them closer to finding the truth about Richard.

But after a few minutes had passed and Jack had still not appeared, Kate wondered if he would show up at all. But then footsteps in the hallway signaled his approach, and Kate squeezed Thatcher's hand once more before letting go. It was time to do what they did best, which was spying, of course.

"Katharine Hadley," Jack said as he came around the corner, and Kate's immediate response was to snort a laugh at the picture he made.

His shirt was half untucked and browner than white from

the layer of dirt that encased it. His trousers were ill fitting and streaked with dirt as well. And if she weren't mistaken, there was a twig of sorts in his hair. But even more oddly, at his feet sat the oddest looking dog. He was longer than he was tall, and outrageously long ears fell on either side of his long snout.

"Are you laughing at me or the dog?" Jack asked, and he was once again the boy who had chased her and her sister about their country home.

"I'm not sure," Kate said. "But it's Katharine Thatcher now, Jack. This is my husband, Matthew."

Thatcher tipped his hat in greeting.

"It's nice to see you again. You look much as you did the other day, except drier."

Kate wondered if the look of hesitation on Jack's face was a result of him calculating who the gentleman was that stood in front of him, or if he sensed something greater afoot. Thatcher's words confirmed that Jack was indeed the man with Lady Folton the other day in the park, and that he was, in fact, a part of the assassination attempt. But what did that mean?

When Jack hesitated a little longer than she thought wise, Kate bent, calling to the dog as a distraction in case the latter should be true.

"Here boy," she said, just as Jack said, "I wouldn't--"

And the odd-looking dog launched himself at her. She would have gone completely over if Thatcher hadn't caught her and pulled her from the dog's overzealous greeting. As it was, she felt the run of slobber down her cheek and patted at it gingerly with her gloved hand. Thatcher handed her a handkerchief.

Jack had caught the dog around the scruff of his neck and was pulling him against his feet. With a command of sit, the dog put his haunches to the floor and stared up at her, the extra folds of skin about his neck falling backward to create an unusually grand collar about his head. He looked rather regal then.

"What is that?" Kate asked, pointing to the dog.

"It's a type of hound being bred largely in France these days. They're calling it a Basset type hound."

Thatcher laughed. "You spend years fighting the French and at the end of the war, you bring one of them home with you?"

Kate couldn't help but smile at her husband's accurate description.

But Jack shrugged. "I didn't bring him home with me. I more or less ended up with him after Uncle Willy didn't want him anymore."

Kate felt a stab of remorse at Jack's words, remembering the reason why her childhood friend had left her so swiftly and the subsequent letters of news from her mother telling of the deaths of Jack's aunt and then of his brother and father.

"I can't imagine Uncle Willy with a dog," Kate said to change the tone of the conversation.

"Precisely. I think that's how I ended up with him. After Roger died and all," he said.

Kate only nodded and, as if sensing her unease, Jack said, "Star gazer lilies."

Her brow wrinkled at his words, and she said, "Star gazer lilies?"

Jack nodded. "The scent you're wearing. It's derived from star gazer lilies, is it not?"

Kate nodded, her brow softening into quiet understanding. "You were always one to know his way around the garden," she said, and Jack smiled softly.

She turned to Thatcher. "I'm not sure if you recall our last meeting, but this is the gentleman that required saving."

Jack raised an eyebrow. "So you're the reason for Kate's distress at our last meeting. She was quite ferocious when she stampeded into our barracks."

Thatcher looked at her, and she looked away before he could see the blush she knew was imminent.

"I believe she demanded a ship of the fleet from a commodore in His Majesty's Navy during an active conflict. You must be very important, Mr. Thatcher," Jack said.

But Thatcher only laughed. "I reckon she just liked to cook for me."

She caught the look of disbelief on Jack's face at Thatcher's words.

"It's a strange world when one is involved in government work, is it not, Jack?"

Something flickered across Jack's face at her words, and she wondered what it was that had triggered such a reaction. She thought perhaps it was too soon after his return for her to speak so flippantly about the recent conflict, but there was something else about his gaze that reminded her too much of her father, Captain Hadley, when he pondered a particularly volatile situation.

And Kate knew what such a look meant. They had overstayed their visit.

"We see that you are still settling in, and we don't wish to keep you from your task," she said then, looping her arm through Thatcher's. "Perhaps you'll come to dinner soon."

The invitation was half-hearted at best, and Kate hoped Jack didn't sense the falseness of her brevity.

"Of course," Jack said in response to her question, but his eyes remained on Thatcher.

It was most definitely time to go.

"It was nice to meet you, little man," she said to the dog, who licked his lips at her.

She pulled Thatcher toward the door.

"Until then, Jack," she called and dragged Thatcher out of the house before he could speak his own goodbyes.

Once they were on the pavement outside, Thatcher adjusted his hat as the sun bore down on them.

"Something's not quite right there," he said.

Kate nodded in agreement.

"But the question is, what is it?"

CHAPTER 7

*H*ow was it that she had gone from a vast selection of proper evening gowns to having not a single thing to wear?

Margaret stood in the middle of her dressing quarters surveying the options of dresses for the Harrison gala that night. Her indecision irritated her like her unsettled nerves had irritated her previously. This was all Viscount Pemberly's doing. Before she had met him, she had been perfectly fine in her existence of both her quiet home in Mayfair and her work with the War Office. As her hand hovered over yet another gown before moving on to the next, she frowned at her own actions.

Had she been truly happy?

Had her existence before she met Viscount Pemberly truly been one of real living?

She thought of Timmons' repeated summons to the breakfast table the morning she had received the invitation for a stroll in the park with Pemberly, and she thought her existence would not have been called lively. It would have simply been termed an existence.

She selected a gown of muted blue hues, pulling it from her dressing quarters and flinging it across the bed in her chamber. She looked at the garment as it was splayed against the plain brown fabric of the duvet on the bed. The blue tones brought out the color of her eyes. That wasn't something she had decided, of course. It was what the dressmaker had said when Margaret had had the gown commissioned. This was the first time she wondered if the statement were true or if the modiste was just trying to make a sale. Margaret went to the corner of the room and rang the bell pull before settling down at her dressing table.

Her lady's maid appeared before she had finished selecting a plain gold chain from the table and an equally plain set of ear bobs. Bethany curtsied as she entered and stopped at the sight of the gown on the bed.

"Excellent choice for this evening, my lady," she said, but Margaret was too busy staring at her own reflection in the mirror.

The yellow gold clashed with the brown hues of her hair making her look like an odd rendition of a person's bodily functions. What made such an odd idea come into her head, she didn't know. Perhaps it was too much time spent in the company of Viscount Pemberly and his drooling dog. She ripped the ear bobs and necklace from her person, turning on the bench to find Bethany straightening the gown on the bed before turning to find appropriate underthings.

"Bethany," Margaret called before the woman could go into the dressing quarters.

Bethany turned, and Margaret realized for the first time that the young woman was quite pretty. Margaret had hired her from a home in Yorkshire, and the girl had said something about wanting to work in the home of an admirable woman.

"Bethany, I believe it's time to take out my mother's

jewels," she said before the words could get stuck in her throat.

* * *

CAPTAIN EDWARDS HAD ASSURED him that he did not look the part of a jester, but Jack did not feel the captain's assessment was trustworthy as he entered the Harrison gala that evening. The new jacket and trousers fit much too perfectly and chafed in the most inappropriate places. He regretted the ruin of his last uniform despite the obvious mob of marriage-minded mamas and their flock of waning daughters that stood before him. It was the end of the season, and by all purposes, the season was actually over once Parliament adjourned. The families still left in town were those with daughters they still needed to unload, having not secured a marriage proposal by the end of June. It had come to Jack's attention that the Harrison gala was the prime event at which this occurred. He had only learned this at Reynolds' obvious shock that his employer should wish to attend such an event.

But Jack had already told Lady Folton that he would be attending, and he had already accepted the invitation. He wouldn't mind backing out on the last part, but the first part was not something he would even think of denying. And so, in his too tight clothes, he stepped proudly into the gala and hoped not to drown under the girth of a smothering mama.

The room was packed, and Jack wondered if there was even space in it for him. The ballroom was grandly lit with a battalion of chandeliers and lamps, and the sheer glow of the satiny fabrics of the gowns crushed onto the dance floor. The room buzzed with the energy of music and too much drink, and Jack snatched a champagne flute from the nearest waiter hoping that joining in the festivities would reduce the volume of said festivities.

He had only been standing there a few moments when the first of the heads began to turn in his direction, and he knew the moment the marriage-minded mamas had seen him. So this was it. This was to be his end after everything. After numerous campaigns across numerous seas, his end would come in an overheated ballroom. And in that end for a perverse moment, Jack smiled. Perhaps his luck was finally changing.

And then the most peculiar thing happened.

It was as if there was a collective gasp from the crowd, and everyone stepped back.

This, of course, was not what actually occurred, but more that Jack sensed it happening like a deer sensed the approach of a hunter. His senses went on alert as he anticipated assault at any moment. His eyes made a quick scan of the doors and his nearest possibility of escape. And that's when he heard the voice of his assailant.

"Good evening, my lord," it said, sounding oddly like Lady Folton.

He turned, and his breath seized in his lungs, the movement so wrenching he thought he might lose the forgotten glass of champagne in his hand.

She was beautiful.

He had always thought her presence mystifying, but tonight she was just radiant. That was all that he could think, and in the time he should have replied with an equally polite greeting, he instead stood there, staring at her until she let out the softest sigh of capitulation he had ever heard. It was an odd noise, and one that seemed completely out of place. What was it she was resigning herself to?

"Pemberly, I feel I must tell you something before this night gets any odder for you," she said as if she could read his mind. "I'm a bit of an enigma in society, and my presence here tonight may have people turning their heads at you if we're seen together. I'll understand if you wish us not to converse any longer."

It took Jack a moment to understand everything that she had just said, and in that time, she turned as if to leave. And it was then that he, John Lynwood, commodore of His Majesty's Navy and most recently the Viscount Pemberly, committed the biggest social scandal of the season without so much as a single thought of awareness.

He grabbed Lady Folton's arm, stopping her progress.

Once again, Jack felt the collectively drawn intake of air from the occupants of the room, felt the lethal sting of their gazes, and yet, he felt nothing at all. His gaze remained locked on Lady Folton at his side, and in that moment, she softened, as if the edges of her very body lost their hardness and before him stood a woman, a real woman for the first time. She was dressed in blue, and her eyes sparked with the color of it. Jewels of dazzling greens and turquoise strung about her neck and ears, letting off a brilliance not to be outmatched by the light of her gaze.

And it was then that he knew he had to make her his.

"I don't think you're a clerk for the government," he said and nearly cut out his own tongue at the impossibly untimely pronouncement.

But Lady Folton did not hesitate. "Margaret," she said. "It's probably time you called me Margaret."

"Then I suppose you should call me Jack," he said.

Discarding the champagne glass on the nearest table, he turned back to her.

"Shall we dance, Maggie?" he said and pulled her onto the floor before she could object to the pet name or the dance.

* * *

"ONLY FOUR FOOTMEN? TRULY? AMATEURS," Nora scoffed while Nathan glared at her.

She was once more outfitted in what he was coming to call her gentleman's regalia, over-large hat, baggy jacket, and ill-fitting trousers, now made even more ill-fitting by her growing stomach. He had not wanted her on this assignment, preferring she stay in the safe keeping of Lofton House and Hathaway's merciless guard, but Jane had been right, as she always had been. If anyone were to sneak Nathan into the staff of a large gala like that which the Harrisons hosted, they would need Nora to slip him in at the right time. Her role was minimal, and he latched onto that to keep himself from imagining all sorts of horrors.

"I'll feel more at ease when you are tethered to home with a babe that must be fed regularly," he said, and enjoyed the scathing look she cast in his direction.

"Well, until then, I hope you can endure my expertise," she said. "Come along."

They made their way farther down the alley that ran along the backside of the homes in this part of Mayfair, their well-worn boots making no noise on the uneven cobblestones. They arrived at the Harrisons' mews just as the four footmen in question returned to the inside of the residence, whatever task they had been sent outside to complete having been necessarily finished.

Before the kitchen door could close, Nora slipped a hand between it and the jamb, successfully keeping the lock from clicking and allowing them both to enter the darkened, low-ceiling hallway that led into the bowels of Harrison Place. Nora gestured to a light at the end of the corridor and made the motion of eating. She pointed to the right and made the motion of fixing a cravat. That was where he would find livery then. Likely a laundry room or a place where the maids brought their mending. She gave him a beautiful smile, kissed him softly once, and slipped back out the door before he could say anything else.

He made certain the door was properly shut before moving deeper into the house. He slid to the right, stepping carefully into a room glowing with the light of the moon outside. It was indeed a mending room, and there on a rack on the wall was a footman's garb. He pulled it down, holding it against him to measure for fit. It would do for his night's endeavors. He shed his own clothes, rolling them carefully into a parcel before fitting himself into the footman's jacket and colors. He made his way deeper into the room, searching for where they might keep the shoes that needed shining. He was not disappointed when he came across a rack of newly shined shoes, and a pair that fit his feet perfectly. He turned about but before leaving the room as a newly outfitted foot-man, he slipped the bundle of his clothes through the only window in the room. He heard the muffled thud as it was caught on the other side of the sash. He imagined Nora disappearing into the night, his bundle of clothes in her arms.

SHE TRIPPED, the movement so subtle she doubted Jack had noticed.

It was a waltz, and as though she had never made a debut at Almack's, or anywhere else for that matter, society allowed her to partake in the daring dance due to her unusual circumstances. One need only whisper the Breck-enshire daughter in the general direction of a society matron, and the entire room would be abuzz as it was tonight. For a moment she pitied Jack and felt a twinge of guilt at his ignorance. She should tell him the truth. Or at least, tell him the truth about her parents. She had meant to do just that nearly a week ago in the park when they had nearly been killed.

Remembering that day in the park righted her senses once more, and she focused on the thing that had caused her to trip in the first place.

The Earl of Stryden, standing on the periphery of the dance floor and winking at her, in clear display of his defiance of a direct War Office order.

And winking at her.

Didn't he have a wife? Sarah something or other. Where was she?

"Is something wrong?" Jack asked, the warmth of his breath passing over her ear and utterly distracting her from the assignment at hand.

"No, nothing, perhaps I just need some fresh air," she said, and with quiet precision, Jack moved them in the direction of the refreshment table.

They exited the swirl of dancing couples, and he handed her a glass of lemonade before she could ask for one. Using the distraction of lemonade as an excuse to look back across the ballroom, the Earl of Stryden had disappeared. She swiveled her head from side to side, trying to take in the room at large but being rather vertically challenged, she either couldn't see much or couldn't turn her body enough to see anything at all without looking like she'd developed a tick.

"May I take your glass, my lady?"

Margaret turned toward the footman, extending her glass. It wasn't until the container left her hand that she let out an undignified squeak. She stared at the footman, his square features and angular jaw, his broad shoulders and incredible height. She swung around in the other direction, looking across the ballroom where the Earl of Stryden had stood winking at her, and then swung back to the footman who had just taken her glass. Surely, the Earl of Stryden was not dressed as some footman. Was he playing some horrid game with her? She would report him immediately if that were the case. But the footman only looked at her quizzically.

"Are you all right, my lady?" he said, his tone sincere, and she pushed away her ridiculous thoughts.

"Yes, are you all right?" this from Jack, who stood beside her eyeing her cautiously.

"Quite," she said, moving her lips into what she hoped looked like a smile. "Just a touch overheated."

She batted her hand toward her face as if to support her statement. Her ineffectual hand did little to move the air about her in the stifling ballroom, and for an instance, she really did wish for some fresh air. But somewhere in this ballroom, the Earl of Stryden was clearly defying orders, and she needed to find out why. He could put her entire assignment in jeopardy.

"My God, Lynwood, is that you?"

She watched as Jack turned and looked down nearly a foot and a half to the small man who approached them from out of the crowd. He was balding, the remainder of his hair creating a halo about his head. His over-large ears fanned out from his face, supporting a pair of weighty, round spectacles perched high on his nose. His graying whiskers sprung out from his face in a disarray that challenged the rest of his haphazard appearance of mismatched waistcoat and cravat all smudged with...dirt? But to make his appearance even more confusing, the little man was unusually fit. Margaret would even go so far as to say he might be one of those gentleman who attended Jackson's Saloon with great regularity.

"Sir Toby," Jack said, executing a neat bow to the little man beside him.

"Dear Jack, how good it is to see you again so soon. Hadn't thought we'd see much of the society this late into the season. How are those cone flowers faring?"

Margaret looked between the little man and Jack, wondering what sort of connection there was between the two, when she remembered the state of Jack's clothes the first time they had met. And what had Sir Toby said about a society? Did the two of them belong to some sort of gardening club?

"The cone flowers look exactly perfect next to the salvia. I am glad you changed my mind on those. You will need to come round when the garden is finished."

Sir Toby shook his head. "I am still amazed you managed to snatch that property up. You're not the first member of the society to covet that house for the garden. Are the rumors true though? Did the previous owners let the gardens go to neglect?"

Jack shook his head. "I'm afraid it was worse than that, Sir Toby. There was a great deal of experimentation underway when I arrived."

Sir Toby's face took on a measure of disbelief. "Unknowledgeable experimentation?"

Jack nodded. "Precisely that kind."

The little man actually cringed outwardly, screwing up his face and bringing his arms into his chest as if to defy Jack's claims. "Terrible, terrible."

Sir Toby suddenly seemed to notice Margaret standing there.

"Oh where are my manners. Who is this lovely young woman, Jack boy?"

Sir Toby bowed in her direction before Jack could say, "Lady Margaret Folton, I'd like you to meet Sir Tobias Hall, master gardener of the Gardening Society."

Somewhere in her distant memory she heard the familiarity of the name, but then, as was always the case when someone was introduced to her that may have at one time known her parents, Sir Toby stood straight up and began making his apologies.

"Oh my dear, I am so sorry," he said, taking one of her hands in his without her permission. "Your parents, dear. Such a tragedy. Very sorry, my dear."

"Quite," she said and plastered on her most polite smile. "What is this I hear about you being a master gardener?"

As she had hoped, Sir Toby's face changed from one of sadness to absolute joy.

"Do you not just love a pretty bouquet, my lady?" he said, and while he still held her hand, he pressed it against his heart.

Feeling more awkward than when she had been attacked in a drooling fit of kisses from a six-inch-high dog, Margaret looked to Jack for help, who quickly stepped in and extracted her hand from Sir Toby's grasp.

"Yes, Sir Toby is a master. Developed his own hybrid of roses."

Sir Toby interjected, "I called them Martha roses. After my sister."

Margaret thought she saw a tear come to his eye, but then his gaze averted, drawing to the other side of the room.

"Are those gardenias in an arrangement with hydrangeas? Oh no, that will not do. Who is in charge here?"

And with that, Sir Toby was gone.

"What an interesting little man," she said as Sir Toby walked away.

"Yes, indeed. With a rather unfortunate past I'm afraid," Jack said.

Margaret looked at him, a question wiggling in the back of her mind.

But then Jack asked, "What was that he was saying about your parents?"

She didn't have time to answer as the Earl of Stryden stepped in front of her.

* * *

"My LORD," she said, but he smiled at her, winking again to see if it threw her off as it did before.

"Ah, but it's your grace now, isn't it?" Alec countered and watched her lips go thin.

"I guess you're correct," Lady Folton said. "Again, I'm terribly sorry about your loss."

He could bet she was. He bowed to the gentleman beside her whom he now understood to be Viscount Pemberly, formerly Commodore John Lynwood. Kate had said he carried himself like a sailor, and it was evident in his rigid posture and proper stance beside Lady Folton.

"And I understand you are a viscount now," Alec said to the man.

Pemberly nodded as Lady Folton made to introduce them.

"Viscount Pemberly this is the Earl of Stryden - er..."

He smiled again at her simply, because her annoyance was giving him great pleasure. This woman held the secret behind his father's supposed death. He was not going to let her get away so easily.

"Or the Duke of Lofton as it were," she corrected.

Alec finished bowing to the viscount and upon straightening said, "I understand you're good friends with an old acquaintance of mine. Katharine Cavanaugh, recently Thatcher?"

Alec saw the moment recognition crossed the other man's face, and he pondered at what nerve he had struck. Was it merely Katharine's name as a friend from another life or was it something more meaningful than that? Was Kate right when she had indicated that their call on Pemberly had unnerved him somehow? Alec watched the man now and saw what Kate must have seen then. It was subtle, and if any other man had been watching him, nothing would seem amiss. But Alec knew the signs of a man carefully cataloging the moves of those around him.

Alec raised a hand to scratch at his chin. He saw Sarah detach herself from the crowd beside him at his signal, appearing like a water sprite from a pond.

"Darling, I've been looking everywhere for you," she said, stepping up to slide her arm into his.

He smiled down at her. "Right here, dear," he said with unnecessary drawl and obnoxious smiling. "My dear, allow me to introduce you to Lady Margaret Folton and Viscount Pemberly."

Sarah curtsied in turn to each of them. "Viscount Pemberly," she said, "Are you the gentleman commodore returned from the Mediterranean? I've heard rumors of your exploits on the front. Be a peach and tell me they are all true."

Alec almost burst into a fit of school girl giggles at his wife's overtly coquettish manner. Lady Stryden was anything but coquettish. Alec himself had applied the terms bullheaded, stubborn, and obstinate, but never coquettish. But at her words or tone, Pemberly seemed to dissolve, becoming once more a gentleman at a social gathering and not a military leader on point.

"I'm afraid they are just tales," he said to Sarah. "My adventures on the front were much more grand than the rumors they tell of me."

He smiled, but Alec saw that the smile did not reach his eyes. Sarah laughed in response to his statement, though, as the viscount likely anticipated.

"He's terribly modest," Lady Folton mumbled, and Alec observed that she, too, smiled falsely.

His mind traveled, wondering just what it was that Lady Folton and Viscount Pemberly were hiding. He hoped Nathan was having a bit of luck below stairs. Neither of these two was likely to give him anything. He laid a hand over the one Sarah had tucked into his arm, and she immediately raised a hand, calling to an invisible friend on the other side of the crowd.

"Nora!" she called. "Oh darling, we must go and speak to Nora. Come along, dear."

She tugged on his arm.

"Pleasure to have met you, my lord."

He scraped a bow and let his wife haul him away, dissolving into the crowd without so much as a backward glance.

"Those two are up to something," Sarah whispered into his ear when they were far enough away.

"I believe you are correct, lady wife," Alec said. "Perhaps there is a certain footman about who can provide something more than a watered-down drink."

* * *

MARGARET DID NOT REMOVE her eyes from the Earl of Stryden's back.

"Jack, would you excuse me a moment? I must see to some personal needs."

She didn't wait for his answer. Scooping up a handful of skirt, she followed the Earl and Countess of Stryden as they weaved through the crush of the ballroom. By the time she burst her way through a barrier of fashionably dressed ladies, she had lost sight of the pair. They could not have gone far in this crush though, and she made her way to the outskirts of the room, hoping to find a better vantage point.

What she found instead was a gaggle of matrons speaking at unusually loud tones about the new Viscount Pemberly.

"That's not what I heard," one of the matrons said. "I heard he's got himself some bit of fluff. Not here more than a month's time, and already he's settling in like a real rake. Thin scrap of a girl, too."

Margaret froze. Were they speaking about her?

"Bit of fluff? Is that what you call the daughter of the Earl and Countess of Breckenshire?"

The gasp of shock that sprang from the group was louder than any of the single voices. Margaret wanted to fade into the woodwork around her, but she thought that a physical impossibility.

"The new Viscount Pemberly has taken up with Lady Folton?" another matron said, and the matron that had made the pronouncement nodded in affirmation.

A third said, "How odd. I didn't think that girl had a heart."

The heart in question flinched.

"Not have a heart?" another matron interjected. "How can you say such a thing? Do you know what that girl went through? It's lucky she's alive at all. You should give her heart a little leeway in the matter."

Precisely, Margaret thought, and then she moved on, her eyes scanning the crowd for the Earl and Countess of Stryden.

She had only made it a few more feet when her eyes spotted him. It was only a glimpse through a smattering of people, but she recognized the width of shoulder and the turn of head. She sprang forward, pushing her way through the masses until she fell out into a corridor. She looked about her, but he was nowhere to be seen. There was only a footman disappearing farther along the corridor.

Margaret turned about to go back inside when she stopped, swiveled on her heel, and chased after the disappearing footman.

It wasn't the Earl of Stryden she'd seen. It was the mysterious footman who looked like him. And what a remarkable resemblance it was. Surely, that couldn't have been accidental. Something was not right with this Black family, and Margaret was going to find out what it was. The family should have been in mourning, not prancing about at galas. And now a footman that looked like an earl. How could they possibly even suspect that the Duke of Lofton was not dead? They couldn't. There must be something else at work here. Would the duke's own family make an attempt on his life?

Margaret rounded the corner where the footman had disappeared only to see him pass through a door at the end of the connecting corridor. She pursued, her slippered feet carrying her swiftly down the hall. Coming to the door, she opened it, carefully peeking inside to find a flight of stairs leading down. She supposed this was one of the servants' staircases leading to the working floors below. Easing herself back out, Margaret looked about her. There was no one to witness her movements, so she plunged through the door, nearly falling down the first stair in her haste to get through the door and close it before anyone should see her.

The staircase was only dimly lit, and she picked up her skirts to keep them from making noise against the wooden treads. Stepping carefully, she made her way down the stairs, stopping to pause on the bottom most step. There was nothing but darkness around her. She peered from side to side, hearing voices and seeing lights in the distance. Listening carefully, she surmised that the kitchens were to her left. Only the sound of scurrying steps came to her right, and she decided that there must be corridors connecting the kitchens with other rooms in the house via underground passages. Having never had the cause to travel below stairs in a house this size, she had only her intuition to go on. She turned left, heading in the direction of the kitchen.

If anyone should stumble upon her, she need only inform them that she was a guest, and she had gotten lost on her way to the retiring room. An excuse such as that would be plausible, and if she acted silly enough, believable as well. Perhaps a kind footman or maid would believe she was into her rum punch a little too much. Margaret had no idea what rum punch was, never having consumed the stuff in her life, but it sounded good.

The voices were getting louder now, and she heard the sound of rattling cookery. Footmen carrying trays came into her vision, and she saw them scurrying from the kitchen like rats in a subterranean tunnel, fleeing up staircases to the rooms above. She kept her body pressed close to the wall, hiding in the shadows. As she drew closer, she saw the footmen were picking up trays from a central banquet that stood just outside what must have been the kitchen.

Scullery maids refilled glasses as quickly as they could, and Margaret watched in fascination as the trays disappeared and were replaced with new ones. But the earl's lookalike was not among the footmen. She waited in the shadows for several moments just to make certain she did not miss him, but he never returned to the station. Ducking back down the corridor from whence she had come, she made her way to the stairs that would lead up to the corridor that would return her to the ballroom.

She had only gone a few steps when a man stepped in front of her from one of the connecting corridors. The movement was so sudden, a hand flew to her chest in surprise, and she let out a soft, "Oh."

The man looked at her through hollow eyes, his features wane in the dim light of the corridor. She took a step back, taking in the rest of his contrasting appearance. The man was rather young, she realized, but his sparse hair, sunken eyes, and hollow cheeks made him appear much older than he was.

"I do beg your pardon," Margaret blurted out. "I seem to have gotten myself lost."

She waited to see what the man would do, and she took the time to both listen to the sounds of the kitchen behind her, faint now that she had traveled some distance down the corridor, but close enough that they may hear her scream should it become necessary to do so, and also to take in the sight of the man's uniform. For although he clearly wore one, she noticed subtle differences about it that suggested he was not a servant of the house. Something in her tickled with suspicion, but the man only raised an arm, pointing to the other end of the corridor.

"You'll find the staircase to the main floor just there, my lady," he said.

She did not wait for further instruction, simply bowing and giving her thanks before moving down the corridor. She did not give the unusual man the pleasure of a backward glance, however, and found the stairs, carefully making her way up them. She was less cautious about making noise now, for if there were someone in the corridor above, it was unlikely they would think it was anyone other than a servant.

Opening the door slowly, she peered into the torchlit hallway beyond, its colors muted in the glow of the candles, reds fading into browns. She stepped onto the rug, closing the door behind her with a soft click.

And that was when Jack spoke from behind her.

"I think it's about time you told me what's really going on here."

CHAPTER 8

*J*ack kept his grip on Margaret's arm as he pushed their way through the ballroom to the opposite side where large doors opened onto what Jack hoped were some sort of gardens that would provide them with a touch more privacy for a conversation he was anxious to have.

The air was no better when they breached the doors to the garden, but he sucked in a lungful anyway, the need to breathe clawing at him. The terrace was littered with couples, nearly as crowded as the ballroom they had just left. The heat was stifling, and he was sure everyone was trying to get more air. They would need to go farther into the gardens. It was the only thing to be done.

He took the stairs quickly, not pausing to see if Margaret kept pace with him. He heard nothing from her as he took the path to the right at the bottom of the stairs, pulling her deeper into the night. At the first alcove he found, he tucked them inside, setting Margaret on the stone bench that set back in its depth, shielded on all sides by tall shrubs.

"This will have to do," he said, crossing his arms and

staring down at the mysterious woman who had suddenly appeared in his life only a week ago. "Who are you, Maggie?"

She looked up at him, the moon lit her eyes like a beacon through the darkness, shimmering pools of iridescent blue.

"I'm a spy for the War Office," she said plainly, her voice neutral and without feeling.

He stared at her. "I beg your pardon?" he finally asked, because he wasn't sure how one responded to that statement.

She did not give any indication that his question annoyed her. Her hands remained softly folded in her lap, her entire person unnaturally still.

"I am an agent for the War Office. A spy to be precise. I'm in the domestic unit, so I cover--"

"How much of this should you be telling me?" he interjected, visions of him being captured and tortured for information running through his mind.

She shrugged, the motion so hideously casual in a moment that was anything but, that he felt his stomach roll. How long had she been a spy, as she had called it, that the topic had become mundane?

"I shouldn't tell you any of it, considering you're the mark. Civilians usually don't handle that type of news well, so we try to keep mum on it. Especially around the subject in question, but you seem adamant to know. So there it is."

He swallowed. "Did you say mark?"

She nodded. "Yes, I'm afraid someone is trying to kill you."

He sat down on the bench next to her. "I beg your pardon," he said for the second time in so many minutes.

"Someone is trying to kill you," she restated, turning her head to look at him. "I'm sorry to say you were granted a title created by the War Office as a ruse for luring out a suspected mole, an assassin that has been targeting agents of the Office."

"An assassin?"

Margaret nodded. "He's already taken action against a very valuable agent. Fortunately, he was not successful in his attempt."

Jack looked at her. "Valuable agent?" he asked.

Margaret seemed to think on it for a moment before saying, "Richard Black, the Duke of Lofton."

Jack's mind traveled back to the awkward exchange between Margaret and the Earl of Stryden, presumably the newest Duke of Lofton.

"Richard Black is not dead then," he said.

Margaret shook her head. "No, the assassin failed in his attempt, but the War Office has prevented him from learning this information by hiding Richard Black in a safe house."

Jack raised an eyebrow and said, "Safe house? Is that really necessary?"

Margaret looked at him. "The assassin also tried to run you over with a curricle."

Jack straightened. "That wasn't an accident," he said, referring to the incident in the park.

She shook her head. "Of course not. We were just lucky to have been so close to the Serpentine. I'm not sure what I would have done if we hadn't been."

Jack looked at the woman beside him, her stature so small she looked as if a strong breeze would carry her away in the night.

She had saved his life.

"Thank you," he said, his voice going soft.

She smiled that unfeeling smile she had that never reached her eyes. "You needn't thank me," she said. "Only carrying out orders."

He watched her face, at once an unforgiving mask, blocking him from seeing anything occurring behind it, like breathing or thinking or emotion. He wondered again how long she had been doing this to make her so objective.

His mind suddenly flashed back to the moment she had stepped beside him in the ballroom. The crowd, seeming to sense she had arrived, drawing back from her as if she were some sort of pariah. What had happened to Lady Margaret Folton? What was so awful to make her this shell of a person that she was now?

Jack bent forward, his elbows on his knees. "So now there's someone trying to kill me?" he asked, to restart the conversation.

Margaret nodded. "And the War Office is doing everything in its power to protect you. I can assure you--"

"You," he interrupted her. "The War Office doing everything in its power to protect me is them sending you. Why is that?"

She looked at him out of the corner of her eye but otherwise, didn't respond to the question. He wondered suddenly how much of the truth she was telling him, how much others knew of her that he didn't. He had been away from London and the happenings of the ton for too long. He didn't know the first thing about this woman sitting next to him, and it seemed the rest of bloody society knew everything. At least he knew she'd never had a dog before in her life, but that she wasn't afraid of them, if her reaction to the captain's intimate greeting were any indication.

"Yes, they sent me. As an agent for the domestic unit, it's my--"

He had to cut her off again. "I think I would prefer it if you didn't explain to me the inner workings of a confidential government agency. Perhaps just the highlights in the event that I'm kidnapped and tortured, I can honestly say I don't know anything."

This brought that odd smile to her lips once more, and he felt unspeakably proud for having done it.

"Very well," she said. "Then simply yes, the War Office sent me to protect you."

He tilted his head at her. "You must be incredibly skilled to have been the agent chosen."

She watched him for a moment, and he had the oddest sense that she wished to say something. But in the end, she didn't. "I believe it was just luck," she said.

It was his turn to smile. "I'm not really an admirer of luck," he said.

She cocked her head. "I suppose I can understand. Given your current circumstances."

Jack blinked at her. "I'm sorry?" he asked.

She gestured a hand between them as if to highlight the situation.

"Luck brought a target to your back, so I assumed that was why you were not an admirer of luck."

He let her statement sink in, his mind racing through the events of his life that all involved a degree of luck that had brought him something, taking away others in return. He stared at her, her face pale in the moonlight, a perfect heart shape from her wide eyes to her small mouth with its unusual smile.

She was right.

His entire life had been filled with events that had kept him alive out of sheer luck and nothing more. His intelligence and wit had gone unused as life handed him things from a mysterious well of gratitude. But now luck had brought him something else.

A death sentence.

He felt happiness begin to bubble from deep within him.

"Oh my god," he whispered.

And then he did the only thing he could think of in that moment.

He kissed her.

To say she was startled would put it mildly. She squeaked in surprise, her hands flying up to his chest. But she didn't push him away. The kiss was unlike the one they'd shared in the sitting room of his townhouse. This was something much more intimate, more robust with feeling, making a connection that ran deeper than the casual touch of lips. This was a kiss, and it drove a pillar of heat straight into the bubble of happiness percolating in his core.

And then Margaret fell off the bench.

One moment she was angled beneath him, their bodies connected in the most basic way possible, and in the next moment, she was gone. He faltered for a moment, his body leaning into the space that Margaret had so recently occupied. Catching himself on the edge of the bench, he looked over the surface to where she now lay sprawled on the garden floor. The blues of her dress shimmered against the black of the surrounding ground and shrubs.

"I do beg your pardon," she said. "I don't believe I was quite ready for that."

* * *

She thought she should feel mortified, or at the very least embarrassed, but instead, Margaret felt nothing at all. She lay on the ground, mercifully dry and not spongy with dew or rain, and felt nothing. Or nearly nothing.

Whilst kissing Viscount Pemberly, she had felt rather astounded if that were the word for it. She enjoyed the kiss. She actually enjoyed it, and it was probably this enjoyment, which had caused her to fall off the bench.

The kiss was not like that of the previous one in his sitting room. That was a mere touching of bodies, and that alone had been enough to send her quite silly. But this. This had been much more. And when she had leaned back, trying to get a breath, or perhaps space or strength to absorb it all, she had fallen. It was as simple as that.

And so now she looked up at this man who had suddenly stirred in her feelings she had thought long vanished, or by chance had never had the opportunity to blossom in her at all, and wondered if perhaps he would kiss her again. Kiss her even though it appeared she disappeared at so much as a hint of advance from him.

He reached down a hand to her. "I suppose you weren't," he said, as he pulled her back up on the bench next to him.

She noticed how he was careful to put space between them, his arms crossing his chest as soon as he released her hand. She wondered why she felt a pang of loss at his distance, but she knew him to be quite right about it.

"Am I to assume you are glad that someone is trying to kill you?" she asked, referring to his obvious elation at her words.

"Oh quite," he said, nodding his head. "I have been waiting a very long time for my luck to turn. It appears you have brought me the very thing I've sought the entire of my life."

She frowned at him. "That seems an odd thing to be delighted over," she said.

He frowned, too. "I suppose it is, but if you knew the history of it, you would agree," he said.

She recalled their conversation from the park and his long litany of people he had lost in his life while he seemed to continue on, moving, if not advancing, through life while he lost those that mattered to him. But to base such a thing on luck seemed absurd.

"Do you honestly think luck is what has brought you this far?" she asked, watching his face in the moonlight.

His arms remained crossed over his chest, the stance drawing attention to the white of his cravat.

For the first time, she took note of his dress and suddenly blurted, "Did you hire on a valet?"

His mouth had been open, and she noticed the hesitation, as her next question seemed to arrest his line of thinking.

"Yes on both counts, I suppose," he finished with a nod.

She sorted his answer in her mind and realized he both believed luck had brought him to his current station, and that he had indeed hired a valet. She pondered which was of more import.

"And you've paid a visit to your tailor," she said, choosing the subject of more practicality.

He grinned. "Or rather my new valet's tailor. Having not been in London for quite some time, I went on his recommendation."

Margaret tilted her head at that. "It seems rather odd to just accept a newly hired servant's word on such a matter."

Jack shook his head at her confusion. "I've known the man for quite some time. He's only just returned from the front, and I hired him on as soon as I received word he was in London."

Margaret felt a ripple of unease at this. She wasn't sure why, but the notion that someone from Pemberly's past had suddenly returned to London and was now working under the viscount's roof seemed rather unwise to her. She couldn't place her finger on a specific reason, but her instincts as an agent were rankled.

"I see," she said. "Did you have the honor of serving with this man?"

Jack nodded. "He was with me through the majority of it. Mayhew by name. I'm glad to have him back in London."

Margaret rolled the name over in her head, committing it to memory so she could have the man researched by a clerk at the War Office. She couldn't be too careful. An attempt on Jack's life may have been taken before the arrival of this

Mayhew fellow, but she could never be too certain of Jack's safety.

"What do you think it is if it wasn't luck?" Jack asked then.

It took Margaret a moment to ascertain of what he spoke. She recalled what had started this conversation and blinked her eyes at the shrubs just beyond his head.

"Any number of things really," she said, her eyes continuing to blink as her mind raced for something more plausible than a bit of fluff. "Perhaps your ingenuity, your intelligence, your determination. Those are all things over which a person has much greater control. Those are the things that would determine a man's outcome in life. Luck just seems so frivolous and inconsequential."

Jack frowned at her, the rays of moonlight striking his wide mouth at an odd angle.

"But that's just it, I'm afraid. I've used none of those things to acquire my station in life. It just always seems that I happen to be in the right place at the exact moment I am supposed to be there."

She thought he meant to say more, but she interrupted. "Did you choose the navy?" she asked.

Jack turned to her, his eyes reflecting in the darkness. He nodded but didn't say anything, so she continued.

"Then how can you say you've reached this spot without having made that decision? Surely, that must stand for something."

"What spot? Here in this garden? I believe I dragged you into this garden, which was my own decision, but I don't see how that's relevant."

She felt herself grow the slightest bit frustrated with the conversation when she noticed Jack's mouth had tilted up slightly at one corner. She hesitated.

"My lord, are you jesting with me?" she asked.

Jack's mouth spread into a wide smile now, his eyes crinkling at the corners.

"Is it such a terrible offense? My attempt to make you laugh."

The air seized in Margaret's lungs.

Laugh?

She could not recall the last time someone had made her laugh this readily. More, she could not recall ever feeling the need to find something over which to laugh. It just wasn't there. She felt her conscious dipping backward, falling and falling into the blackness that made up her body, and when she pulled it back, it was empty, just as it always was.

"No, it's not a terrible offense," she said, but the words only came out as a whisper.

Jack's smile melted from his face. It was slow and deliberate, and Margaret felt a flash of regret. She had not meant to make his happiness disappear thusly. She scrambled for something to say, feeling the need to speak now more than ever, and more importantly, the need to speak something that would bring the smile back to his face.

"When I was a child, my au pair used to have a series of puppets. She would put on shows, and I would laugh."

The sentence was mundane and lacking detail, but she was in such a rush to speak, it was the best that she could do. Jack stared at her and for an awful moment, she thought she had failed. That he would remain withdrawn because of her careless words and forgetful tone. But then Jack's eyes changed. Even in the moonlight she could see the way they darkened in hue even as their movement began to search her face. What they were hoping to find, she couldn't be sure, but she held still as if a movement from her would break the spell.

And then finally Jack said, "Puppets? When you were a child?"

Margaret nodded slowly, the motion matching the path of his searching eyes as she tried to catch his gaze.

"Yes, there were three of them. A mother and a father and their little girl. My au pair would make up stories about them. They were a family."

She realized with a jolt the words she was saying, the way her tone remained flat, void of feeling and substance. She swallowed.

"What happened to you, Lady Margaret Folton?" Jack asked, his words little more than a whisper.

Margaret wanted to answer him. Knew that she should answer him. But suddenly, her tongue lodged into the roof of her mouth as her mind floated to a memory she had long locked away. Sitting on the floor of her nursery, watching her au pair move the puppets about in a pantomime, the sound of her mother's slippers on the floor behind her as she came into the nursery to say good night to Margaret.

And then with the snap of a twig in the surrounding shrubbery, the memory vanished, and the acumen of a spy overtook her body. Her skin prickled in awareness, and she straightened, her ears straining for sound. Footsteps along the path in their direction, one plodding and one prancing.

"Someone's coming," Jack said, before Margaret could speak the words herself.

She looked at Jack, thoughts racing through her head. If they were seen sitting on the bench conversing, the gossip would go about that they had been alone together. But worse, the gossip would say they had been alone together and doing nothing but talking to one another. Margaret recalled the sudden hush in the ballroom as she had entered earlier that evening. Recalled how painful silence could really be.

She sucked in a deep breath, grabbed Jack by the lapels of his jacket, and planted her mouth on his.

* * *

JACK FELT the shock nearly knock him off the bench.

It was the third time his lips had met hers, and he could safely say it was by far the most awkward. The joining had been done in haste by a, presumably, inexperienced Lady Folton. But the contact was all the same. Pure heat cascading through his body like a waterfall of sparks, splintering as they struck only to ricochet further through him. The feeling was astounding, and his mind quickly lost track of everything going on around them.

Her hands gripped his jacket, drawing him into her, and he took advantage of their positions, his arms coming around her to pull her more fully against him. Their hips connected on the stone bench, and thigh matched thigh. He felt the heat of her burn through the many layers of clothing, and he suddenly imagined himself combusting on the spot. Later, poor Harrison was likely to find a pile of ash where once two lovers had conspired. The very word, lovers, spiked an idea in his head, a notion he wallowed in as her lips continued to push against his.

Lovers.

The thought was ridiculous. She was an unwed, virginal woman of society. He did not debauch virgins, and he most certainly was not interested in marriage.

Marriage.

Now the two words combated for space in his head, neither of which he wished to give room, but as the heat of her touch threatened to consume him, he let another word slip through his mind.

Courtship.

This word was equally as dubious as she had just very clearly indicated that her chosen profession was that of government agent, the very nature of which precluded intimate relationships. Or so Jack assumed. But perhaps he could convince her otherwise.

He shifted on the bench, taking control of the kiss even as he felt her bend beneath him. He made certain his arms were carefully around her this time, not wishing to lose her once more to the ground. He angled his head, the movement relinquishing the pressure from her lips, and he felt the instant she understood that he was now kissing her. Her acceptance rattled him, the heady sensation of control rolling through him. She trusted him to do this. She trusted him with her body in such an intimate, carnal fashion. It was more intoxicating than the feel of her lips under his.

He moved his mouth slightly to the right, nipping at the corner of her lips. He heard a soft gasp of surprise, and he would have smiled at her response if his mouth wasn't busy. But he couldn't linger long in one spot, and dipping his head, he traced kisses along the line of her jaw, past her ear, to that sensitive spot of delicate skin right behind her ear. He pressed a single kiss there, feeling the connection of his lips to the delicate flesh. And that's when he felt her tremble. Like a wave passing over the still surface of a pond, the shiver moved from her shoulders down her back and through her legs. He felt it along the length of him, and it dared him to take the kiss further.

So he did.

He pulled the lobe of her ear between his lips, gently biting. The gasp that followed was neither soft nor quiet, and for a moment, he worried they would be caught.

But then he realized that was the point of the entire thing. It was to be caught. Once more he felt a smile tug at his lips, but instead, he moved his mouth downward, following the long line of her white throat. He tipped her back, his arms holding her up against him. He realized she had lost her grip on his jacket at some point, and her head fell backward, exposing the column of her throat. He took advantage of her position and dipped his head to suck at the place where her neck met her bared shoulder.

She made no noise, but her body jerked suddenly in his arms, and he did smile then, a simple, feral smile of pure conquest. It was the first time he had felt such exhilaration when he was with a woman, and it startled him to know they were both still fully clothed.

But he had little time to revel in the moment as voices suddenly carried over the night to his ears. And what they said was enough to douse any ardor.

"It couldn't be her," a feminine voice hissed through the night. "They say she's made of stone."

This exclamation was followed by a series of shuffling noises and the snapping of twigs. He shifted Margaret in his arms, slipping one hand up her neck and burying his grip in her hair, securely holding her head in his hand. He cared nothing of upsetting her hairpins, only the need to hold her more closely as the hurtful words continued their journey over the night air to him. He only hoped he distracted Margaret enough for her not to hear them.

"I heard she makes children cry when they see her, because she's so empty of life," this was a very male voice that had not seen the benefits of a successful adolescent growth period, its pitch high and whiny.

Jack moved his lips to take Margaret's mouth once more in a kiss so passionate he felt the moan as it generated in her chest, passed through her neck, and spilled onto his own lips. The sound was more satisfying than physical response, and he deepened the angle, sealing her lips with his.

"Surely it can't be her. Who on Earth would want to kiss a woman so deadened?"

Now Jack felt the flutter of eyelashes as Margaret likely opened her eyes.

So he grabbed her breast, his hand carefully cupping the supple mound through her gown. Jack opened his own eyes to watch her reaction and was pleased to see her eyes fly open, her mouth go slack as his name slipped through her swollen lips.

"Jack," she whispered, and in her now opened eyes he saw nothing but desire, and he smiled, knowing it had worked to distract her from their onlookers' careless words.

He took her mouth once more, as he kneaded her breast with his hand.

"Oh my," came the dual response from the shrubs beyond them, and then, "Do you suppose the stories about her aren't true after all?"

Jack took that moment to trace the line of Margaret's lips with his tongue. Her hands dug into his back, the pressure welcomed as he shifted her in his arms, drawing her nearly onto his lap.

"We shouldn't be watching this," came from the shrubs.

Sitting upright now, Margaret's head fell so that their foreheads touched. Jack withdrew long enough to look at her face, to understand something of what she was feeling. She may have started this charade to distract intruders, but he had most certainly taken it over in a powerfully intimate way. He wanted to ensure that what he was doing didn't upset her. But when he pulled back, she squirmed, her hands flying up to grab him, pulling his lips back to hers. The sound that came from her throat was something of a growl, and their onlookers commented from the shrubs.

"But I cannot look away from this, Saunders," said the female onlooker.

"I understand, Felicity, but really, it's so--"

"Passionate," said Felicity, her voice wistful.

Jack smiled, his lips lingering on Margaret's as he heard

the intruders trample away from them, disappearing deeper into the Harrison gardens.

Long, agonizing seconds later, Jack finally lifted his head, but he kept his hands around Margaret's waist, liking the feel of her weight against him. She sat fully upright, her shoulders square and her neck long. But her eyes remained closed, and her breath fluttered from her in staggered gulps. Her hair had come undone and fell softly around her shoulders. He picked up a strand and ran it through his fingers, letting the silkiness of it fall away.

"Maggie," he finally said, when she still had not opened her eyes.

"I'm afraid we may have just caused a scandal," she finally said, still not opening her eyes.

For a moment, Jack felt a pang of regret at likely ruining her reputation, but then she did open her eyes.

Desire.

Her eyes were filled with desire, and passion and what Jack thought might be happiness. And the feeling of regret vanished.

"I must apologize, Lady Folton. I meant no such offense," he said.

Margaret shook her head. "I think you might have," she said, and Jack smiled.

Margaret reached up, her hands searching for the fallen clumps of hair.

"Oh dear," she said, "I don't think I shall be returning to the ballroom this evening."

Jack frowned at her. "I am sorry about that. I think I may have gotten carried away."

She smiled at him, looking up at him from under her lashes as she concentrated on gathering her hair behind her head.

"Again, I do not think you feel any measure of apology, my lord."

And then to his amazement, he saw the slightest twitch of her lips as if she wanted to smile but perhaps didn't know how.

"Do you think this gossip will raise the suspicions of my would-be assassin?" Jack asked, feeling a sudden jolt of concern that quickly doused his euphoria.

Margaret finished with her hair and regrettably stood, leaving his body exposed to the sudden rush of night air.

"I'm not certain actually. The set-up of the War Office prevents agents from knowing much about one another. I cannot be certain that the assassin knows I am an agent at all."

Jack frowned but stood. "Perhaps it would be best if we were to stay apart for a while." He said the words even as they stuck in his throat.

He saw the flash of despair cross her features, and he wanted to assure her it was for no other reason than her safety. But before he could speak, she nodded her head, her shoulders squaring themselves into the woman he had come to know as the government agent.

"You're quite right, Jack. We should try to keep our behavior above suspicion. Perhaps I shall call on you in a fortnight. Do you have any reason to leave your residence before then?"

Jack shook his head, thinking of the mayhem that was his garden. "No, I think I can remain safely indoors for the duration."

She nodded in response. "Very good. Remain in your townhouse at all times, and do not accept any callers. No matter who they are."

Her tone was so very abrupt that Jack smiled at its

disparity to the woman who had so recently melted with passion in his arms.

"Understood, my lady," he said, and then offered her his arm.

She shook her head at him. "I shall not be leaving by way of the front door, I'm afraid," she said.

Jack frowned at her.

"I don't want to risk being seen with you," she said flatly, and picked up her skirts to move when she must have noticed the look on his face. "Oh, I did not mean it like that," she said.

He laughed, the sound and the feeling ridiculous in a conversation so wrought with tension, but it was there nonetheless.

"How is it that you plan to leave then?" he asked.

Her eyes sparkled in the moonlight.

"That is a state secret, I'm afraid," she said and, before he could say anything else, she disappeared into the night.

CHAPTER 9

*J*ane swirled the brandy in her glass, watching the light from the lamps fracture in the liquid and against the etching of glass surrounding it.

"So she followed you," she said then, looking up at Nathan who sat across from her in the Lofton House library.

Nathan, Nora, Alec and Sarah had only just returned from their mission at the Harrison gala to uncover any information they could about the relationship between Lady Margaret Folton and Commodore John Lynwood, recently Viscount Pemberly. Nathan nodded now at her statement.

"But why would she follow you?" Jane asked.

Sarah replied with, "Perhaps it is the resemblance between Alec and Nathan. She seemed startled when Alec approached her."

Jane looked about the room at the assembly of so many talented agents for the War Office and remembered a time when it would have been just her and Richard. With a sudden inhale, she thought of Richard and wondered where he was just then. For three horrible days, she had believed him dead. Believed he had left her until she would see him again in the next life. But now, knowing he was alive some-where, in danger somewhere, this pain was even worse than thinking him dead.

For she could not help him. If she made the wrong step, took the wrong path of action, she could put him in greater danger. And then mayhap, he really would be dead. She swallowed.

"Does Lady Folton not know of Nathan?" Jane asked as Sarah shook her head.

"The Office is very careful about not revealing the identi-ties of agents. Even more so since that disaster in '12."

Jane narrowed her eyes in question.

"It was a matter of possible treason in the war against the American states. The Office is much more stringent about the secrecy of agent identities."

Jane frowned. For the past few years, she had been assigned work on the front mostly, and left Office matters to Richard. She hadn't realized how polluted the place had become. How the need for confidentiality had become so critical to an agent's safety.

"If she doesn't know of Nathan, then why would she follow him?"

"Because I could be the assassin," Nathan said from where he stood, one hand resting on the mantelpiece of the dormant fireplace, much in the stance of his father.

"Why?" Nora asked.

Jane looked over to the young woman now as she sat in the chair nearest the fireplace, her hands absently rubbing her rounded stomach. With a pinch, Jane wondered if Richard would be back in time to see the birth of his first grandchild, and with this thought came swiftly the possi-bility of Richard never returning at all. Jane pushed the thought away and concentrated on the matter at hand.

"I obviously look unusually like Alec and therefore, may

be a bastard son of the Duke of Lofton. Perhaps I'm seeking my revenge for being cast aside."

Alec raised his glass as if to gather their attention. "For one," he began. "You are a bastard son. And for two, why would you seek revenge on the War Office? It would seem the matter would be taken much more closely to the family."

Nathan seemed to ponder this, as Jane said, "Unless he knew how much the mission of the War Office meant to Richard."

Sarah picked up this line of thinking. "And then perhaps not only get his revenge on the man who cast him aside, but put into question his very contribution to the War Office effort."

"Well, I reckon that would look mighty awkward."

Jane looked to the other side of the seating area where Thatcher sat, his hand entwined with Kate's, as his wife sat next to him. The gesture was one so familiar to Jane that she felt the sting of tears at the back of her eyes before she could force it away.

"While that's a lovely theory, I think we're missing the point of what this means," Nora said, and all eyes turned to her as she continued. "If Lady Folton knows what happened to Richard, knows that someone tried to kill, or maybe is still trying to kill him, then Lady Folton is the only one who can help him."

"And her attention is focused on the wrong man," Alec finished as Nora nodded in approval.

"Bullocks," Jane muttered, sitting back in her chair. "What do we do about that?"

"We can't allow Nathan to lie low. He's a valuable member of this team," Alec was quick to say, and Jane smiled at the brotherly bond that had the younger sibling defending the older one.

"Whoever it is that is behind this entire thing is trying to kill Viscount Pemberly. That much is clear," Kate said.

"So we focus on Pemberly?" Alec asked.

"I reckon I could take to following them, but I'm afraid I'm rather noticeable," Thatcher said in his overtly American accent, his characteristic charming grin on his face.

"No, I suppose that would not be prudent," Jane said. "But you could be useful in other ways," she added.

"How so?" Thatcher asked.

Jane smiled. "No one at the War Office knows who you are. We could use you if we ever need someone to gain information from another agent."

Thatcher's eyes crinkled in confusion. "You mean if we need someone to spy on a spy, Duchess?"

Jane smiled harder. "I mean precisely that."

Thatcher grinned even more, and his wife quietly rolled her eyes beside him.

"Then I think from here we need to make a plan as to how we are going to focus on Pemberly," Nathan said.

"And keep the poor bastard alive," Jane added.

"$\mathcal{I}$ think your suggestion of the begonias is accurate, Captain," Jack said, fisting his dirty hands on his hips as he surveyed the recently planted flowers in question. He had added them to the formerly tropical garden bed to add a dimension of height variation, and the small, flowering plants worked perfectly along the border of the bed. The captain dozed in his flowerpot, not offering a comment.

He let the sweat ripple down his back, soaking his already ruined shirt to pool in the waist of his trousers. Tilting his head back, he scanned the horizon for the telltale line of gray clouds that hovered in the distance. Spotted just after dawn that morning, he had a reasonably high degree of hope that the heat wave that had held London in its grip would soon break with the coming shower. If only the gray clouds would move closer, but instead, they merely hung on the horizon, taunting him with their proximity.

He would work on the various rose bushes that afternoon, as long as the rain kept at bay. He let his hands fall as he dropped his gaze to the surrounding sprays of roses.

Typical varieties there, thankfully, and Jack wondered why the previous owner had not taken a gamble on a new strand of the flower. Jack thought for a moment that perhaps Sir Toby would part with one of his beloved Martha roses plants, but as soon as the thought came, he pushed it away. Sir Toby was terribly protective of his Martha roses, growing them only in a single bed in the garden of his London residence, not even allowing the gardeners of his vast estate in Cornwall to touch them. No, Sir Toby would not be parting with a single sprout of the flower.

But perhaps Jack would have the chance to view them once more. Sir Toby had presented them once at a meeting of the Gardening Society, and Jack had immediately been taken by their unusually strong scent. Sir Toby had used two very fragrant strands of roses to create the Martha rose, and it was evident in their pungent, exhilarating aroma. Jack drew in a deep breath as he stood surrounded by three different varieties of roses and smelled absolutely nothing.

"I suppose their beauty will have to suffice," he said to the captain, who let out a groan as he adjusted his squat body in the flowerpot.

Jack bent to retrieve his basket of gardening tools, swiping at his forehead as he did so, but before he had time to straighten, the captain rolled himself out of his pot, the crockery falling away as the hound took off for the house like the fires of hell licked at his tail.

"Not again," Jack murmured as he dropped his gardening basket and took off in the direction of the fleeing hound.

When he reached the front drawing room, Jack paused on the threshold, his chest heaving as he tried to catch his breath in the thickness of the humidity.

"Now put your rump on the ground, or I shall not be giving you this tasty morsel," Margaret said to the captain.

Jack took in the scene with a measure of amusement. The

hound sat slightly askew on his haunches, head tilted up in unending adoration for the woman who pointed a very directing finger in his face with one hand and held a hidden treat up in the fingers of her other hand. The treat looked to be a morsel of ham, and Jack watched the drool begin to pool along the captain's jowls. He waited for streams of the stuff to start dripping in the direction of the worn carpets, but before the flooring could be put in danger, Margaret bent and carefully placed the bit of ham into the captain's mouth.

No chewing occurred when the morsel entered the hound's mouth, and Jack watched as the dog swallowed quickly and looked up expectantly.

Margaret shook her head. "What did it taste like?" she asked, her small mouth pursed into a look of disappointment.

"Like the beginning of a very delicious treat. Only he's wondering where the rest of it went," Jack said.

Margaret looked up, and her frown deepened. Jack felt the hairs on the back of his neck go up.

"I presume you bring tidings of ill news as it has only been ten days since the Harrison gala, and we had agreed on a fortnight of separation."

It had been a brutally long ten days, and Jack hoped she would not suggest they remain apart for any substantial length of time again. Like, for instance, a day or an hour. His body knew the taste of her kiss, the feel of her every curve, the sounds she made when he pleasured her. And for ten days, there had been no outlet for this knowledge. No way for him to expend his desires. And now, just the sight of her in his drawing room was enough to quell much of the restlessness that had consumed him for the past ten days.

"I'm afraid it is, in fact, ill news," she said, reaching into the reticule dangling at her wrist.

He watched as she pulled a folded square of parchment

from it and held it out to him. He waited a moment before approaching, worrying what might be on that piece of parchment that had brought her to him earlier than her stated fortnight. For he was certain, Lady Margaret Folton was not one to change plans when it came to an assignment from the War Office.

He took the parchment and opened it, steeling himself for some kind of startling missive or correspondence revealing the name of the assassin. But it was worse than that.

"It's a gossip rag," he said, looking up from the newssheet in his hand.

Margaret nodded. "It's a very popular rag, and I'm afraid it's mentioned us."

Jack quickly looked back down at the newssheet, his eyes scanning for any mention of their names.

"It's been ten days since the Harrison gala. Surely, our not entirely covert romantic interlude would have been leaked and bantered about before now."

Margaret shook her head, and he caught sight of the movement out of the corner of his eye just as his gaze found their names. Or rather, what were likely their names. For he doubted any other attendants at the Harrison gala could be called Lord P., formerly of the Sea, and Lady M., thought dead. He frowned at the last moniker, and once more felt a niggle of guilt at not knowing more about Margaret when very clearly everyone else in the godforsaken ton did.

He quickly scanned the paragraph and looked up. "This rag blatantly accuses us of being lovers."

The sentence felt odd to say even to him, but it was the fact of the matter. The news sheet did not only articulate the embrace they had shared in the Harrison gardens, but it went on to fabricate all manner of lies, including that the pair had been lovers since Jack's return to London.

"Well, the fact that you advised your butler to always

allow me entrance, should I call upon you, does support that accusation." She said this with a perfectly straight face, not a muscle moving to betray the sarcasm he knew lurked beneath her words.

"I thought it more convenient if you had free access to the residence," he returned, but she frowned almost immediately.

"I advised you not to accept callers," she said.

"I haven't accepted any callers. I've accepted you," he said and smiled, which brought a rise of color to her face.

"Very well, but what are we to do about this matter?" she said, gesturing toward the rag.

He looked again at the parchment in his hand. "I'm not certain if this is a good or bad thing really," he said and looked up at Margaret. "What do you think the assassin will think of us being lovers?"

He noted then the crispness of her hair, pulled tightly in a bun at the nape of her neck, the stiffness of the collar of her dress, enclosing fully about her neck, so terribly unlike the fashions he had seen on other women in the town, but something he suspected Margaret desired. However, he also wondered if the woman was at all affected by any of her environment, for she looked exactly the same as she had the day she had called upon him in the guise of a government clerk. He wanted to chuckle then, realizing that she had never lied to him. She was a government clerk, just not the kind he had thought she was.

And in that same thought came the understanding that he had thoroughly ravished this plain, unassuming woman of incredibly small stature standing before him, and yet she still looked as virginal as the day she had appeared in his life. Even now, he could take her in his arms and have his way with her on one of the various dust cloth-covered sofas in the room, and she would likely appear just as unaffected. Something about the notion upset him, but he didn't have time to over think on the matter, because just then there was a noise in the distance, and Margaret frowned.

"Was that thunder?" she asked.

And then the captain began to bay.

MARGARET DIDN'T KNOW whether to look at the poor hound, standing on all fours at attention, his head thrown back as monstrous bays erupted from his tiny body, or to follow Jack about the room as he pushed through cloth-covered furniture and moving crates to get to the nearest window shrouded in moldy, dust-covered draperies. The sight of a once again not entirely dressed Viscount Pemberly making his way over moving crates and around tables and chairs was a compelling sight, especially given that she knew exactly what it felt like to be pressed against that body, but the obvious distress of the dog had her on her knees, her arms flailing uselessly at her sides.

She had not a single clue what to do for the poor animal as his bays grew increasingly worrisome and robust. Suddenly, there was a terrific crashing noise as the sound of a tremendous clap of thunder met the sound of Pemberly pushing aside a set of drapes just as the dog yipped one final time and threw himself under the nearest sofa, squeezing his large, short body under the furniture.

"Captain Edwards!" Jack called sharply.

Margaret looked up at him, her heart racing at the sound of his scolding voice, but when she saw his face was folded into a frown, she frowned as well. Jack stood encased by the light of the now exposed windows, the sky having suddenly turned black with the menace of a tremendous summer storm. Her first thought was that she hoped Lofton was all right in his rickety room in White Chapel and her second being that she hoped it broke the massive heat spell that had gripped the City for so long. And then she noticed what a striking figure Jack made standing there as lightning lit the sky behind him. She had now seen this man encased in moonlight and illuminated by lightning, and she felt an odd thrill race up her spine.

But quickly, she thought of poor Captain Edwards and turned to the sofa under which he had sought cover.

"What should we do for him? He sounds so scared," she said, staring at the spot where he had disappeared.

"He's not scared," Jack grumbled from his place by the window.

She looked up at him in puzzlement. "He's not?" she asked.

Her familiarity with dogs was on a level with her familiarity with ostriches, so she couldn't say what the baying had meant. Only that it had sounded terrifyingly awful.

"He thinks the hunt is on. The thunder reminds him of gunshot. He's taking to the brush to flush out the hare," Jack finished on a murmur as he began picking up the dust cloths and looking under them. "The last time he did this it took me six hours to find him. He's relentless when it comes to the hunt."

Jack straightened, his fisted hands on his hips. "With a storm this size, I'm likely not to find him for days."

Just then a crack of lightning split the sky as thunder shook the panes of the window behind Pemberly.

"And I am likely not to make it home," Margaret said, not realizing she had spoken aloud until she saw Jack's face sink into a mask of resigned disbelief.

"I think this is somehow bad for your reputation," he said, looking about them as if to indicate that they were alone in the house. Except for Reynolds and Mayhew, of course. "But it will do wonders for the writers of this news sheet," he said, holding up the parchment he still clutched in his hand.

Margaret had the sudden and complete understanding that her reputation mattered very little. When she had first seen the paragraph about her encounter with Jack in the Harrison gardens, she thought of the implications it would have on her assignment. She had not thought at all of its implications on her reputation. This should have been cause for her to reflect on her priorities, but it just did not matter.

She needn't play by society's rules. She hadn't been forced to do so since her parents' death. When that had occurred, everything had changed for her, and with it, all of the rules. So she smiled at Jack to ease his conscience.

"I assure you, Jack, you needn't worry about my standing in society. My reputation will be just fine. And it's not as if I am here for scandalous reasons." She looked again at the parchment in his hand. "Well, perhaps that may be the truth, but society may see it differently."

Thunder sounded then as if to support her point, and her mind fled back to that night, recalled the feeling of being lost in Jack's embrace. And for a moment, Margaret remembered the real reason she had come today. She had to tell Jack the truth.

That night in the Harrison gardens had been unexpected and unusual, and Margaret thought it unlikely to happen again. But the fact that it had happened at all was concerning. The intruders on the scene had had the right of it. She was dead inside. Empty and emotionless, and she had no right being in Jack's arms.

He deserved a woman who could love him, who was capable of feeling love. Who was capable of feeling anything. She had to tell him. She had to tell him what had happened to her, and then he would understand.

"I am merely an acquaintance stuck in awful circumstances," she said. "And you are offering me shelter. That is quite understandable."

"Then I don't suppose I could convince the Lady Folton into helping me find a hound on the hunt for a hare?"

She smiled. "I think perhaps you could," she said.

He smiled. "All right, Maggie, let's be off then."

She frowned at his retreating back. "It's Margaret," she muttered, but there was no one there to hear her.

* * *

"Do you think we should try another scrap of food? Perhaps some cheese this time?"

Jack looked over to where Margaret sat on the floor in a rather unladylike sprawl of limbs, skirts and discarded dust cloths.

"I'm not sure what Cook has in the larder," Jack said absently as another clap of thunder sounded from beyond the walls of the room.

In the nearly four hours since Captain Edwards had first disappeared under the sofa in the first floor drawing room, their search had taken them to the second floor sewing room. At least, that's what Jack believed it to be from the remnants of furniture in the room. There were some small tables and chairs that implied a work area for ladies at their embroidery, but it was the loom and the spinning wheel that really suggested the room had been used for endeavors in textile.

"Do you think he will eventually surface?" Margaret asked, picking herself up from the floor, carefully avoiding dust cloths and scattered crates.

Seeing the crates reminded him that he really needed to unpack at some point. He had been lucky that, with the hiring of Mayhew, at least his personal possessions had been seen to. But it was all of the family memorabilia that Uncle Willy had sent to him that remained in boxes, as if waiting for something Jack knew was coming but could not name.

In the weak light of the room, Jack had a sudden vision of Margaret unpacking the crates in her position as lady of the house. The notion was ridiculous, and he pushed it away, but even as he did so, he wondered if it truly was ridiculous.

"He eventually does, but I worry about him being lost amongst all of these...things," he finished when he could not dredge up a better word for the disarray that surrounded them.

Margaret nodded as she found a seat on one of the sofa-shaped blobs of white cloth. Dust rose up about her, but she didn't seem to notice. Jack struggled to his feet as well, abandoning his search under the stack of tables in the corner of the room. In the dim, he made his way carefully over to Margaret. He paused beside what looked to be a lamp. Carefully tugging at its cover, he pulled the dust cloth free to reveal a brilliantly gaudy lamp of pink and orange crystals and turquoise-painted plates of metal.

"Dear God," Jack said before he could stop himself.

"Indeed," Margaret said from the sofa.

Jack rummaged in the drawer of the table on which the lamp set before finding a flint. He lit the lamp without mishap, and light flooded the small space of the room they occupied. There wasn't much to be seen, and the light did little more than solidify the shapes of stored objects.

Jack thought briefly of attempting to make it to a window to see the condition of the sky beyond, but the way was a shambles of crates and furniture. So instead he took a seat on the sofa next to Margaret.

"So we're lovers then," he said, by way of restarting the conversation they had been having before the captain's untimely departure on the hunt.

Margaret looked at him. "It appears that way. I'm not sure if that aids us in our deception or not," she said.

"What deception would that be?" Jack asked, returning her gaze.

The lamplight angled across her features in such a way as to light her face just under her eyes, casting her gaze in shadow. He wondered what she was thinking, as they sat there discussing the topic of being lovers.

"The one where we seek out the assassin while attempting to appear as innocent members of society," Margaret said.

"I am an innocent member of society," Jack said and watched as Margaret's face folded into a small smile.

"I suppose you're right," she said. "I apologize. I'm just used to working with agents of the Office. It's hard to remember when you're with civilians sometimes."

Jack barked a laugh. "I'm hardly a civilian," he said, and a kaleidoscope of memories from the war spilled through his mind in an inarticulate blur of sound, smell, and sight.

"I suppose that's correct," she said, and in the indirect light of the lamp, he saw a ghost of something flash across her face.

The look, if it had really been there, was gone before he could discern it. He thought of their conversation in the park the day they had almost been run over by the assassin in the curricle and wondered if she thought on his terrible telling of his black history. It came to him then that she could have been killed that day, too. And here both of them sat, quite calmly, in the dim sewing room listening to the chain of storms pass them outside, hoping a hound emerged from a dust cloth-covered piece of furniture.

She could have been killed. She could be killed yet, and all because he was the one to receive the wrong title. A title created specifically to ensnare the focus of this assassin. She could be killed because of him. A parade of faces pranced before his mind's eye. His mother and brother, his aunt Dottie, his father and his last brother. All of them gone while he still lived.

He stood up and paced to the other side of the room. Or rather, walked around crates and furniture and paced when space allowed. But he suddenly needed a distance between him and this compelling mixture of a woman that had suddenly taken such a demanding grip of his life.

"So do we use this scandal to our advantage?" he said, hoping to keep the conversation on one of strict business.

"I believe we do," Margaret said. "It may work to our favor."

"For instance?" Jack prompted.

"It would explain my presence. I'm not exactly a believable prospect for marriage for a viscount, and our acquaintance would be questioned. But if I were merely your lover, then our association would go unnoticed." She seemed to rethink this. "Or rather, it will go unnoticed by the assassin. The rest of society can choose to do with it what it will."

Jack had stopped pacing at her mention of marriage, and a slice of pain raced over him at her conclusion that she was an unlikely candidate for the position of his wife. He studied her as she sat there, her small frame swallowed by the sofa, and he thought her not unsuitable at all. He rather liked the idea of her as his wife.

It was frivolous of him to stand there in his sewing room and ponder the likely qualities of his future wife when he had no intentions of marrying in the near future. Whether it be Margaret or some other woman, perhaps a debutante left-over from the most recent season. The thought of another woman brought an acrid taste to his mouth, and he swallowed.

"Then we use this gossip to our advantage, and it explains

our relationship without alerting the assassin that you are, in fact, working to protect me," Jack said.

His pacing had brought him back to the sofa by way of loom, spinning wheel, and crates of unpacked books. Resuming his seat on the sofa, he picked up Margaret's hand, placing a delicate kiss on the backs of her fingers. He didn't know what had prompted him to do it, but he had the sudden urge to properly introduce themselves to one another, and placing a kiss on her hand seemed to fit the moment. But when his lips touched her skin, the flash of heat seared him, striking deep into his bone where it held without sway.

He looked up at her face, turned in his direction now so he could see her eyes.

And that was when he saw it. That hidden burst of passion within her. Passion so far buried, he was certain she didn't know it was there or even when it surfaced, so secretly there in her eyes only he could see.

"That settles it then," he said, his voice thick as his body responded to her nearness, responded to the unrealized desire in her gaze. "We're lovers."

He watched her lips part, saw the glint of lamplight as her tongue peeked out to moisten them. His body tightened at the sight, the air thinning in his lungs.

"I'm so sorry," she whispered.

For a moment, he didn't understand what she had said. His body was strung so tightly with wanting her that he didn't understand anything at all. He only wondered why she was still not in his arms, why she was sitting there, the fires of passion banked in her eyes as something overcame them, as something drove out the heat in her.

"I need to tell you the truth, Jack," she said, and with her words, the fire in him died.

* * *

"WHAT IS IT, MAGGIE?"

She wanted to correct him on her name, saying that it was Margaret, but a part of her liked the sound of it. His voice calling her a name she had never been called before, not even as a child. But even more it didn't seem pertinent right then as her body betrayed her, yearning towards something she didn't know how to understand.

"I watched them die," she whispered, her eyes focused so intently on his face that she didn't really know what she was saying. "I watched them die, Jack. They tortured them, and I watched. And now, I can't feel anything."

Jack's face showed nothing of what her words meant to him, how they affected him, but she felt the pull from deep in her core.

She had never said those words aloud. Never. Not once. Not when the agents retrieved her from the chateau in Lycée, not when she had arrived in London, not when she had been placed in her uncle's home under the care of a governess who worked as an agent for the Office. In those first few months, she had said nothing for she had not been required to. The story had traveled swiftly, word reaching the remaining agents in France before the week was out. The Earl and Countess of Breckenshire had been killed, and the French operatives had forced their young daughter to watch. Margaret had not needed to say anything, because the tale was all too horrid and real.

And then having said nothing, her silence persisted until no one spoke of it any more.

Until now. Sitting here with Jack, she had spoken the words that had stayed inside of her like a treasured secret for more than twenty years. She waited for Jack to say something, but he made no noise that he had even heard her. But then his hand slipped from her wrist, sliding down until his fingers entwined with hers.

"I think you need to start at the beginning, Maggie. If you can," he said.

His voice was so firm, she thought she might have been a child he was scolding. But it wasn't that. His voice was firm in reassurance, and with his grip on her hand, words poured out her.

"I lived in France as a child," she said, the sentence rather banal.

Jack nodded, indicating that he was listening, but he did not try to push her on. For a moment she let her mind drift, remembering the streets of Paris as they walked through them, she holding her mother's hand. All that she could recall was the scent of lilac water. Her fingers moved to the place at her neck where she now dabbed lilac water every morning as part of her toilette. She didn't know why she did it, only that when she had grown old enough to assume her inheritance and become an independent woman, she had adopted the mannerisms of her mother, whether consciously or subconsciously. But her fingers stroked the place where the lilac water lay.

And then Jack was lifting her fidgeting hand away from her throat. He took her hand into his, sliding his fingers between hers until their palms rested together. He held both of her hands in his lap. She looked at him, the lamplight striking golden lightning into his dark hair, much as lightning streaked the sky beyond their secluded haven of the sewing room.

"What happened, Maggie?" Jack asked, his voice still firm and, while coaxing, it did not prod her to continue.

"I don't feel anything, Jack," she said, her voice cracking on the words.

Her pitch was low, and tears filled her voice while none sprang from her eyes. But Jack only held her hands in his.

"I can't feel anything," she continued. "They died, and I saw it, and I didn't cry, and I can't cry, Jack, because then they'll know I'm weak, and they'll try to hurt me." She shut her mouth on the words, feeling them strike against the curl of her tongue as she stared at this man she had only known for a few weeks, the only man who had made her feel anything.

She expected him to mock her, shake his head at her, stand up and leave her sitting on the sofa with her nonsense, but he only sat there holding her hands until he said, "No one is going to hurt you, Maggie. I'm here."

The words were so simple and yet their meaning blasted through her. Jack was there. He was sitting next to her. She could feel the heat of his body where it connected to hers, but--

"I'm supposed to protect you," she whispered.

Jack moved his head in agreement, and she thought he would speak, but instead he only kissed her. It was a kiss unlike the one in the garden. That kiss had been about fire and fervency. This was a touching of lips, a caress of skin that told her he was there when no words could. He leaned back much too soon, and the words spilled unhindered from her lips.

"My parents were the Earl and Countess of Breckenshire. They were agents of the Office and were stationed in Paris. They were discovered to be spies. The French government had them tortured and killed. And they made me watch."

It had been such a tumultuous, altering event in her life and yet, she had relayed the entire tale in but a few simple sentences. She didn't think it possible. Her voice wobbled, but her eyes remained eerily dry.

"I can't feel anything, Jack. I don't know why. I thought it would come back after a time, but there's just nothing left inside of me."

Jack's eyes narrowed, and she thought he would ask something of her. But his eyes cleared, and she knew the questions would come later.

Instead, he said, "Do you trust me, Maggie?"

The words washed over her like the gentle stroke of assurance and quiet calm. She felt the shiver of her past slide through her body before lifting away.

"Yes," she said, and then she said nothing more as Jack kissed her.

CHAPTER 11

*J*ack kissed her softly at first, the weight of her words still pressing in on him.

He had finally learned what everyone else had known about Lady Margaret Folton, and he wished he had never found out. While the ton was not one to take matters of impropriety lightly, it was stunningly capable of glossing over the missteps of one of its members. So when the mere presence of Lady Margaret Folton had caused the entire tone of a gala to turn sour, he had known that it was something more than a misstep in her past.

He only wished he had been wrong.

But he knew words could not fix what was so obviously wrong. Her crumpled voice and lack of tears told him something her words never would, and thus, it could not be fixed with words. This was not something that one treated with sympathetic words and pats on the hand. This ran deeper than that.

The scars were not visible, but they were there. And he somehow knew that talking could not heal them. Words could not even begin to touch them. He was certain that words had been said at the time it had happened. She had been a child. Surely, an adult had taken her into custody. Had told her that everything would be all right.

But everything hadn't been all right. His mind flashed to the puppets and a little girl watching their play as she laughed. It was the last time she had been happy, she had said.

No, words could not fix this. But he knew something that would.

He had to make her feel again. On some basic level, he understood that. It was not words of reassurance. It was not an understanding that she was an adult now. That she was safe, and if her performance in the park were any indication, she could fend for herself.

But this was not about that. This was about trust. She needed to feel trust again. Perhaps, trusting in herself, she could begin to feel again. And only something physical could make that happen. And Jack could be the one to make it happen.

Only he wouldn't do it without knowing that she trusted him first. Her revelation was still settling into him, but something in him knew that he had to act now, while the confession was still raw on her lips. He didn't know why, but he sensed that now was the time to plunge forward, for if he didn't, he may not have the chance again.

So he kissed her, her lips soft against his, his touch restrained. He recalled the moment on the bench when his excitement over the realization of his turning luck had overwhelmed her, and she'd fallen from the bench. Now he would practice restraint. Now he would show her what sensual lovemaking was like.

He trailed his lips to the corner of her mouth, his tongue darting out to take the barest of tastes. He heard a resounding gasp of surprise from her, and he kept going, blazing kisses along the line of her jaw as if sipping from her, drawing in the very essence of her desire. Finally, he reached that spot behind her ear, the cool, pale skin beckoning his kiss. But he backed away, and he watched her eyelids flutter in confusion. But before she could fully open them, he pressed his lips to that spot, felt the shudder course through her body, and he reveled in her reaction to him.

Jack moved slightly, drawing her closer, pivoting so that he leaned into her. Her head slid along the back of the sofa until it fell loose, her neck exposed to him. Pausing again, he just looked at her. The graceful lines of her throat, the careful angles of her face. In the dim light of the lamp, she looked almost ethereal, as if she were not quite of this earth. And in that moment, he almost believed it.

For his good luck had never brought him a woman quite like Margaret. Had never brought him anything that may bring him pleasure the way she did. But it was something more than just fleeting pleasure that he found in her arms. It ran deeper than that, hotter than that, and he feared that it may never go away. Looking at her then in the flickering light, he asked himself if he had ever truly imagined taking a wife. And then on that thought came another. Could he live without her? Could he live without Margaret?

Without answering himself, he leaned forward, licking his way down the long, white column of her throat. She exhaled, and he felt the rush of her arousal as it shimmered into him. Her hands gripped his upper arms, and he knew she hung onto him, clinging as if she might fall if she let go.

Reaching the delicate curve of neck melting into shoulder, he scooped her onto his lap, tilting her all the way back into the crook of his bent elbow. She rested there, safe within his grasp, and he felt her response almost immediately. Her body went loose about him, her hands coming free of his arms to slide inward, trailing along his chest until they pressed into his core. He felt the heat of her skin through his shirt. He thanked whatever deity it was that made him garden in only a lawn shirt for he did not think he could take the disappointment of so many layers of clothes between them.

His lips had reached the high collar of her dress and, carefully adjusting so he could still hold her upright, he reached behind her to undo the upper most buttons of her gown. For a brief moment, he thought he felt startled hesitation in her, but he pressed a kiss to her lips, his touch gentle but firm, and the hesitation he thought he had felt disappeared. The collar fell away as he slipped two buttons free, and he reached back around to her front, pulling the fabric away until he could kiss the very spot where her neck gracefully traveled into the curve of her shoulder. He pressed further, licking his way to the curve of her shoulder and back along the line of her collarbone.

It was then that he suddenly realized the height of his own passion, so absorbed in pleasing her that he had not noticed his own body's reaction. He burned for her, his skin growing damp with sweat, his heart beating a staccato in his chest. He needed more than just kisses, and yet he knew that he could not push her this time. That he could not take more from her than she wanted to give.

But he yearned for it, and in his mind, he pictured a time when he would have more. But not now. Not today. Today was about teaching Margaret that she could trust herself. Today was about showing her that it wasn't that she couldn't feel, for time and again she had shown him that she could. It was that she wouldn't let herself feel. And though it may brand him as a tyrant, he would give her no choice in the matter. He would give her something that she had no ability to deny.

Turning once more, he slipped out from under her,

settling her back against what may have been the cushions of the sofa under the dust cloth. Slipping his arm from beneath her, he sat up, waiting until she blinked up at him.

When her eyes were fully open, he said, "Do you truly trust me, Maggie?"

She didn't answer right away, her large eyes simply blinking as if she couldn't quite get him into focus. But she did not pull away from him. She did not recoil. She simply lay there, her face relaxed, her chest rising and falling with her labored breath.

"Yes."

The word was only a whisper, but Jack took it as a solemn oath, moving out from the fall of her skirts until he knelt on the floor, the worn carpet cushioning his knees against the hard floor.

Outside the storm raged, and as Jack slipped his hands beneath Margaret's skirts, gripping her ankles and feeling the small bones pressing into his palms through the silk of her stockings, a clap of thunder sounded somewhere in the distance, and its sound reminded Jack that this was really happening. That he was here with Margaret, in a cluttered, forgotten room in the townhouse he had purchased as the requirement of suddenly being a viscount. It should have seemed surreal, but his ears strained, hearing another clap of thunder and the pelting rain against the windows behind the shroud of dusty drapes that clung to the outer walls of the room.

And it was real then, and Jack moved his hands up Margaret's legs, the curve of her calves filling his palms, tracing the rigid outline of her knees, until he found the delicate softness of the skin of her inner thigh. His hands stilled, only his fingertips moving to take in the unbelievable softness of that place on her body.

Jack moved quickly then, a surge of lust rocketing

through his body so unexpectedly that he flipped her skirts up without ceremony, displaying her sprawled legs for him. Her stockings were pure white and outlined every curve and nuance of her legs. The garments were tied at the top with a delicate white garter, and his fingers trailed over the bows. He tugged at the string of one of her garters, letting it fall loose about her thigh, and her stocking sagged, but only in the slightest, given her position.

His gaze traveled to the still untouched garter, and again, he felt something unknown tug at him. And he left that garter still tied in the pristine bow that he imagined Margaret tying off that morning when she dressed.

Again, an image flashed in his mind, and he wondered if he would ever have occasion of seeing Margaret dress in the morning. If he would ever have the pleasure of waking up next to her. The image was of such banal and normal happenings that certainly occurred to many fortunate people every morning, and yet he coveted that picture like a thirsty bed of hydrangeas coveted water, only perking up after having their fill of the liquid.

His eyes traveled up the length of her to find her watching him, and he felt another surge of lust spike through him. She did not look away when he caught her, and it fueled the fire within him. This diminutive, carefully controlled woman did things to him no other woman ever had.

"Do you trust me, Maggie?" he said, and this time her consent was firm and concise.

"Yes, Jack," she said, and in her eyes, he saw no hesitancy, no wish to suspend their activities.

So Jack reached up, shifting her skirts until they pooled about her waist. And then he saw her. All of her. The very center of her womanhood. His hands still gripped her skirts, and he let his hands fall, his fingertips gliding over the tops of her thighs, the crease between leg and torso, and he felt her jerk against him. He looked up, but her eyes were closed now, her head pressed back into the cushions, her chest heaving.

He smiled and continued to caress her, his fingers traveling so close to her core before drifting away. She squirmed now, her hips coming up off the sofa, driving her into him, but he pulled his hands away, using them to hold him up as he leaned over her.

Nestling his lips next to her ear, he whispered, "Patience, darling."

And she moaned, her hips coming up then, pressing her hot center against his aching groin. The movement very nearly undid him, and he sat back, quickly resting once more on his knees between her splayed legs. Finally, unable to bear the torture himself for any longer, he leaned forward and pressed his mouth to her.

He felt her sit up, her hands plunging through his hair and gripping his skull.

"Jack," she said, the name a strangled cry from her lips.

He reached up, pushing her back down against the cushions, never releasing his kiss from her intimate mound. He felt her fall away, and he turned his attentions to the intricate folds of her.

She was wet for him, and the realization startled him with how much it pleased him. Carefully, he licked his way into her delicate folds, tasting her wetness, pulling her scent into him. She continued to squirm, her hips moving beneath his attentions, and he reached up, gripping her in his hands until she stilled. And then he moved, lapping his tongue gently at her opening.

"Jack," she said again, but he wouldn't let her distract him, moving his tongue in and out of her opening, slowly, deliberately, and he felt her legs squeezing in on him, as if she wanted to bring him closer but didn't know how.

He would be closer one day. He knew that. But today was not about him. Today was about her. Right now, he wanted to show her everything that she could feel. He backed away, moving until his mouth found the very spot where her thigh met her body, and he bit down on the sensitive joint.

"Oh my God, Jack, no," she said, sitting up once more and pushing now against his head. "Jack, it's...it's..."

She never finished the sentence, and her hands were soon pulling his head into her, driving him to lick the flesh he had just tortured. He moved to the other side, his teeth scraping at the sensitive flesh.

"Please, Jack."

Her voice was nothing more than a whimper now, and he knew that he had her. She was coming apart in his arms, and he knew he had only to touch her, and she would find the very thing he wanted her to realize.

Shifting again, he settled once more on her mound, his tongue separating her folds until he found her sensitive nub. Her legs came up, the slippers of her feet striking his shoulders, and he thought she may have tried to say his name again, but it only came out as a strangled moan.

He caressed her with his tongue, lapping at her nub in slow, painful strokes. Her body tensed all around him, her muscles contracting until they centered into the spot he tormented.

"Jack," she said one final time, and then she came apart.

He felt her climax hit her, and not in some basic, sensual way, but in the pounding of her slippered feet against his back, the spasm of her release gripping her until she no longer had control of her limbs, and Jack made a note to remove her slippers the next they made love.

And watching her then as she realized her completion, he knew there would be a next time. He had only begun to teach Lady Margaret Folton how to feel.

* * *

AWARENESS SEEPED into her like red wine staining a white tablecloth. There was something soft against her back, soft yet slightly stuffy as if left untouched for a great length of time. Pulses of light flicked across her eyelids as if she lay beneath a lamp. Somewhere came the pulse of a distant thunderclap, and with the noise, she remembered where she was.

Her eyes snapped open, expecting to see Jack looming over her. But instead, she saw...nothing.

She sat up, using the back of the sofa to pull herself upright and quickly scan the room. But Jack was nowhere. The sewing room sat much as it had when they had first entered it in search of Captain Edwards. Dust cloth shrouded furniture scattered between piles of unpacked moving crates. She looked at the drapes, hanging in dismal silence over the windows, and she wondered what time it was. Looking about the room, she could see no clock nor hear anything ticking within her vicinity.

Slowly, she pulled back her thoughts, remembering why she was there and what was happening. With a rush, her memories of Jack paraded through her, and heat blossomed on her face. Her hands went to her cheeks as if to suspend her reaction to her wayward thoughts, but it was no use. Only then did she become aware of a stickiness between her thighs, a dampness in her most private parts.

"Jack."

She said his name as if in blame, but blame for what she didn't know. He had asked her if she trusted him, and she did. But what he had done to her, she had not expected, and she couldn't be certain if what he had done startled her or her own reaction to it had.

For she had felt.

She had felt everything. She had felt his touch, his kiss, his deliberate attentions. But she had felt more than that. She had felt desire, lust, passion, and more, she had felt Jack's in return. She had felt everything. For one intense moment, she had been swamped with sensation, her nerves riding a wave that threatened to consume her. Yet so overwhelmed by it, she had not realized it was happening.

And now, now she felt...nothing.

She pressed her hands to her stomach, pushing her body into itself as if to recover from whatever it was that she had just endured. And where heat had flooded her face, a cold realization that she once more felt like the reserved, untouched Lady Margaret Folton banished the heated memories from her mind.

Margaret bit down on her lower lip, the gesture so unlike her, she nearly bit too hard.

It hadn't worked.

Whatever Jack had meant by his actions, it hadn't worked.

She prodded at the recesses of her mind, at the most remote caverns of her senses, and she found nothing. There was nothing there, but the black void that had become so familiar to her. Panic began to well in her chest, and she moved her hands to her throat, lest the panic spill over into insensible blathering.

Jack had said he could make her feel. He had said he could help her. But she felt exactly the same. She pulled in deep breaths, the air filling her lungs, but still she scrambled for more air.

And then she stopped, the panic that had so quickly gripped her pooling away as her senses once more took in the room about her.

Where was Jack?

While she had registered the fact that the room was indeed empty, she had not taken the next step in her thinking to realize this should be odd as Jack surely must have been there. He had been the one to--

She couldn't finish the thought. It wasn't that she was a sheltered miss, a young lady who on her wedding night sought the advice of a stodgy old matron of a mother. But even so, she was no cultured woman when it came to the relations between a man and a woman, and what Jack had done to her was shocking in the very least.

So where had he gone?

And as if the universe could hear her inner thoughts, the door to the sewing room opened, light from the corridor spilling into the room as Jack maneuvered his way in, his arms full of a tea tray, brimming with cups and sandwiches. He must not have noticed her sitting there, watching him, for when he came fully inside he stopped suddenly, a sheepish grin coming to his lips.

"I was hoping to make it back before you awoke," he said. "It is rather impolite of a person to step out for a sandwich after giving another pleasure for the first time."

Margaret felt her cheeks heat at the easy way he spoke of what had just happened between them, and her hands once more flew to her face. "Jack, I--"

But he waved at her as he relinquished the tea tray to the shrouded table in front of the sofa on which she still perched.

"We mustn't speak of it if you do not wish to," he said, and then looked up to focus on her with a stare so intense, she was glad her hands hid her over-warm cheeks. "But I promise I will not be abandoning this challenge you have set before me. That you must understand."

Confused, she wrinkled her brow. "Challenge?"

Jack nodded. "Yes, I intend to make you feel what you just felt many more times to come," he said, filling two cups with steaming hot liquid.

Margaret shook her head. "Jack, that is the very problem,"

she said, and Jack stopped his movements with the tea, his head snapping up at her.

"Problem?" he asked. "There did not seem to be a problem earlier."

His grin then was rather feral, filled with masculine gloating, and Margaret could only frown at him.

"No, not what it was that you...I...we did," she said once she had found the correct word. "It's rather what I feel now."

Jack still hovered over the tea tray, and for the first time, she noticed he looked exactly as he had when he had come in from the garden when she had called earlier that afternoon. Seeing him so made her hands move to her own person, inspecting her clothing by touch as if to see if she, too, remained in the same condition as before their lovemaking. It seemed somehow impossible to her that she should not be unchanged somehow by the act, but it appeared to be so.

"How do you feel now?" Jack asked.

She looked at him, her hands coming to rest on her stomach as they paused in mid-search. "I feel rather the same unfortunately," she said.

And Jack laughed.

The sound was startling in the small, quiet space of the sewing room, and Margaret had visions of jesters popping up from between packing crates as if to mock her.

"I beg your pardon," she said to Jack as he sat down beside her, holding out a cup of tea.

She took the tea but waited for an explanation from him as to the reason why laughter was called for at the moment she felt nothing but panic.

"Maggie, darling, one moment of passion is not enough to undo years of emptiness," Jack said, his movements casual as his words weighed on her.

He picked up a sandwich from the tray and held it up, carefully placing the foodstuff between her lips until she absently took a bite. Taking a bite of the sandwich himself, he reached for his tea.

She chewed, the bread sticking to the roof of her mouth.

Finally swallowing, she said, "Truly?"

Jack looked at her over the rim of his teacup. Swallowing as well, he said, "Of course, it's true."

Something on her face must have told him she was not convinced, because he leaned over, putting aside the sandwich and teacup and, straightening, cupped her face in his hands.

"Maggie, I cannot say that I understand what you went through. I cannot say that I can even imagine what it must have been like for such a small girl to endure something like that. But I can tell you this. No matter what it is that you're feeling or not feeling in here," he said, as he moved one hand to her chest, her heart beating against his palm, "I'll still be here." He returned his hand to her face then, his thumb brushing over the curve of her cheek, and before she could help it her head tilted into the comforting embrace.

"May we try again then?" she asked, and Jack laughed once more, the sound doing strange things to her.

She wasn't sure when last she had made someone laugh. Jack dropped his hands, picking up the sandwich to make her take another bite of it.

"I promise we will try again soon, darling, but not now. Things take time, and we have an assassin to catch."

At his words, Margaret felt the familiarity of working an assignment sweep over her like the glide of a familiar blanket over one's skin.

"I suppose that's true, my lord," she said, and then took the remainder of the sandwich from him.

He stared for a moment at his empty hand but soon reached for a second sandwich from the tray.

"I suppose you did not come here today only to advise me of our current status as lovers in the eyes of the ton."

Margaret shook her head.

"I've been contacting my associates still left in the field. The War Office has been pulling back many of its domestic agents. It's difficult to find anyone left who has heard of any goings on in the ton."

"I take it you found someone," he said, finishing off his sandwich and reaching for more tea.

Margaret nodded.

"I have a colleague who wants to meet as soon as possible," she said. "In fact, his note was rather urgent. I'm afraid he's noticed the pull back of the agents and is rather concerned."

Jack looked at her, another half of a sandwich forgotten in his hand.

"Why would he be concerned? Isn't he an agent privy to the actions of the Office?"

Margaret shook her head and nudged aside the teapot on the tray where she suspected a plate of biscuits hid. She met with success as she uncovered a platter of lemon drop biscuits. Picking up the plate, she offered it to Jack and carefully selected the one with the most sugar crystals on top for herself.

"He is not an agent, I'm afraid, but rather a man who has completed many noble assignments for the Office."

Jack raised an eyebrow.

"What qualifies an assignment as noble?" he asked.

Margaret licked her lips where sugar crystals coated them and was not too slow to notice the look on Jack's face at her actions. She paused, taking in the heat from his scrutiny, and felt a wonderful cascade of power fall through her. She did that to him. And in that quiet moment, she felt the edges of the black void recede, and she wondered if Jack was right. If it really would take time.

"As he is not an agent for the Office, he has no obligation to fulfill any requests from said agency. However, he has, shall we say, specialized talents that sometimes can be of use to the War Office."

Jack's eyes darkened, and Margaret wondered what it was he was thinking.

"Specialized talents?" he asked.

And Margaret raised an eyebrow to his darkened gaze. "It's not really what I think you're imagining, my lord," she said.

Jack leaned in, his gaze growing even darker if it were possible. "What is it that you think I'm imagining?"

Margaret leaned in herself, narrowing her eyes as she got close enough for their breaths to mingle. When she thought she was close enough, she whispered, "He can kill you before you even know he's there."

Jack blinked, and she saw the muscles about his mouth tense. Margaret leaned back, letting out a laugh so vibrant she nearly startled herself. When she regained her composure, she found Jack had fully straightened, the expression on his face one of displeased humor.

"What sorts of people do you believe I associate with, my lord?" she asked, reaching for another lemon biscuit.

Jack took a sip of his tea and also reached for a lemon biscuit.

"When it comes to you, darling, I am not certain what I can assume and what is best left to the imagination."

"I assure you, my contact is nothing at all in the extreme. He merely has some information he wishes to pass on to me."

"Did he indicate what sort of information?"

She shook her head, dabbing at the corner of her mouth where she felt a stuck crystal of sugar.

"No, he did not," she said. "His message was rather cryptic, which leads me to believe what he has to say is pertinent to the request I put out."

"What did the request entail exactly?"

"I have my suspicions about the gentleman from the Harrison gala. The one who resembled the Earl of Stryden to too great a degree."

Jack raised an eyebrow.

"You think he has something to do with this?"

"I'm not sure, but I think my associate can shed some light on the matter."

She hesitated, her mind traveling back to the night of the Harrison gala and the strange man she had met below stairs with the mismatched uniform. She looked at Jack and decided it was likely best to tell him everything.

"There's another piece to this puzzle that concerns me, I'm afraid," she said. "The night I followed the Earl of Stryden's look alike, I encountered a man below stairs in the Harrison house. He was rather odd in appearance, but more than that, he wore a uniform that did not match those of the Harrison staff."

Jack regarded her quietly. "Perhaps it was another household's servant, staying at the house for the gala?"

Jack's explanation was plausible, but something about it still did not sit right with Margaret.

She nodded though and said, "Perhaps."

Jack finished the last of his lemon biscuit before standing.

"When are we likely to arrange a meeting with this associate of yours then?" Jack asked and turned to her as he stretched. "As much as I enjoy remaining within the walls of my garden, it is getting rather tedious. It would be nice to go about once in a while, even if it is only to meetings of the Gardening Society."

Margaret stood as well, brushing out the now wrinkled

mess of her skirts. "I'm terribly sorry you are going through this, Jack," she said looking up at him, but he only shrugged.

"It is the least I can do for my country."

His grin was wry, and she felt herself smiling back at him.

"Do you suppose Captain Edwards will surface soon?" she asked, looking once more about the mounds of shrouded furniture in the room.

She hadn't any idea of the time, but she suspected hours had passed, the dog still unfound.

Jack shrugged again.

"One can only hope, but I suppose the search must go on."

They began to pick their way through the room, dodging crates and the loom and spinning wheel.

"Maggie, what is the name of this associate you're going to meet?"

Picking up her skirts to avoid a large crate of books, she said, "Poison Peter," and heard Jack curse behind her.

CHAPTER 12

"They call him what again?" Jack asked as the carriage bounced over another hole in the road.

"Poison Peter. I'm not certain why, but he's rather reliable despite the name," Margaret said.

Jack looked at her sitting next to him on the bench, her appearance once more the very picture of perfection with not a single hair out of place or a single wrinkle in her dress. He wanted to push her skirts up and take her right there in the carriage just as he looked at her. He blinked and looked away, willing his ardor to regress.

It had been an entire week since that afternoon in the sewing room. A week since he had even seen her, smelled the wispy scent of lilac that draped about her, watched as her face translated her understanding of her surroundings. An entire week since he'd kissed her. When she had left that night, he had not expected them to be apart for as long as it had been, but she was trying to keep him safe. And in keeping him safe, she had to learn the identity of the assassin.

Thus the reason for their trip that day. He had insisted on accompanying her to the coffee house. A coffee house. Gad, he could not believe it. What rabble he expected them to find there. He was certainly not allowing Margaret to go alone to such an establishment. So he was escorting her to meet her contact. One Poison Peter by trade.

"And how is it that you had the opportunity to make an acquaintance with the name of Poison Peter?" he asked, already girding himself for the answer before she responded.

"I met him in a duel," she said, her gaze wandering along the landscape of London beyond the carriage window.

"I beg your pardon?" he asked, feeling his mind surge at the idea that she should be in a duel.

She glanced over at him, and apparently his face belied his feelings, for that small smile appeared on her lips.

"Don't worry. I won the duel," she said, her eyes wrinkling in concern for him. "Did you really think me not capable of it?"

Jack shook his head. "It's not your capability that I ponder. It's the fact of circumstance. Why ever were you in a duel in the first place?"

She shrugged. "I was masquerading as the lover of the Countess of Staffordshire," she said.

He blinked. "You were masquerading as a man?" he asked.

She nodded. "In the domestic unit, an agent is required to take on any number of guises to complete a task. In this case, I was a man. Unfortunately I was caught by the Earl of Staffordshire, who is rather enamored of his wife, and although she denied any existence of me, the Earl demanded the slight be addressed."

She didn't continue, and her gaze traveled back out the window.

"And what happened?" he prodded.

She blinked as she returned her focus to him. "The duel was to first blood. I shot him in the arm."

Her face remained passive as she said the words, and Jack

could only stare at her. "You shot a man out of no reason other than mistaken identity?"

She shrugged. "I was following orders."

The carriage slowed then, and he knew they approached their destination on Marlborough. But before she could alight, he laid a hand on her arm.

"Would you be so kind in future to discuss any orders you receive concerning my person before you carry them out?"

Her eyes showed her confusion, but she nodded. "I suppose," she said, and turned to step down from the conveyance.

Marlborough was an interesting mix of commerce, and its varied clientele was what had brought in the establishment of a coffee house. It was rumored to be the place for intellectuals to gather, but he had fought enough wars over the arguments of intellectuals to not feel much trust or favor for the place. He took Margaret's arm and together they entered the squat building, dodging errand boys and peddlers as they made their way from the carriage to the door.

Inside, the room was crowded with tables and various groups of men scattered about them like forgotten clumps of sawdust after the logger has moved on. Jack frowned.

"There was a time when women were banned from coffee houses," he said under his breath.

"And women once attempted to ban coffee altogether, so I'm not sure there is a point to any of that," she said and pulled them into the thick of the crowd.

They found a table on the other side of the room, placing their backs to the wall as they watched the door. A woman came to their table with a tray set with a press of coffee and a single cup.

"Oh, I beg your pardon, my lady. It's not yer usual to show up 'ere with a gent."

As the woman spoke, she revealed a row of tattered teeth, gaps of black showing where a tooth once stood.

Margaret nodded. "This is Lord Pemberly, Sally. He's an acquaintance from the Gardening Society," Margaret said without pause.

Jack wanted to raise an eyebrow at her lie but kept his face neutral. "Just another cup then, Sally," Jack said, giving her a grin that he had once heard called devastating.

Poor Sally nearly dropped the tray, so it apparently worked. The woman disappeared off into the crowd without another word, presumably to fetch him a cup.

"You visit this place with alarming frequency then?" Jack asked, looking about the room with the eye of a man who had been responsible for the backs of too many men.

"I wouldn't say it was alarming," Margaret answered, pouring herself a cup of the thick, black liquid.

Steam rose from her cup, and without pausing to put cream or sugar in it, she raised the cup to her lips. Jack watched, fascinated, as Margaret sipped the black concoction, the look of splendid bliss spreading across her face, her eyes closing with the ecstasy of it.

"Perfect," he heard her whisper and felt himself blink.

"You also enjoy coffee," he said inanely.

Margaret looked at him and then back at the cup in her hands. "Have you never tried it?" she asked.

Jack frowned. "Of course, I've tried it," he said. "It was in Constantinople actually at a place much like this."

His words seemed to have garnered Margaret's attention away from the cup of coffee, for she looked squarely at him. "Constantinople?" she asked. "What ever were you doing there?"

"A storm had cast the fleet off course. It was a terrible day for His Majesty's Navy."

He felt his face fold into grim lines and knew his expression must convey more than his words.

"That must have been quite the storm," she said, and then turned her gaze toward the door as a gentleman entered carrying a black walking stick with some sort of ornate topper that flashed in the light from the windows.

The man appeared finely attired, with tight black breeches disappearing into highly polished Hessians. His waistcoat and cravat were of a matching cranberry hue while his jacket bore the same blackness as his trousers. While the look was austere, it was also fashionable. The rest of the man was rather average looking, as he had close-cropped brown hair and square features about his plain face. Even his eyes were rather dull. If not for his impeccable dress, Jack would not have remarked upon the man at all.

But when he approached their table, a smile coming to the man's face as he saw Margaret, Jack felt an odd tug of jealousy pull at him. And then Margaret stood as the man reached their table.

"Peter," she said, taking his outstretched hand, "Thank you for coming on such short notice."

Jack watched the exchange, so surprised by the appearance of Poison Peter as a fashionably dressed gentleman that he forgot to stand. Only when Margaret gestured to him did he remember to rise to his feet. He bowed in the man's direction as Margaret made the introductions.

"Lord Pemberly, I would like you to meet the Earl of Wickshire, Peter Grafton."

The Earl of Wickshire was known to the War Office as Poison Peter?

Jack looked at Margaret as they resumed their seats at the table, and Peter took the one across from them.

"Margaret, it has been ages, love. Whatever have you been

keeping yourself busy with?" Peter asked, a smile broadening his mouth.

Jack thought he saw a flush of color creep up Margaret's face at the other man's attention, and the tug of jealousy he had felt earlier turned into a shove.

"The Office keeps me very busy indeed, Peter."

That was most definitely a blush. Jack cleared his throat, and Margaret cast a blank glance in his direction before looking back at Poison Peter.

"I wonder if you could tell us what you've been hearing lately, Peter. You know how the gossips are in academia," Margaret said, a heavy emphasis falling on the word academia.

A flash of awareness struck him then as he realized the Earl of Wickshire was some sort of academic fellow. Odd for a titled gentleman, but Jack remained silent, waiting to hear what it was that had brought them to Poison Peter in the first place.

"While there's the usual mutterings of finding the elixir of life, or some such nonsense, from the radicals and the staunchly conservative groups looking for a cure for gout."

Sally arrived at the table with another tray of coffee for the gentleman and cup for Jack.

"Why if it isn't Peter, 'imself. 'Aven't seen you in 'ere in a bit, 'ave we?"

"I've been unjustly absent, Sally, my love. Please forgive me."

Jack did raise an eyebrow then at Poison Peter's outlandish pattern of speech. In that moment, Jack recalled what Margaret had said about meeting Poison Peter in a duel. A duel in which she had been masquerading as a man. Jack surveyed Peter's overly meticulous dress once more with a critical eye, feeling the tug of jealousy ease from him, slinking off like a reprimanded dog.

Sally sauntered off on her way to the next table as Jack reached for the press of coffee.

"Funny thing is, there's been talk of some gents leaving the City. Gents that never leave the City for fear of missing a development. Right odd, that is. I can't seem to figure out what would make them leave so quickly."

Peter's words were flippant while his gaze was direct. Jack set down the coffee press, his senses focused on the conversation before them.

"I'm afraid it's terrible, Peter," Margaret said, but she did not elaborate.

Peter nodded. "Thought as much," he said. "But the rumor has it that there's a bloke that's asking many a question about the City. Rather brash type. Asking questions about different families. Seems he's looking for something."

Jack absorbed this information, trying to find a place where it would fit in with what they already knew. He looked over to Margaret to see her nod once. The information had made a connection for her it seemed.

"And this bloke that's looking for information. Have you seen him?"

Peter shook his head and took a sip of his coffee, tasting it for sweetness most likely, as the man had already put in three spoonfuls of sugar.

"No, I've never seen him. I've only heard tell of his questions from the gentlemen that's been leaving town. I did hear one rumor that he was privileged to a rather low title himself. But I'd only heard that from one gent. Not confident on the authenticity of it but wanted to be sure not to leave it out."

Margaret nodded, the slightest purse coming to her lips. So this gentleman may or may not be titled. Jack wondered what that said about the assassin. Could it be a fellow spy gone rogue? Or could it be as Margaret theorized, a relation of the Duke of Lofton, a possible bastard child, bent on revenge against the organization his father held in such import?

"He's asking about families, you said? Familial connections, perhaps?" Margaret asked then, and Jack could feel where her thoughts were going.

Peter nodded, but something didn't sit right with Jack. They didn't know who this stranger was that bore such a striking resemblance to the legitimate son of the Duke of Lofton. He felt uneasy pushing this new evidence into the mold that Margaret had already designed.

And what of the other man Margaret had encountered in the bowels of Harrison house? Jack's mind began to swirl with suspects, and he wondered how Margaret could maintain focus in such a situation.

"That's right. Mighty suspicious, if you ask me. Seems as if a man should know who his family is. Shouldn't need to go about asking every Tom and Harry. Isn't that right, love?"

He said this last bit with a wink and took a final gulp of his coffee. Setting down his empty cup, he stood abruptly. "I hope you don't mind this short visit. But the duty of the crown calls, my dear. I do hope you call on me sometime." Straightening his jacket, he turned to Jack, saying, "Pemberly, a pleasure."

He winked once more at Margaret, and with a jaunty salute, he picked up his walking stick and headed for the door. In a flash of light from the windows outside, Jack finally saw the topper on the man's cane. It was a griffin.

* * *

MARGARET REMAINED SEATED although she wanted to rise at once and leave the coffee house, so she could follow the lead Peter had just given them.

A man, possibly titled, asking questions about familial connections. She sipped casually at her coffee, keeping her hand steady as she felt the lick of anticipation of moving another step closer to discovering the assassin. Her mind briefly flashed to Richard, still ensconced in the safe house in White Chapel. Although the heat had broken, it was still a hovel. And more, he had been separated from his family for weeks.

When this entire escapade had started, she had hoped to have been further along by now. In truth, she had assumed she would have the assignment completed. But as Jack took a sip of his own coffee next to her, grimacing slightly as the thick black liquid reached his mouth, she understood that there had been a level of distraction to the assignment.

Her face flamed before she could prevent it, her wandering mind betraying her. But she couldn't help it. The memories from that afternoon in the sewing room remained emblazoned on her mind. She hoped the intensity of the memory would never fade, but Jack had promised her it was only the beginning. Could it get any better though, she wondered. She gazed into her cup as she contemplated just that.

Because she had felt.

She had felt something in his arms.

She had felt ecstasy.

That was the only word that seemed even remotely adequate. Everything else just did not merit. For the first time in her life, she had understood what it meant to be consumed. To be completely overpowered by a feeling that could not be named or grasped.

And she had reveled in it.

But then it was over.

It was as simple as that. He touched her, and she flamed. He stepped back, and the shield that had fallen over her so many years ago slid back into place. Once again, she was just Lady Margaret Folton. She grimaced at the grounds in the bottom of her empty cup and wondered if Jack could be right. If they continued to be lovers, could he help her? Could he make her feel?

The word lovers lodged in her throat, causing a physical cough to erupt from her mouth. Jack's hand came to her shoulder, and she nearly dropped her cup.

"I beg your pardon," she said, setting her cup neatly on the table. "Grounds," she murmured, as if Jack would believe her.

"Indeed," Jack said and took another sip from his cup. "Poison Peter turned out to be rather a surprise."

Margaret looked at him. "How do you mean?" she asked.

Jack shrugged, setting his now empty cup down. "With a name involving a chemical substance, I was expecting a gentleman of a less refined nature."

Margaret nodded. "Yes, the moniker is rather misleading. But I believe it is something to do with his subject of study."

Jack raised an eyebrow, and she said, "Chemistry. The man studies chemistry. There was talk once that he developed an untraceable poison that was used in an attempt on Napoleon's life."

She watched Jack's face change to one of rapt attention.

"And?" he prompted her.

Margaret shrugged. "The poison was so lethal the assassin accidentally killed himself before administering the substance."

She picked up the coffee press and poured herself the last of the coffee. Jack was silent beside her, but she felt his eyes on her. Picking up the cup to inhale the aroma of the thick liquid, she looked sideways at Jack. "I said I wasn't sure how Poison Peter got the name. I'm only saying that was one of the rumors."

Jack eyed his now empty coffee cup, and Margaret felt a laugh burbling inside of her. She paused suddenly, her cup going back to the table in front of them. She pressed a hand to her chest as if to stop the feeling with a physical touch, suspend it inside her chest. She looked at Jack, but his eyes were on the crowd about them. The air in her lungs had stalled, and she felt the beginnings of a faint press in on her vision. Coughing, she sucked in air and blinked, the moment drifting away from her. But her mind still lingered on her reaction.

Jack looked at her now. "You should be more careful about those grounds," he said.

Margaret saw the humorous glint in his eye and wondered when he had started making her laugh. She was sure it had happened before then, but now everything about Jack came with sharper angles and more intense impacts. She didn't know exactly when it had happened, but she was fairly confident to take a guess.

"Do you think perhaps we should continue in our investigation now that we have this new information?" she asked, feeling her nerves settle as she returned to the assignment at hand.

Jack nodded, but his gaze remained fixed at a spot across the room. "Indeed," he said, "But how do we use this rumor of a possibly titled gentleman asking questions of familial connection about the ton?"

Margaret said, "The stranger who so closely resembles the Earl of Stryden, obviously. He must have something to do with this, Jack. Peter's information supports--"

Jack looked at her with an expression on his face she had not seen before then. She wasn't sure if it were recrimination or simple scolding, but she felt its lash on her skin, and she shut her mouth.

Momentarily at least.

"You believe I am drawing conclusions before we have all of the facts," she said, and Jack's face softened.

"I think we had best see how this plays out before we start making accusations," he said and straightened in his seat to lean closer to her, his voice low, the smell of coffee on his breath drifting towards her.

She shivered at such an intimate contact and wondered how her body knew to make such a reaction.

"I think we need to get him out in the open," Jack said. "This stranger that resembles the Duke of Lofton's male family members. If we drew him out, we could question him, and we may be surprised by what we find."

But Margaret felt her head already shaking. "I cannot allow that to happen, Jack," she said. "It's too dangerous, and I am sworn to protect you. If anything should happen to you--"

She felt the end of the sentence hanging between them like the tower of Pisa about to collapse on them both.

What would she feel if anything were to happen to him? There was the obvious that she would fail her mission for the War Office, and she would feel disappointment at this. But the feeling was so minuscule and irrelevant that her mind skipped ahead to what she had truly meant when she had started that sentence.

"I couldn't bear it," she whispered, and Jack's eyes flashed with something she couldn't name.

"Then I guess I'd better not get myself killed," Jack whispered back to her.

They stayed that way, heads bent together, the air between them vibrating with the whispers that had carried so much weight. And it was at that moment that Sally returned with a fresh press of coffee.

"You'll be 'aving another, I see," she said, setting the press down as she picked up the used one.

Margaret straightened as she heard Jack mutter something under his breath that sounded suspiciously like a curse.

"Thank you, Sally," she said and reached for the coffee press.

Her fingers froze, nearly curled about the handle of the press.

"I can't imagine a woman consuming so much of that stuff in a single setting," Jack said from beside her, as he, too, straightened. "There should at least be some kind of warning language about the stuff."

"Jack," Margaret whispered as if they were not sitting in the middle of a crowded coffee house, and her actions would be noticed by every member in the room, thus the need to speak quietly.

When in fact, they were nearly surrounded by two intensely argumentative groups, both taking up most of the tables in front of them as if forming a kind of barricade of intellectual debate. But beyond the barricade, Margaret saw him. Or his reflection rather. He had taken a seat at such an angle that she knew he could see them through the barricade, but they would not be able to see him. Not until they had been in the coffee house long enough for the direction on the windowpanes at the front of the house to reflect back the images of the occupants in front of it.

"Jack, it's him," she whispered again.

She felt the words seep from her and suddenly realized her hand was still on the coffee press. She had not moved in seconds, and very likely, looked as guilty as if she'd been caught stealing biscuits from Cook's larder.

"Kiss me, Jack," she said, "Quickly."

She needn't ask twice as Jack turned her toward him and kissed her, his mouth firm against hers. It was as yet another kind of kiss, unlike any they had shared before then, but she supposed the coffee house was a far less romantic setting and the reason for the kiss a much less ardent one.

She murmured against Jack's lips. "By the window."

She felt the flutter of Jack's eyelashes as he presumably looked in the direction of the stranger that so resembled the Black family men, and she soon heard a resounding grunt in agreement. Jack broke the kiss, but only enough to draw his head back to look at her and speak coherently.

"What is it you'd like us to do, spy lady?" he asked, his mouth twisting up into a grin.

She wanted to wipe the grin from his face. "This is not a matter to be taken lightly, my lord," she said. "This man may want you dead."

"But not in a coffee house," he said, his words oozing confidence that made her want to wipe something else from his face.

Jack eased back a bit, and Margaret saw his eyes travel once more to the reflection she was sure he saw in the coffee house windows.

"I think we should talk to him," Jack said, his voice low and close, the words vibrating against her skin.

Again, Margaret felt the odd flair of something inside of her, and she pressed a hand to her stomach as if to stop it. She would think later on what this man was doing to her, but for now, she needed to get him safely out of the coffee house.

"Jack, I do not wish to do this, but if you insist on putting yourself in danger, I must order you to remove yourself from this establishment."

Jack laughed then, all pretense of subterfuge gone as his head tipped back and his mouth opened with a burst of amusement. When he had seemingly calmed himself enough to resume their conversation, he looked at her and said, "You will be ordering me, my lady? Tell me. Have you heard the rumor about me being a commodore in His Majesty's Navy?"

Margaret felt the flush start at the base of her neck, spreading wildly to her face.

"I do not take orders," Jack finished, all humor having fled from his voice.

And before she could say anything further, he stood and moved around their table, walking in the direction of the stranger.

* * *

JACK IMAGINED ALL of the names Lady Margaret Folton was calling him just then, but he did not pay the notion any heed. She could call him all sorts of terrible things, but he knew that what he was doing must be done. He could not allow her to seize on this idea that their mysterious stranger was the culprit, and all facts subsequently learned must lead in that direction. He forgave Margaret her sudden cloudy judgment, as he suspected it was his fault, or at least, it was largely his fault.

He approached the first table of men that cocooned their table at the rear of the coffee house. Based on the angle in which he viewed the reflection of the man from their table, Jack knew the man had to be sitting to the left, ensconced in the front portion of the coffee house beyond this rabble of conversing men. There were two tables quite close together with men sitting, standing, and leaning around them, their voices raised in a zealous debate. Papers were strewn about both surfaces, and discarded coffee urns lay like forgotten dirty stockings about the tabletops. Pipes were being both smoked and upended into trays on the table. The entire babble was disconcerting, but for Jack, it lent the perfect cover for his move in the direction of the mysterious man.

As Jack drew closer to the first table, he crossed his arms over his chest, resting his chin in one hand, bending his head forward to hide his face. The stance allowed him to be absorbed by the crowd in front of him, and he let himself look up at the windowpanes at the front of the coffee house. The man still sat there, his face clearly seen from his lack of hat. The man appeared to be reading something, a newspaper likely, and a coffee press sat untouched next to him. Jack shifted, bringing him a step closer to rounding the first table.

Sally appeared then, her tray filled with new coffee presses, and Jack tucked his head, hoping he would go unnoticed. The woman moved her rotund body about the tables, her worn skirts swishing in between chairs, tables, and standing men. Eventually, she careened in their direction, depositing coffee presses as she went. It seemed she had a thing to say to each of the men at the table, asking after their welfare and if there was anything else she could get for them. Jack thought he was safe as Sally turned as if to head toward the back of the coffee house when a bloke bumped into her, knocking her tray to the floor. The woman made a grand fuss of it, and Jack felt every head in the room turn in their direction.

Sally stood only three feet from him, and Jack rounded his shoulders, shrinking as best he could to blend with the men around him. But then Sally bent and fetched her tray, and upon straightening, her eyes fell on Jack.

"Viscount Pemberly, what are you doing over here?" she called, her hands going up into the air as if to emphasize her point, tray and all.

The loud call went out above the cacophony of the men about him, and the conversation in the room suddenly died, all eyes now traveling to him. He straightened, knowing rounded shoulders would do him no good at this point.

And then several things happened at one time.

The first of which was the mystery man rising from his

seat, discarding the newspaper he was reading and taking long strides in the direction of the door. The second of which made his blood boil.

Margaret bolted from her seat behind him, her legs carrying her faster than he thought possible in the direction of the fleeing mystery man.

"Stop!" Margaret called. "In the name of His Majesty, stop that man!"

And then she, too, was gone through the door after the mystery man. Jack deflated, frowning in the direction of the door, where the woman he cared so much for had just given chase after a man they suspected of murdering government agents.

Jack sighed, the feeling so intense they left him drained. Pulling some notes from his pocket, he tossed them to Sally. "I beg your pardon, my dear, but it appears we will be leaving rather abruptly."

And with that, Jack ran out the door in pursuit of a government spy and a suspected assassin.

$\mathcal{M}$arlborough was crowded at this time of day. Shoppers strolled about the thoroughfare, stopping to look into shop windows or converse with a friend met accidentally on the way. Peddlers littered the pavement, acting as obstacles that were not needed just then. Margaret hauled up her skirts past the point of decency and ran.

The mystery man was only yards in front of her, his progress impeded by the very peddlers she simply pushed out of her way. She was in pursuit of an assassin of spies for the British crown. She would not allow a match vendor to get in her way. Dimly, she became aware of running footfalls behind her and deduced that they must belong to Jack. She wanted to turn her head to confirm this fact, but doing so would slow her down. And such an action may cause her to overrun a poor peddler, which was not something she wished to do at all. Removing them from her path was all that was necessary. Complete destruction was overdone.

Up ahead, the mystery man rounded the corner onto Kingly Street. She picked up her pace, her kid boots striking the pavement with solid thuds as her speed increased. For a brief moment, she was thankful the heat had broken, for she was certain she would not have been able to breathe at this moment had the humidity continued to grip the City.

But when Margaret made the corner, her legs stopped as her brain scrambled to catch up.

The man was gone.

He had just vanished into nothing.

Her gaze swept the scene in front of her, moving left to right, taking in the passing carriages, hacks, peddlers, and ladies about their shopping. There was nothing unusual about the scene at all except that the man was gone.

She felt frustration like a splintering wedge in her chest. Her lungs fought for air, both from exertion and the suffocating sense of failure. She didn't know how long she was standing there when she heard the heavy, rapid foot falls of someone running behind her, and then Jack stood next to her, his own chest heaving as he sucked in air.

"I take it he has escaped us," Jack said in between breaths.

She turned to look at him, swatting a piece of damp hair from her forehead. "It would appear so," she said, and then she turned, raising her hand to hail a hackney. "But he has not escaped us for long."

Jack shuffled over to where she had moved to the edge of the street, leaning to the side to gain the attention of a passing cab. "And how is that?" Jack asked.

Margaret lowered her arm as a hackney pulled to the curb. "Because we're going to visit someone we haven't spoken to yet," she said to Jack, and then turning to the driver of the hackney. "Number 17 Park, please. Lofton House."

* * *

"You plan to question the Duchess of Lofton?" Jack asked as the hackney bounced over yet another rut in the road.

As far as hacks went, this one was fairly clean, but it was still of a degree that Jack kept from touching as much of it as he could.

"Yes, that is exactly what I plan to do," Margaret said.

Jack blinked at her. "You know what the woman is like, don't you? Even I have heard the stories, and I haven't been in London in ages before now," he said, but Margaret's gaze remained fixed on the passing world outside the hack.

Jack got to his feet and shifted to the opposite bench, taking one of Margaret's hands in his own. The heat of her skin traveled through both layers of gloves until he felt it like a hot iron being branded into his skin.

"Maggie, perhaps we're going about this all wrong," he said and was pleased that he had gotten her attention by calling her by the shortened name he was keen to use. "What if this mysterious man has nothing at all to do with the matter? What if it's that strange man you met the night of the Harrison gala?"

Margaret shook her head. "Unlikely, I'm afraid. Someone begins assassinating agents of the War Office--"

Jack held up a finger to stop her. "Attempted assassination, remember," he said, and then waved his hand for her to continue.

"Right," she said. "Attempted assassination."

She paused as if she expected him to interrupt her again. He merely raised an eyebrow, indicating she could go on safely.

"And at the same time, a man who happens to resemble the men of the Black family appears in the same location as us."

"Yes, precisely, he happens to resemble them."

Margaret shook her head again. "The resemblance is

stunning, Jack," she said. "We can't simply disregard it, no matter how much we would wish to."

Jack felt the need to sigh but restrained himself before the sound had a chance to escape. "So we question the Duchess of Lofton. What is it that we ask her?"

Margaret opened her mouth but nothing came out. She swallowed and after a moment she was finally able to say, "I don't really know actually. I guess it would be rather impolite of me to ask if her deceased husband had had an illegitimate child with his lover."

Jack raised both eyebrows. "Quite," he said. "Especially considering the fact that her husband is not dead. That would be rather awkward when he comes back around, don't you think? I would hate to be the one involved in that conversation."

Margaret frowned at him. "I suppose it would be awkward," she said. "Then we must go about this another way."

Jack nodded. "And what would that be?"

Margaret looked back out the window. "It would not be too late to call with our condolences," Margaret said, but Jack wasn't sure if she were speaking to him or the passing buildings beyond the windows.

She turned back to him. "Or perhaps I can claim, what is the word for it?"

Her face screwed up into an expression of deep thinking, one Jack had never seen on her face before. It almost made him laugh, but he thought she was being serious. His laughter would be unwarranted.

"Word for what?" he asked, instead of laughing.

Her face relaxed so she could look at him. "The word for when you know what a person is going through at the moment," she said.

Jack paused, thinking about what her confusion revealed

about her person. "Perhaps empathy is the word you are looking for," he said.

Margaret held up a hand as if in triumph. "Yes, that's the word," she said. "I could say that I'm there to express my empathy for her situation."

It was Jack's turn to adopt an expression of confusion. "I'm not sure one calls on another to express empathy in the literal sense," he said.

Margaret blinked at him. "No?" she asked, simply.

"No," Jack returned, "But you could say that you are there to let her know that should she have any questions or just needs a friendly ear, you are there for her."

Jack waited, wondering what effect his words would have on her. He had only just begun his personal quest to see the vibrant woman he knew was inside of this quiet, serene lady come out, and he didn't know how far he could take what he needed to say. What he needed to tell her. But she seemed to absorb what he said, because her face softened in thought.

"Yes, I could say that," she said, her voice a whisper as if she were talking to herself.

But then her expression hardened and she looked at him directly. "Do you think she'll believe that, though?" Margaret asked. "I mean given her reputation."

Just at that moment, the hack eased to a stop. Jack leaned forward to look out the window at the townhouse that rose up in front of them. Its facade was as stately and intimidating as was the woman they were about to find inside.

Jack absently shook his head. "I think that's a bet on which I'm not willing to wager."

* * *

THE DRAWING ROOM into which they were shown was graciously appointed, and Margaret observed the absolute state of cleanliness that shrouded the place. Even the draperies seemed freshly beaten, and the entire room smelled of a mixture of fragrances that gave her pause to consider on their origin but did not intrude enough so as to interrupt the experience of peace she felt within the room.

It was an odd reaction to have to a drawing room, but Margaret considered it may have been overly exaggerated based on the low expectations she held for this meeting. And at this thought, her senses as an agent sharpened. Was the room purposely made to lull the unexpected visitor into submission? The thought seemed ludicrous, or it would have if Margaret did not know into whose home she had come. Richard was a renowned agent for the Office, and if any gentleman of the ton were to install subliminal submission messages in his interior decor, it would be Richard Black, the Duke of Lofton.

But this thought brought another, and Margaret scanned the room once more with keener interest. There had been rumors circulating about the War Office about a possible secret passage the duke had had installed after his home had been invaded during an assignment. Margaret had always dismissed the rumors as folly, but now, seeing the interior of Lofton House for the first time, the rumors suddenly became rather more intriguing.

She sat up straighter on the sofa onto which she and Jack had retreated. The butler, one Hathaway, Margaret had overheard, seemed rather old to be in employ, but Margaret would not question it. Perhaps he was a splendidly good butler, and good help was always difficult to acquire.

"It seems friendly enough in here," Jack said to her under his breath, leaning in so she could hear him.

The first thing she registered was his smell, fresh earth and soap. The scents invaded her in a confusing contradiction, and she had to shake her head to think clearly once more. The second thing she registered was his words.

"That's precisely what has me worried," she whispered back.

Jack looked at her, one eyebrow raised. "Are they trying to win over our trust?"

Margaret nodded. "It would seem so," she said, just as Hathaway returned.

"Her grace shall be down momentarily. She has requested tea," he said, and then he said nothing more, but he also did not leave.

Margaret watched him, a casual and slightly gracious smile on her face. But still the butler did not leave. He remained standing just inside the door, his back turned so that he watched not only the corridor beyond but all parts of the room as well. Again, Margaret's instincts told her this behavior was unusual, but another part of her told her to take it with reason. Perhaps, the Duke and Duchess of Lofton trained their butler to behave thusly.

She wanted to remark on it or any other matter, to see if she could illicit a response from the man, when the woman they had come to see entered. Jane Black, the Duchess of Lofton, or perhaps, the dowager now, Margaret forced herself to recall, did not look to be the sixty some years her age would suggest.

She had black hair streaked with gray that lent her an air of sophistication. Her features were angular and well proportioned, and she carried herself with the proper degree of composure and confidence. She was everything every debutante was taught to aspire to when entering society as a lady.

And Margaret found the entire thing incredibly suspicious.

"Your grace," Margaret said as she and Jack stood.

Margaret curtsied politely while Jack bowed in Lady Lofton's direction. When the woman was close enough, Margaret extended a hand.

"Lady Folton," the duchess said, extending her own hand to take Margaret's. "What an unexpected surprise."

Margaret took the offered hand and squeezed it in what she hoped was - what was that word Jack had used? Empathy.

Smiling with the slightest hint of sadness, Margaret said, "Your grace, I hope we are not intruding on your time of mourning."

Lady Lofton made no sign that Margaret had even said anything, so she continued.

"I had only wished to extend my condolences."

Lady Lofton nodded now, the movement so precise and exacting, Margaret felt as if the woman were scolding her with a simple gesture.

"Do sit," Lofton said, indicating the sofa. "Tea will be brought in shortly."

Margaret and Jack resumed their seats, and Margaret took the opportunity to ascertain the location of the butler. There was something about him, perhaps his rigid and commanding bearing, but Margaret wanted to be sure of his location at all times. Her gaze swept carefully to the right, and that was where he stood. Exactly where he had been before, back slightly turned in the opened doorway so as to have a view of not only the room but also the corridor beyond.

What was he watching for?

Margaret swallowed and returned her attention quickly to Lady Lofton.

"Viscount Pemberly," Lofton was saying when Margaret picked up the conversation. "I have heard rumors of your exploits in the Mediterranean."

Margaret looked at Jack to find a cast of unease over his face. She wondered at that, and then recalled his belief that luck had brought him all of his gains in his professional and personal life. She wondered if that belief also made him uncomfortable speaking of it.

"Yes, your grace, I suppose word of the actions of the fleet in the Mediterranean would have reached the drawing rooms of London."

Lady Lofton waved a hand as if to bat away his modest reply, but the movement was once again so exact, Margaret sat back as if the woman meant to slap her.

"Your humility is unwarranted, my lord," she said. "The adventures of Commodore Lynwood have already been told to such an extreme that you are likely never to recover from it."

Jack smiled sheepishly, and Margaret wondered just how much his mislaid beliefs affected his outlook on what was in all reality a brilliant military career.

"I suppose I could attempt to live up to the tales," Jack said, but his eyes were not cast in the duchess' direction.

If anything, he stared at the wall beyond the duchess, and that was when Margaret noticed his hands pressed firmly together in his lap.

She wanted to place her own hands over his, thinking the touch would ease his tension. The thought had blinked into her mind with the suddenness of wind along the Thames, and Margaret swallowed as if to push that and any thoughts like it from her mind. She had never exhibited a sympathetic tendency before now, but it would appear that something had been damaged inside of her. Perhaps Jack was right. Perhaps he could make her feel again.

Margaret snapped her gaze back to the Duchess of Lofton, or dowager as it were, and firmly pushed her personal thoughts away. Now was not the time to analyze her relationship with the man who sat beside her, nor its effect on her feelings.

"Your grace, I came here today out of respect for your family," Margaret said, and the dowager's gaze turned in her direction, the eyes so intense, Margaret wished once more to lean back as if to escape their impact.

"My family?" Lofton asked.

Margaret nodded and opened her mouth to continue, but just as she did, the teacart was wheeled in. She looked up to note the maid wheeling in the teacart and was startled to find the woman heavy with child. Margaret blinked, but the fact remained the same. The maid was quite pregnant and still in service it appeared.

For a brief moment, Margaret wondered if she shouldn't stand to assist the woman, but then she surmised that if the maid was still working, she was likely still capable of doing so. Perhaps Margaret would offend the servant with an offer of assistance.

"I shall pour, Nora," Lofton said, and once more raised her hand in that exacting motion. "But perhaps you can ask Cook for those lavender biscuits. I do so very much enjoy those."

The maid, Nora, it would seem, looked the duchess directly in the eye, her chin held up and shoulders back, her spine ramrod straight despite what must have been a heavy girth of child.

"The lavender biscuits, your grace?" the maid asked.

Briefly, Margaret thought the duchess would scold the maid for questioning her in front of guests, but the duchess did not.

She simply said, "Yes, the lavender ones."

And then she turned to Margaret and Jack. "There's an old tale that lavender biscuits provoke the telling of truths from the consumer. What an audacious tale."

While Margaret sat stunned on the sofa, the duchess turned once more to the maid. "The lavender biscuits, dear."

"Very good, your grace," the maid said, and curtsied before taking her leave.

Margaret watched the woman as she carefully exited the drawing room, but even as the woman disappeared through the door, her mind remained fixated on her.

A butler who did not leave, a maid in an advanced pregnancy, and lavender truth-invoking biscuits.

Something was not right here, and Margaret could feel it like an ill-fitting chemise, uncomfortable yet invisible to the eye.

"How is it you take your tea, my lady?" the duchess asked, but Margaret's gaze remained fixed on the door where the pregnant maid had just disappeared.

"She takes hers with just cream," Jack answered beside her. "And I'll take both cream and sugar, your grace."

Margaret finally returned her gaze to the duchess to find a cup and saucer being extended in her direction. She took the proffered cup and sipped at the hot sweet liquid, so pungently tart after the thick, dark coffee she had consumed hours earlier.

"You were speaking of my family," the duchess said, and Margaret recalled what she had been saying before the teacart had arrived.

"Yes," she said, swallowing another sip of tea, "I have come in regards to your family."

She set down her cup, folding her hands in her lap as if to assume the most polite, serene, and sympathetic pose possible. She saw Jack look at her out of the corner of his eye, and for a moment, she thought he may be grinning at her.

But she continued with, "I'm sure you have heard the stories of my own terrible tale. I had wanted to come here today to express my understanding. And should you ever need someone with whom you can speak, I would be honored to be that person."

The duchess made no sign that she had even heard Margaret as the older woman sipped at her tea.

"Your own terrible tale?" the duchess said when she finally spoke, and briefly, Margaret felt a ripple of something pass over her skin as if she had walked through a spider web.

She had never spoken before of what had happened to her as a child. There had never been any need to. Everyone of the ton had heard of the awful things done to the Earl and Countess of Breckenshire and what their daughter had been forced to endure. But when she had heard the words relayed back to her, it all became suddenly...unimportant.

Margaret blinked as if to clear her thoughts with the motion, but she couldn't shake the understanding within her. Had too many years passed for her to no longer remain objective when it came to her relation with the past? The void that had once been her reaction to the story of her parents' death was now filled in with nothingness. She wasn't sure how she could determine the difference, but it was more something that she felt.

And with this, she coughed slightly, her eyes once more sweeping to Jack in a sidelong glance, wondering briefly what he was doing to her.

"Yes, my parents were tortured and killed by French revolutionists," Margaret said, and once more the words carried weight and depth, no longer suspended in a vacuum.

Although they held weight, Margaret did not fear them or feel saddened by them. They just were, and it was a part of her history that she had accepted at some point without really understanding how.

Still the duchess made no outward sign that these words had any effect, and Margaret waited, wondering what the woman must be thinking.

It was then, sitting on the sofa in the drawing room of Lofton House, that Margaret suddenly recalled telling Alec Black, the Earl of Stryden, and Richard's son, of the man's death. At the time, it had been a simple enough procedure, and she had carried out orders as specified by the Office. Now she paused and thought on what she had done.

The War Office had been adamant in telling the family that Richard had been killed while carrying out an assignment for the Office. They had not outwardly stated that Richard had been an agent, but they may as well have. And this gave Margaret pause now, as she watched the unnoticeable reactions of his widow. First the son was told, then the story relayed to the wife and stepmother.

Her mind flashed to another scene, the night at the ball when the now Duke and Duchess of Lofton had approached Margaret, their faces one of masked social kindness with just a hint of something unusual. Not at all as if they were in mourning. Before her, the duchess sat quietly, her gown a deep shade of lavender, a color usually seen months if not years after a husband's death.

And that was when the pieces snapped together with a resounding click.

The Duchess of Lofton knew her husband was not dead.

Margaret sucked in a breath as the realization settled on her. Her eyes flew to the butler still standing poised by the doorway as if standing guard. The image of the pregnant maid looming up over the duchess, her stance confident, almost authoritative. The truth-invoking biscuits.

The Duchess of Lofton knew her husband was not dead, and she wanted Margaret to know it. But even more than that, the woman had armed herself with a battalion of protection in the bodyguard butler and the pregnant woman. Margaret faltered on this one, her mind unable to grasp how a pregnant woman would be of use, but there was something about how the woman stood, her chin held much too high for a servant.

"That's quite unfortunate what happened to your parents," Lofton said now, and Margaret tried to focus on the conversation at hand, although she felt all attempts at getting the woman to speak would be futile now.

Just then the maid returned, a tray of biscuits in hand. Once more, Margaret carefully watched the woman as she delivered the tray, her hands going to the small of her back as soon as she straightened, her posture that of a commanding officer, surely.

"Will that be all, your grace?" the maid asked.

Lady Lofton nodded. "Quite, thank you, Nora," she said, but her gaze never left Margaret's. If anything, her eyes hardened as if the older woman were inviting Margaret to make her next move.

And so Margaret did.

"Your grace, did you ever feel that there were things you did not know about your husband?"

Margaret asked the slightly impolite question in the presence of the maid, knowing that she would either receive no answer at all or that she would receive a fabricated one. Either of which would do them no good in finding the truth behind the mystery man that continued to torment them.

The duchess finally showed a reaction in a single raised eyebrow.

"That seems a rather unusual question to ask," the duchess said, and still the maid did not excuse herself.

Margaret continued anyway. "It is just that I learned so much about my parents after their death, and there was no one to whom I could speak. I just wish there had been someone," she said, and for the slightest moment, she worried the words were true.

But the duchess stood, and propriety demanded they stand as well, and Margaret knew the audience was over.

"I did not learn anything unusual about my husband after his death," the duchess said. "Now you must excuse me. My nerves are overwrought."

Her last words dripped with a sarcasm so real, Margaret thought she could touch the stuff. They were being dismissed, and Lady Lofton wanted her rejection of them to be obvious. And she had swiftly done just that.

"I thank you for seeing us," Margaret said, curtsying to the dowager.

Jack bowed beside her. "It's been a pleasure, your grace. I'm sorry for your loss," he said and then took Margaret's arm.

The butler, standing still as a boulder by the door during this entire conversation, straightened and gestured to the corridor. When Margaret and Jack passed him, he stepped out behind them, nearly shoving them in the direction of the door.

"Fitzwilliam will see you out," he said, his voice like gravel.

Margaret picked up her pace, pulling Jack along with her. They descended to the ground floor, expecting to see a footman by the name of Fitzwilliam, when she saw a man at the door wearing the uniform of a butler. Margaret's step slowed, and she took in the man's exceptionally watery features. Her stomach pinched as she realized she was looking at the strange man from the Harrison gala. He opened the door without a word, but Margaret felt the burn of his gaze on the back of her neck as she and Jack fled from the home. It wasn't until they were out on the street hailing a hackney that Margaret released her breath.

* * *

JACK STOOD ON THE CURB, his arm raised to signal a cab.

Too many things clogged her mind, and Margaret struggled to think of what to say first.

So she blurted, "That was the strange man from the Harrison gala. The footman who just let us out. Fitzwilliam, I think he was called."

Jack turned to her, momentarily abandoning his quest for a hackney.

"The oddly placed second butler?" he asked.

"Yes," she said. "You noticed it, too?"

"What house has two butlers?" Jack asked. "The uniform the man at the door was wearing was most clearly that of a butler."

Margaret shook her head, letting the evidence fall where it may. But there were more pressing matters to discuss.

"She knows," Margaret murmured, looking back at the intimidating house on Park, her thoughts traveling to their moments within the structure.

"I know," Jack said.

Margaret spun around. "You do?" she asked, her eyes growing wide.

A hackney slowed in the street, maneuvering itself to the curb. Jack reached for her hand to help her into the conveyance. "Yes, I do know," he said, and then called up to the driver. "Number 13 Claremont," he said, before following Margaret into the hackney.

Jack settled on the bench opposite her, and Margaret waited for him to continue.

"Well?" she said, when Jack did not speak, but continued to stare out the window at the house from which they had just fled.

Finally, Jack looked at her. "Mrs. Katharine Thatcher," he said.

Margaret shook her head. "I beg your pardon?" she asked.

"An old friend, Katharine Cavanaugh, the Countess of Stirling, the last I met her, and now Mrs. Thatcher, paid me a visit the other week at my townhouse," he said.

Margaret nodded, urging him to continue when the words didn't seem to be enough.

"Her husband is the American who so conveniently rescued us that day in the park," he said, and the breath seized in her chest.

"The American?"

Jack nodded.

"That's rather unusual, but what does that have to do with Lady Lofton?"

"Kate wears a rare scent. It's a perfume derived from star gazer lilies," he said, and Margaret felt her head tilt in confusion.

"The drawing room where we met with the duchess reeked of the stuff."

Margaret fell back against her seat, the clues that she had thought connected in her mind suddenly scattered like the bits of colored glass in a kaleidoscope.

"The American who rescued us in the park is married to a woman whose scent was in the drawing room of Lofton House?"

Jack nodded.

"That seems rather odd, but I don't know how it fits into the puzzle."

Jack's face turned grim. "It's worse than that," he said.

Margaret straightened, bouncing as the hackney made its way through the streets. "How?"

Jack leaned forward, elbows on his knees. "The last time I saw Katharine Cavanaugh, she demanded a ship of the fleet to rescue the American from a mercenary trader in Naples, Italy."

Margaret blinked. "Demanded a ship of the fleet?"

Jack nodded. "During war time. And the order was granted by a very important person at the War Office."

Margaret waited, her mouth going dry. "Who was it?" she asked when she could bear the anticipation no longer.

"Richard Black, the Duke of Lofton."

CHAPTER 14

*R*ichard had a sudden vision of a little girl, about six or seven years old, in a pristine, starched pinafore and stockings, black boots shining with polish. Her braided hair a perfectly smooth trail down her back, and her eerily empty smile framed by a dusting of freckles across her nose as she told him who it was that had betrayed England.

And that young girl had been far more composed than the Lady Margaret Folton that stood before him then. He had never seen the woman so agitated in his life, and a smile came unbidden to his lips as her agitation brought him a perverse sense of joy. Her hair had come loose from its pins, tendrils falling about her ears and along her neck under her bonnet. Her dress was wrinkled where she had clearly pressed it with her hands in her agitation, and her reticule swung wildly from her arm as she fired her questions at him.

"Richard, your very life depends on the answers that you give me at this moment, and right now, I am not finding your answer at all agreeable," she said, her voice never rising above a perfectly cultured level of propriety.

He wondered then what it would take to get her angry

enough to raise her voice, and then he wondered if he could ever achieve such a feat. He smiled harder, which only served to fuel her agitation.

"Really, Richard, is that all you can do? Smile at me like you're some sort of innocent?"

Her words were cutting, and Richard thought they were meant to make him feel guilty. But they did nothing of the sort for he answered every question she asked honestly and with as much depth as he could provide. The problem was simply that she asked the wrong questions.

He had been surprised by her visit, and even more surprised when she had erupted into the room after he removed the bureau from the door, her agitation clear in her body language. Expecting her to relay some foul news on her search to find the assassin, he was rather startled when she asked rather bluntly if he had ever had a mistress during his marriage to Lady Lofton and if he had gotten said mistress with child.

His mind had immediately gone to Nathan, and he wondered what the boy was up to. Whatever it was it must have been great enough to raise the ire of the impenetrable Lady Margaret Folton, and this had only started Richard smiling that afternoon. Lady Folton's continued agitation helped keep that smile alive.

But he had answered Lady Folton truthfully as he had not had a mistress in the entire length of his marriage, and he had no intentions on acquiring one now. And thus while he had remained honest, his answer served only to make matters worse.

Richard thought that perhaps he should clarify for Lady Folton where her mistake was made, but he could not bring himself to do it. He had sent that chestnut roaster to Jane with a purpose, a warning for her to keep safe and be watchful. It appeared that the gesture had worked well, for his son was obviously about something that had an agent for the War Office suspicious.

Richard's mind raced through the connections of Nathan to Lady Margaret Folton and found none. The War Office was particularly careful about keeping the identities of agents separate, including the details of any familial connections. It was not unusual for Lady Folton to be asking questions then of his potential for extraneous family members as she would know nothing of his family or their extent as fellow agents for the Office.

But then, Richard only wondered what it was that Nathan was up to. It must have been something rather active as it had driven Lady Folton to seek Richard out, a dangerous move as he was in hiding from a would-be assassin. His mind drifted to Jane, and Richard hoped that whatever his son was discovering, he had left a guard around Jane to keep her safe.

"I'm sorry, Lady Folton, but I can safely say that I have never strayed from the vows of my marriage," he said simply. "But perhaps it is something else that you are seeking."

If Nathan had attracted the attention of Lady Folton, it also meant that she was searching for the wrong person. Nathan was obviously not the assassin, which meant the man was still out there and still a danger to every agent in the War Office. Richard wondered how the man had been able to target so many agents when all the intelligence they had suggested the registry of agents had gone untouched. Something just did not make sense.

"Perhaps it's someone that the War Office has helped," Richard said before the thought had finished forming.

Lady Folton placed her fisted hands on her hips, looming over him. "I beg your pardon," she said.

And Richard focused on her face as the thought continued to form in his mind.

"Perhaps we've been targeting the wrong source of information," he said. "We've been focused on the registry, but perhaps that is not how the assassin discovered who so many of the agents are."

Richard watched the tension flow from Lady Folton's body, and he wondered if she were truly accepting what he was saying. If he were ever to get out of this prison and get back to Jane, he needed her to believe him. He needed her to stop focusing on his son and find the real assassin.

"The War Office has interceded in a number of cases when it came to civilian matters. What if the assassin is someone the War Office has worked with? Perhaps this person remembered who it was that had come to their aid and is now seeking vengeance."

Lady Folton shook her head. "Why would someone seek vengeance on someone who provided aid?"

Richard frowned. "Because the War Office has not always been successful in providing that aid."

Lady Folton's body stilled, and Richard knew he had struck a nerve. He hoped the blow had not been too great, as he watched the memories of her own past flash across her face. The War Office had not been able to help her parents. Only she could understand what that could mean to a person, what it could drive them to do.

For Lady Folton, it had been a positive reaction. She had entered the service of the War Office as a child, aiding the Office in its mission since the time of her parents' death. But for others, the reaction may not have been as good.

Lady Folton's arms slid down until they hung limply at her sides, and she nodded. "I will look into the matter," she said, and then turned toward the door.

She stopped with her hand on the knob and looked back at him.

"Are you sure you do not have any bastard children who may want to see you dead?" she asked.

Richard thought of Nathan, of his coming grandchild, of his precious family.

And he answered Lady Folton honestly.

"No, I do not," he said.

* * *

JACK WONDERED NOT for the first time what Margaret was discovering from the Duke of Lofton.

As soon as the revelation had left his mouth, he had seen the spy in her engage, coming to life like a great bird of prey, wings spreading ready to take flight, its conquest in sight.

And then she had said, "That bastard knows more than he's letting on."

And at that, Jack had smiled, and he smiled again now at the memory, as he sat in one of the overly worn chairs used at the meetings of the Gardening Society.

Lady Margaret Folton was not one to be undermined when it came to an assignment from the War Office. He only hoped the bastard in question did not crumble under the woman's wrath.

Jack's thoughts turned to the meeting at Lofton House, the Duchess of Lofton's calculated reception of them. The woman had been cool certainly, but she had also held herself with a certain degree of respect almost welcoming a challenge from anyone she encountered. Her presence had been rather unsettling, and Jack realized the source of the rumors regarding her reputation.

But his mind soon traveled to the other aspects of the visit that had unsettled him. The demanding presence of the pregnant maid, the butler who never left his post at the door to the corridor, and even more suspiciously, the strange man from Harrison house, Fitzwilliam. He had not had a chance to discuss these aspects of his uneasiness with Margaret as his revelation of Kate's scent in the room and her association with the Duke of Lofton had precluded such discussion. But there was something about the look of disdain on the second butler's face when they had left that lingered in Jack's mind. What was he doing at Harrison house the night Margaret had followed their mystery man?

Lionel Weatherby, the Earl of St. John, was droning on about soil composition and the addition of manure to one's field to cultivate abundant blooms. It was a topic that Jack felt had been over researched when it came to personal gardeners' attempts at creating rich soil, but perhaps, Jack had just mastered his own mixture to his satisfaction. He saw a few new chaps in the group that afternoon, and he hoped they were learning something from the exhausting lecture.

It had taken him nearly an hour of argument with Margaret and not a few kisses to convince her to allow him to come to this meeting. He had promised to be on his best behavior and cognizant of his surroundings at all times. She had wanted to send a guard with him, a Bow Street runner if she could contract one out to do the assignment, but he had refused. A commodore of His Majesty's Navy did not go about with a guard. It was rather unmanly.

She had relented in the end, and now, he sat as his rear went slowly numb from the over worn chair and wished he had not pressed her so hard for permission to attend the meeting. He should have thought it rather odd that he had felt the need to ask her for permission in the first place, but it seemed the most important thing to do just then. He trusted Margaret when it came to his life, and even more, he trusted her to be a good spy. And in that case, he would listen to her if she told him to stay within the safety of his home.

Jack had thought briefly of bringing Mayhew, his new valet and former fellow sailor, but he thought the appearance of one's valet in society would be rather out of the ordinary.

He did not want to raise the suspicions of the assassin and throw him off his plan.

After the meeting with Poison Peter, Jack felt that they were closing in on the assassin. The confirmation that there was a familial connection to these attempts on the agents' lives as well as the appearance of their mystery man had clicked something in his head that made him believe Margaret was not following the right trail. There were too many coincidences to be considered coincidences any longer. And his mind could still not dismiss the strange second butler, Fitzwilliam.

No, he must continue to act as normally as possible and hope that Margaret would pull more information from the Duke of Lofton. And so he listened to manure ratios and moisture content lectures. When he thought he would surely fall asleep, Weatherby finished his talk and stepped down from the lectern. Sir Toby Hall stepped up, taking the man's place, and as president of the Gardening Society adjourned the meeting. Jack let out a sign of relief and stood, mixing with the other members of the society as they made their way to the front hall of the converted townhouse where the society met.

The first floor had been divided into several meeting halls that connected along the length of a single corridor that ran from the front to the back of the house. The corridor was unusually large, but as the house in its entirety was known for its unusual architecture, it went unnoticed by the members of the society. That is, unnoticed by everyone but Jack, who had always felt unsettled by the townhouse's odd use of gargoyles and angels. Representations of the creatures in stone hung all about the place in the oddest locations, leaving the observer to feel as though there was always a set of eyes upon him.

Jack ran a finger under his collar as he moved with the

flow of the gentlemen as they exited the meeting hall. He had stepped into the corridor with its bare walls and perched sentinels of gargoyles and angels when Sir Toby caught up to him.

"Splendid lecture, eh, Lynwood?" he said, pushing up at his round spectacles.

Jack smiled, hoping it did not look too much like a grimace.

"Indeed," he said to the smaller man. "I found Weatherby's hypothesis on the types of manures used in soil composition rather original."

Sir Toby nodded in agreement. "I am so glad so many members of the society are still in town at this late date in the year. The lectures have never been more arousing."

Jack took his gaze away from a particularly menacing group of gargoyles that sat directly above his head in an alcove along the balcony of the second floor and looked at the little man. Sir Toby nearly vibrated with excited energy as he watched the members of the society mill about, speaking with one another and gesticulating with their hands.

"Arousing, yes," Jack said, hoping he kept the sarcasm from his voice.

He actually wanted to return to his walled garden and its shabby, unkempt flowerbeds. He had been making progress with a particularly overgrown section and thought he had unearthed an entire patch of moonbeams, but he couldn't be certain. There were still thickets of brambles all about the patch, and he wanted to work them loose today. But as Sir Toby droned on, Jack felt his patience waning.

Until finally, Sir Toby waved a hand at someone behind Jack's shoulder, calling, "Clifford, old man! A word!" And then to Jack, "Pardon me, Lynwood. I must speak with Clifford about his daffodil hybrid."

And with that, the little man slipped into the crowd leaving Jack to gratefully head in the direction of the door. He shouldered his way between two young blokes when he caught sight of a familiar face. Because his mind had just been focused on the very same face, the recognition startled him more than he thought it should, stopping him in his tracks. The second butler from Lofton House stood not ten feet from him. The man's sour expression spoke to him from across the crowded hall. And just as quickly as he saw him, the man disappeared.

Jack picked up his feet to follow the man, but just as he was about to take a step forward, he heard a noise above the din of conversation filling the corridor. He looked about him for the source of the sound at the same time he tried to decipher what the sound was. It was unlike anything he had heard before, and he wondered if the men about him heard it as well.

But as he scanned the room, he noticed the men continued to speak, engrossed in conversations that Jack could only imagine involved manure and moisture content. The sound came again, louder this time, and Jack looked up, thinking it had come from above him. And that's when he saw it.

The mass of gargoyles that sat hunched, suspended just over his head as if they swung from the second floor balcony appeared to be moving. Jack blinked, thinking he was seeing things, but when he refocused on the sculpture, he saw that it was in fact swaying, and then it lurched forward with a terrific groan and began to fall.

In that moment, many things flashed through Jack's mind, the first of which was Margaret. He couldn't leave her. He couldn't do this to her. He had only started helping her to feel again, and he knew his death by gargoyle sculpture would put an end to any hope of her feeling alive once more.

But quickly on the heels of this thought, he wondered about the irony of his good luck and his eventual death by a bunch of gargoyles. And while these thoughts traveled through his mind in less than an entire breath, he suddenly understood that when faced with perilous danger, a person could not react for his body had gone completely numb at the sight of the giant sculpture falling through the air toward him.

And before he could fully understand this thought, the cold marble of the floor smashed into his face, a great mass of a body covering his, pressing him into the floor. The air had been knocked from his lungs, and his chest burned with the effort to draw in breath. The room about him was a chaotic mass of refined gentlemen running for the nearest exit as the gargoyle sculpture hit the floor, mere feet from his face, in a resounding crash of stone against stone. The gargoyles shattered, limbs and wings and faces careening about the marble floor, and he closed his eyes against the spray of broken rock.

The body that pressed against him shifted, moving until he felt whomever it was gain his feet. He wanted to look up, but he could feel the rain of stone against his face as the room settled into the uneasy rhythm of aftermath. Footsteps sounded then as the man who had pushed him out of the way of the falling sculpture began to retreat. Jack's mind raced with implications. Why would this man flee? He had saved Jack's life.

Finally, air made its way into his lungs, and he swiped at his face, clearing it of debris before he turned his head in the direction of his savior's retreating footsteps. He saw a man in a billowing greatcoat moving swiftly in the direction of the rear exit, his head devoid of any hat. Jack's stomach clenched as he watched the man near the end of the corridor where it turned to exit through the alley that ran along the back of the townhouses. He didn't know he was holding his breath until the exhale rushed out of him as the man turned around, casting a knowing grin in Jack's direction before disappearing around the corner.

Their mystery man had just saved his life.

"Well, bollocks," Jack muttered and started to pull himself up from the rubble.

* * *

MARGARET SEETHED as the hackney made its way across the City, weaving from street to street as it traveled from White Chapel to the more fashionable parts of town near the park. Richard's words rolled over in her head, and she pondered them each at a time, fighting with the incongruity she felt but could not find proof to dislike.

Richard had denied any illegitimate offspring. She could assume he was lying, but there was something about his manner that suggested he was answering her questions truthfully. But as a seasoned agent for the War Office, Margaret knew to question what a real answer was and what a truthful answer was. A tickling at the back of her neck suggested Richard's answer was one of the latter kind.

She wasn't sure what had set her on that notion, but Richard's suggestion that she investigate the families that had been aided by the War Office was evidence to the contrariness of his answers. Richard wanted to send her off the path of her current investigation.

But why?

The hackney rolled to a stop at the entrance to Hyde Park as she had instructed it to do so, and she alighted, stepping onto the pavement and heading into the park until the hackney pulled away. As soon as the driver was out of eyesight, Margaret turned, walking along the edge of the park in the direction of the Serpentine and Kensington

Gardens. Knightsbridge was busy that time of day, and she dodged busy strollers, rapt in conversations with familiars. Bending her head so as to conceal as much of her face as she could beneath her bonnet, she reached the intersecting street and stepped off the pavement, turning away from the throng on Knightsbridge and into a more domestic section along the thoroughfare until she reached a particularly imperious gate.

The guard at the gate had been dozing, however, and Margaret frowned at the rather unimpressive sight.

"Pardon me," she said, loudly enough to rouse the guard.

The man straightened, his uniform falling haphazardly about him as he came away from the wall against which he had perched himself.

"If you wouldn't mind," she said, gesturing toward the gate.

The man blinked at her, and for a moment, she saw a look of disbelief and outrage pass over his face. She straightened as well, allowing the sun to find her features, and the man choked on what was likely an indignant reply.

And then he spluttered, "Why, yes, of course, Lady Folton. I beg your pardon."

He scrambled to remove the keys from his belt, inserting a large iron key into the gate and swinging it loose. Margaret walked through the gate and into Kensington Palace.

The palace was quieter these days, with only the Princess of Wales in attendance, and it rather nicely served as residence to another item of importance, one of which Lady Folton was determined to ascertain the integrity of herself. If she were to receive nothing but half-truths from her contacts, she would go directly to the source of the matter.

In this case, the book of agents kept ever so obviously in nearly the most protected residence in all the kingdom. Reaching the kitchen door, Lady Folton knocked once sharply and was admitted by the overheated scullery maid.

"My lady," the maid said, curtsying as Margaret entered.

"Bridget," Margaret returned. "I am here to see Miss Beaupre."

"Of course, my lady," Bridget said, straightening. "I'll have one of the footman escort you up."

Margaret followed the appointed footman through the maze of tunnels below the ground floor of Kensington Palace, her skirts swishing in the quiet of the palace, the footman's boots making no noise on the floor. For a moment, Margaret wondered what sort of training a footman required to serve royalty and thought of her own tendency to not fully notice her own actions. She thought she'd likely fail at the occupation.

The footman reached a narrow set of stairs and went up, opening the solid wooden door at the top. Light spilled through the opening, and Margaret drew in a deep breath, filling her lungs with fresh air as she rid them of the stale air of the underground caverns. The room into which the footman had led her was a different one than the one she had been escorted to when she had last had occasion to deliver correspondence to Miss Beaupre. This room was more grandly decorated than the last, and Margaret wondered for a moment if the Prince Regent had ordered the rooms in Kensington Palace redecorated. Given his unhealthy relationship with his wife, the only occupant of the palace currently, Margaret rather doubted it.

The room Miss Beaupre and her little book occupied changed frequently, and if any members of the staff inquired, it was told that Miss Brie Beaupre was a personal secretary to the Princess of Wales, and in that capacity, she was strictly off limits to the other members of the staff and was to be left alone. In actuality, Miss Beaupre spent her days guarding a book of names written in code by passing the time reading Gothic novels.

And that is how Margaret found her, seated at the rose-wood desk in the corner of the room, her arms folded over the edge of the desk as she leaned over her latest sordid novel. Miss Beaupre was an unassuming woman, which made her an excellent choice for the position. Everything about her was average, and her naturally handsome appearance allowed her to go without remark. She was simply Miss Beaupre, the lovely lady secretary to the Princess of Wales.

And no one ever suspected that she was French by birth.

"Lady Folton," Miss Beaupre said, rising from her seat before Margaret had made it three steps into the room.

Miss Beaupre may have been unassuming, but her personality was in stark contrast to her looks. She was bold and intelligent, two traits noteworthy of a spy, and ones that had been the root of her survival. For Miss Beaupre had much in common with Margaret. Only Margaret's parents had been English spies when they had been captured and tortured, whereas Miss Beaupre's parents had been nothing more than polite gentry in Paris when they had been taken and killed. It was only out of luck that another agent of the War Office was in acquaintance with Miss Beaupre's parents and brought her to England after their death.

Margaret extended a hand as she approached Miss Beaupre.

"Miss Beaupre, how are you?" she asked.

The other woman's grip was firm. "Splendid, Lady Folton, and yourself?"

Miss Beaupre's accent had faded into one of unrecognizable continental flair, and no one would suspect the woman was of French origins. Margaret smiled not only at her friend but also at the sometimes unthinkable workings of the War Office.

"I am well," she said. "But I seem to be having a problem with that stitch you showed me how to perform last time."

At these words, Margaret pretended to rummage in her bag as if looking for embroidery things, and as she never embroidered anything in her life, she did not know what it was she might be looking for or if it would even fit into one's reticule. But as she only had to pretend for as long as it took to hear the click of the door behind the retreating footman, she did not bother with pure authenticity in her actions. When the solid wooden door from the underground caverns clicked back into place, Margaret dropped her hands from her reticule, letting it swing at her wrist.

"There's a matter about the book, I'm afraid," Margaret said without preamble.

Miss Beaupre did not make any sign of hesitation. Her features remained set and her hands calmly folded against the dove gray of her gown.

"I see," she said. "I had heard some murmurings that something was going on. What is it?"

Margaret thought about how to phrase her question. "Would it be possible for someone to get access to the entire book?" she asked.

Thought wrinkled Miss Beaupre's brow, but otherwise, the woman did not seem perplexed by the question.

"The individual in question would need to know the codes by the commanding agents who then relay the coded missives to the book holder, which is myself. Anyone who tried to steal the book would need to decipher the codes individually before it was of any use."

Margaret frowned. It was the same conclusion she and the Duke of Lofton had determined at the outset of this entire matter. But still, Margaret had to be sure for herself after her uninspiring meeting with the duke earlier that day.

"And no one has made an attempt for the book that you are aware of?"

Miss Beaupre smiled, her head tilting to the side, and

Margaret realized why she had been chosen for this position. There was nothing about Miss Beaupre that suggested she would be anything but sweet when Margaret knew the truth to be the exact opposite.

"No, I'm afraid not. I've confirmed its safe existence in its keeping spot just this morning."

Margaret wanted to look about her as if to locate this secret keeping spot, but the book could be hidden anywhere in Kensington Palace. And it wouldn't do for an agent to go traipsing about the place. It was always much tidier when matters of the War Office did not get tangled in matters of the crown.

"I see," Margaret said, and she knew she had let her voice betray her frustration.

It was uncharacteristic at best, and she frowned, wondering what had suddenly come over her. She had carried out numerous assignments for the War Office and had never had such a reaction to resistance. Why would things be different now?

"Is it bad then?" Miss Beaupre asked, her voice going soft in concern.

Margaret looked at the woman then with her wide brown eyes and soft brown hair, looking so innocent as she stood behind the rosewood desk in the ornately appointed drawing room. This woman had been through so much at such a tender age, and now she served a foreign nation in an equally dangerous position. And for a moment, Margaret wondered why. Why would Miss Beaupre do this?

For likely the same reasons Margaret did. But this realization only served to make her feel more confused, for those reasons did not seem important any longer.

"Worse, I'm afraid," Margaret answered. "Is there anything else you can tell me about the book or why someone may want it?"

Miss Beaupre shrugged. "If deciphered, it could bring the entire spy network to oblivion. But there are so many safeties in place to prevent such a thing from occurring, it would seem a foolish route for someone bent on such an endeavor."

Margaret felt her brow wrinkle at Miss Beaupre's words, for they too closely reflected the conclusion of the Duke of Lofton. It would appear that two agents of the War Office were of the same mind. That it was not the book the assassin had somehow breached, and it was not the target now. Margaret did not like to admit she was pursuing the wrong vein of information, but it appeared she may have to at that moment.

"Has there been anything else out of the ordinary, Miss Beaupre?" Margaret asked as she righted her reticule in preparation to leave.

"Nothing-"

Miss Beaupre stopped short as the door to the underground caverns opened, and the same footman who had escorted Margaret in emerged with a silver platter bearing two envelopes.

"I beg your pardon, miss," the footman said. "But this came to you by way of the kitchen door. It seemed pertinent as only your important visitors come through that way."

Miss Beaupre frowned at the missive the footman extended to her, and Margaret felt the tickling at the back of her neck once more.

Accepting the envelope, Miss Beaupre said, "Thank you, Donald."

And then Donald did the most extraordinary thing. He turned to Margaret and handed her the other missive.

"This came by way of courier to you, my lady," the footman said, and then with nothing more, bowed and exited the room.

Margaret's tickle of suspicion had smoldered into a burning sense of trepidation. Miss Beaupre opened the envelope in her hand, and the most peculiar thing occurred. The quiet woman smiled, and if Margaret could have believe it, she would have said the woman blushed.

"Miss Beaupre?" Margaret prompted, and the other woman looked up from the note.

"Oh, it's nothing," Miss Beaupre said once she saw the question that was likely on Margaret's face. "It's an apology from a gentleman who bumped into me at market last week."

Margaret raised an eyebrow, but Miss Beaupre waved her off. "Oh, it was nothing so sordid as that. We were jostled in the crowd, and he made apologies and took me for a cup of coffee at that place on Marlborough. He was rather nice about it and just talked about pleasantries and such. I could listen to him talk all day really."

"Why is that?" Margaret asked.

Miss Beaupre smiled with a cool hint of womanly fondness. "He has the most incredible American accent," she said and grinned.

Margaret's blood ran cold. She stared at the other woman, the world spinning beneath her foot even as she did not move. Without looking, Margaret tore open her own missive, her eyes blurring the words for several seconds until she commanded herself to focus. When the words finally registered, she had forgotten all about Miss Beaupre's encounter with the American.

She looked up at the woman. "I beg your pardon, Miss Beaupre, but I must leave."

And with that Margaret ran for the door.

CHAPTER 15

*J*ack wondered if this was what a bag at Jackson's Saloon felt like. If he could have encased himself in ice, he would have, but as it were, he sat in a chair on the terrace to his makeshift gardens and contemplated the glass of whiskey in his hand. Strong stuff, and he wasn't taken to drinking, but he figured the situation called for it. And the captain had agreed, so that was how he had found a glass of the stuff in his hand.

Captain Edwards was at his usual post in the flowerpot, ears dangling over the side as Jack took another sip of the fiery liquid. It burned, distracting him from the hurt that radiated from the side of his body that had connected with the marble floor when someone had tried to kill him with a stone gargoyle. When he had had time to think on it, he thought the move rather overdone on the part of the assassin. Were there not plenty of gothic novels that used the same method of killing someone when a hero needed to face some sort of trial? And if they didn't, they ought, because the entire episode had been rather morose.

Jack took another sip and looked at the mound of

bramble he had pulled back from another one of the beds. He would have to dispose of the clippings somehow, and seeing the evidence of his work, his mind began to wander on the possibilities of using the clippings in some sort of compost.

He lingered on this thought for a moment until he saw the captain twitch at his perch, his ears giving the slightest clue that he had awoken. Jack stopped with his glass nearly to his lips and listened. Captain Edwards picked up his head, his cheeks pinching as his powerful nose took in the air about him.

And then the dog was off.

It happened in an instant, and Jack had not had time to grab the hound before he let out a bay and galloped in the direction of the front hall. Absently, Jack thought he heard a lamp crashing to the floor and boxes sliding about, but instead of rising to see to the obvious ruckus, he took another drink of whiskey, letting his arm and ribs pulsate in the dull ache of remembered pain.

"Captain Edwards, I will not allow you to partake of this morsel unless you exhibit the appropriate manners."

Jack tilted his head, his ears picking up the calculating voice of Lady Margaret Folton giving direction to his dog. When the first command had reached his ears, he waited with bated breath for what she might say next as he was fairly certain Captain Edwards was not following orders.

And Jack was rewarded with a firm, "That means put your butt on the floor, sir."

And then a more interesting, "I can see myself in, Reynolds. Thank you."

And this followed by some incoherent rambling from his inordinately short butler. Jack pictured the man in his mind, holding his hands up ineffectually at the departing back of Lady Folton. Setting down the whiskey glass, Jack stood, realizing that somewhere along the way in he'd lost his jacket, waistcoat, cravat, and collar. His shirtsleeves were rolled up, as was the usual when he was in his garden, but he had yet to soil his dress with the dirt of his garden.

Jack thought it likely that the captain obeyed, for shortly after the words were spoken he heard the distinct sound of Margaret's footfalls in the corridor and through the sitting room that led out onto the terrace and into the walled gardens. He readied himself to tell her what had happened at the society meeting, knew he could not leave out a single detail even if it meant enduring the quiet, infused focus of Lady Folton when on assignment.

He prepared himself for her reproach, steeled his nerves against what he was certain would be a resounding scolding on yet another attempt on his life and her very noticeable absence when said attack occurred. He was even prepared to receive a command that he remain indoors until the assassin was caught. This was something he was not at all willing to agree to, as the ache in his body told him quite clearly he was going to catch this bastard, whomever he was. He may have been drawn into this mess by error, but he would see it through to the end. It was his life that was in danger, and he had never before allowed someone to have such control over him. And he wasn't about to let it start now.

When this thought passed through his mind, he recalled Margaret's confusion over his perception of luck in his life, and the collision of these thoughts gave him pause. It was as if a horse had thrown a shoe, going off balance if only for a moment. Something wasn't right about the ideas passing through his mind, but then Margaret came sailing through the terrace doors, running the few remaining steps between them, and then flinging herself at him. He caught her, if only barely, and his arms closed around her as she clung to him. The outward sign of affection was unexpected, and he held onto her, feeling the racing beat of his heart match the rhythm of hers. He held her as he wondered at her reaction. No woman had ever thrown herself at him, and the gesture did odd things to him. But the closeness did not last, as Margaret pulled away, her clenched hands grabbing at her skirts, as she seemed to control a rage that threatened to boil out of her in a great explosion.

"I beg your pardon, Viscount Pemberly, but you are not to leave this house until the matter at hand has been resolved."

The warm, vibrant feelings her greeting had stirred in him vanished with the cold onset of suspicion.

"You know," he said.

Margaret nodded, her mouth pursed. "Of course, I know. You advised the War Office of the attempt on your life, and they sent me a missive instructing me to rendezvous with you here."

Jack closed his eyes, bringing one hand up to pinch the bridge of his nose. It was a gesture that he had often resorted to when commanding a ship of the fleet when pressures during battle gave him a pounding behind his eyes. He had not had the need for such a gesture since his return from the front, but now he could feel the pounding beginning its cadence deep within his head.

"I did not inform the War Office of anything," he said, dropping his hand and returning his gaze to her now confused face. "I wouldn't even know how to inform them of anything."

Margaret's mouth opened once but nothing emerged for some moments.

And then, "You did not inform them of an attempt on your life?"

Jack shook his head. "No, but I can hazard a guess at who might have."

Margaret did not move, her entire being frozen before him, waiting to hear what he would say. Captain Edwards sauntered out onto the terrace, coming to land at Margaret's feet, sagging his heavy body against her legs. She did not flinch as the solid dog came to rest, and Jack wondered if she knew the dog was there.

"Oh God, Jack," Margaret whispered then, and he watched, mesmerized, as something transformed her face.

He couldn't say what it was, but something about the emptiness shrouding her came into sharper focus, zeroing in on a point somewhere in the distance that Jack could not see. It sounded absurd even to his own mind, but it was all that he could fathom in his head. It was as if the empty well of feeling within her was struck with a rain storm so great it could not absorb the water, and the dry ground pushed it back away, flooding the area about it, drowning all in its wake.

"Maggie," he said, his voice so unlike his own, as if it, too, were drowning in the storm.

And then Maggie's arms were around him again, her lips pressed to his, her body molding against his own. His body grew hot, his hands finding purchase at her back as he pulled her closer. She kissed him with abandon, her mouth open against his as she plunged. For a woman who was so new to intimacy, she learned fast, as her tongue glided over the line of his lips, the curve of his mouth. He shivered in response, his fists bunching the fabric at the back of her gown.

"Maggie," Jack whispered, and she pulled away from him, her hands going to frame his face as if to physically capture his attention.

"Make love to me, Jack," she said, her voice harsh with emotion.

Something stopped short in his chest, rendering his speech immobile. The color of her eyes danced between dark and sparking blues as he saw the very desire in her float up to her face. The tips of her fingers speared his hair, capturing him against her in a feral and basic way. His body ached for her and yet his mind could not make him take another step.

"Maggie," he started, but her hands tightened against the sides of his face.

"Please, Jack," she said.

And in the slanting rays of the dying afternoon light that danced shadows across her face, Jack knew he could not say no to her. Jack knew that this was it. This was the part where he pushed her a little farther, dared her to feel a little more. She was ready, and she wanted it. The events of the day obviously had sparked something in her, and he knew he could not turn her back, make her think reasonably about what she was asking.

And standing there in the dimming light of his gardens, Jack knew he was going to make Lady Margaret Folton his wife. It was an odd thought to have when one held a woman in one's arms, a woman begging him to make love to her. And it was an odd thought for Jack to have at all, but what had started as a kind of challenge, a dare almost, to see what he could make Margaret feel, had turned into something far greater than even he could understand.

"All right," he said, and he bent, scooping her into his arms and heading in the direction of the house.

The darkness of the house encased them as they entered through the terrace doors, through the sitting room, and out to the stairs to the upper floors. Jack wondered briefly if Mayhew or Reynolds were about and even more briefly of what this may look like. He was, in plain fact, about to debauch a perfectly respectable woman of the ton. He should be stopped. He should be forced to propose marriage to her right then, and if nothing else, he should have been more careful about his actions, as servants were known to talk. Margaret's reputation was likely to be ruined even before he reached the top of the stairs.

But feeling the slight weight of her over-thin body in his arms, he remembered what she had said, remembered her recollection of the story of her parents' death. The rules of society truly did no longer apply to Margaret. And Jack would make love to her. But this time, it would be in a proper bed.

Gaining the second story landing, Jack turned to the right, moving swiftly to his chamber. Only when they were inside, the door safely shut and locked behind them, did Jack set Margaret on her feet. They stood in the dim shadows of the room, staring at one another for several breaths until Margaret smiled.

"I'm sorry, Jack. I may have asked for this, but I have no idea what is to happen."

Twilight was falling outside, and the large windows along one side of the room cast a warm glow on the objects about them, lending the room an air of fairytales and make believe. It was fitting, as Jack still could not believe this woman existed, that she stood there in front of him, wanting him, willing him to make love to her.

Quietly, he stepped forward, sliding one hand against her cheek, threading his fingers into her hair, until he heard the soft pop of pins as they came free, landing on the carpet at their feet as her long, straight tresses fell down, spreading out against her slight shoulders. He drew his thumb over her lips, catching on the plump of the lower one before sliding down, tilting her chin up until he could kiss her. The kiss was not hurried, passionate or grand. It was a simple kiss, a kiss that he hoped told her what he felt inside. That this was only the beginning of something more. That he would not take her this way and leave her. That this was only the start for them.

Carefully, slowly, he reached behind her, undoing the buttons of her gown much as he had done that afternoon in the sewing room. Only now he did not stop at a few. He kept going until the entire back of her gown was opened, the panels of fabric falling away until he could brush his fingertips up the simple cloth of her chemise. She shivered, her body moving imperceptibly forward until it rested against his.

"Jack," she moaned against his mouth, and he tilted his head, deepening the kiss the barest of fractions.

Peeling the gown from her shoulders, he let it drop to the ground, and he broke the kiss, stepping back to drink in the sight of her.

Her long, pale neck spread into the gently rounded curves of her shoulders, sweeping into the long lines of her arms, melting into the curve of her belly, hips and thighs. The sight of her in only her chemise, stockings, and slippers sent a pulse through his body, and his manhood pressed against the seam of his breeches.

Taking no more time to enjoy the very look of her, Jack stepped forward, brushing the straps of her chemise from her shoulders, letting it fall to the ground. She was completely naked except for her stockings and slippers, but he did not stop to look at her. He bent once more, picking her up to deposit her on the bed, laying her back against the pillows. Only then did he sit back, kneeling on the bed to look at her.

She was beautiful. Her small body lay encased in the softness of the mattress, her long hair spread across the pillows. The defined lines of her collarbones accentuated the plump, small mounds of her breasts, pert and perfect, and he longed to reach out and touch them. But instead, he jerked off the bed, shedding the remainder of his own clothes. Only when he returned to the bed did he wonder if the sight of his naked body would upset her, but he watched her through the growing shadows, saw the fire still burning in her hooded gaze.

Slowly, he moved between her spread legs, easing his larger body over her smaller one. But before his skin could make contact with hers, he stopped.

"Jack?" she asked, her voice filled with hesitation.

But Jack only smiled, before easing back far enough to take one of her slippers in each of his hands. And with a soft tug, he pulled them free and tossed them to the floor.

"That's better," he said, as she raised an eyebrow at his actions.

And then finally he lowered his body to hers, and the heat of her body, the rasping of skin against skin, sent a jolt of scorching lust through him.

"I can't go slowly this time," he said as he felt the pulse of his erection twitch against her stomach.

"I don't think I want you to," she said, and he bent his head, smiling as he kissed her.

Propping himself on one elbow, he reached between them, capturing her sensitive nub between his fingertips, rubbing it gently until her moan vibrated against his lips. He prodded at her folds, slipping one finger into her, finding her already wet and slick. His erection twitched again, and he separated her, positioning the head of his penis against her, but not yet pushing into her.

He leaned back, his lips trailing from hers. Her eyelids fluttered open, her eyes so brown and wide, her lips swollen from his kiss.

"I want to watch you," he said, and without giving her time to respond, he plunged into her in one swift motion, filling her to the hilt.

He wasn't sure what her reaction might be as he did not make a practice of deflowering virgins, but he did have a notion how Margaret would react to anything. But in the moment that he filled her, he had no spare thoughts for anything, as he clung to his resistance, the clinging muscles of her tight sheath nearly driving him over the edge before he had even started. Margaret said nothing, but her face did not convey fear or hesitation or even discomfort.

"Maggie," he said, but it was not a question.

He said her name as means of connection. This was about more than making love. This was about forming a bridge, a safe platform onto which she could explore her feelings, her emotions, her thoughts. He would not let her drift away, fall into the abyss of the physical sensations that were surely swamping her.

But then she reached up a hand, her fingertips gliding over his cheek, and a small smile played at her lips. "Jack," she said.

And he was lost, his hips moving, his body penetrating hers in the most primal of ways. That was when he saw it, that was when he knew that it was working, that his body was speaking to hers, pulling it from a black depth that had consumed it.

"Jack," she said again, shaking as her eyes shuttered closed, her body tensing around him.

Once more, he took her sensitive nub between his fingers, and a spasm shook her.

"Jack," she said, and this time it was barely audible.

He could not hold on much longer, and he wanted her to reach her pleasure first, needed her to feel it, feel what it was like to lose control of one's body if only for a fleeting moment. He plunged deeper, driving into her, rubbing incessantly at her nub. And on a strangled cry, he felt her shatter around him, felt her muscles tighten unbearably around his throbbing penis, pushing him into his own climax. The force of it rocked him, his entire body wracked with tremors as he came apart.

But he kept control of himself, as he still lay pivoted above her. She was so small, and he didn't want to crush her if he came down on top of her. His body trembled in the aftermath of his release, and it was all he could do to pull out of her and roll away, falling beside her so he could cradle her against him. He looked up at her then, needing to know how she felt. But as it had been that afternoon in the sewing room, he found her fast asleep.

* * *

SHE WOKE WITH A START, the second time in as many weeks, her heart racing and her head spinning to catch up with her surroundings. The first thing she realized was that her body ached in ways she had never imagined, pulsing with a deep sense of conquest. It was something she had never felt before, and at first, she was frightened, unable to name what it was that coursed through her body.

And then she heard his voice.

"I think this experiment of trying to get you to feel is causing havoc on your person."

Margaret looked in the direction of the voice, finding Jack not far from the bed, his hands filled with what appeared to be a dressing gown. His hair was mussed, and he wore a satisfied grin on his face, a grin that had her becoming aware of other things. The soreness between her legs, the feel of the sheet against her naked body, the swish of her long hair against her back. And then more. The room about her now lit with candles, and while not cluttered with shipping crates, the furniture in the room appeared as though it were an afterthought with mismatched chairs standing before a dormant fireplace, and a lone table here and there about the room, atop which sat flaming candelabras. To her right, a bank of windows had been shuttered for the night apparently, encased in aged curtains.

She wondered momentarily what time it was, sitting up in bed as her senses came fully awake. And then once more, she felt the pull of the sheets against her naked body, the softness of the mattress beneath her, and Jack standing next to the bed, now holding out the dressing gown to her. Margaret stared at the dressing gown uncomprehendingly, for the only thing her mind focused on in that moment was what she had done.

She had made love with Jack. She had given her virginity to Jack. Some part of her thought she must surely feel regret at such an action or, at the very least, soiled in some way. But she felt none of those things. In truth, she felt rather splendid. There was not an ounce of regret to be found in her, and when she reached out and took the dressing gown, she smiled at Jack.

"Havoc?" she asked.

He nodded. "It seems every time I bring you pleasure, your body's reaction is to fall asleep," he said, perching on the edge of the bed and leaning into her. "It seems to me that you have no problem at all with feeling."

Margaret wrinkled her brow, feeling her smile slip away. "I'm sorry, but I must disagree," she said, but Jack was already shaking his head.

"It's not that you cannot feel, Maggie, but rather, I'm not sure you know what to do with the feelings you do have."

This had her raising an eyebrow. "Know what to do?"

Jack nodded and stood, walking away from her in the direction of the door. She thought he was going to leave, but he stopped at one of the misplaced tables, picking up a tray that had been set there. The room was dim with only the candlelight reaching so far, but it appeared to be another tray of tea and sandwiches. At the sight of food, her stomach made a funny protesting noise, and Margaret pressed a hand to her stomach as if to still it. Turning, Jack stopped and looked at her, but he only raised an eyebrow at her body's betrayal.

"I beg your pardon," she said, pushing her arms into the sleeves of the dressing gown and scooting to the edge of the bed to stand and wrap the gown around her body.

But upon standing she stopped, gazing down the length of her body. "My stockings are still on," she said, looking up to find Jack had bent over the low table between the mismatched chairs, the tray nearly setting down on the table's surface when her words seemed to stop him.

"Yes, they are," he said, "But I did manage to remove your slippers this time."

Margaret finished tying the robe about her waist and bent, undoing her garters and slipping the silk stockings down her legs. She tossed the garments aside and straightened to find Jack staring at her. She looked behind her where she had thrown the stockings on the bed and then looked back at Jack.

"Did you find that appealing?" she asked. "When I removed my stockings just there?"

Jack swallowed. She could see the movement in his throat even from where she was standing.

"Yes, quite," he finally said, and she felt the smile return to her face.

Margaret padded over to him, her toes sinking into the plush weave of the carpet, and she looked down, noticing for the first time the vibrant hues of wool weaved into an intricate pattern of contrasting swirls and lines.

"This certainly did not come with the house," she said, stepping back to see as much of the design as possible.

"No, it did not," Jack said, and she heard the clink of

teapot to cups as he presumably poured. "I acquired that from a pirate actually."

Margaret looked up quickly. "A pirate?"

Jack nodded as he arranged her cup of tea with only cream on a saucer opposite him. "I saved his son from an opposing legion of pirates, and the rug was given to me in gratitude. It was a fine rug, so I wasn't going refuse it."

Margaret finished making her way to the chairs and took the one opposite Jack, tucking her legs beneath her. "You're allowed to accept gifts from pirates?" she asked.

Jack raised an eyebrow at her. "He never told me he was a pirate, so in that case, I felt the exchange was more than ethical."

Margaret picked up her tea, but before sipping, she said, "I suppose that would be accurate. Now explain to me how it is that you've developed this theory of me being able to feel, because I have rather intimate knowledge on the subject and have come to a starkly different conclusion."

"You're perfectly capable of feeling, but your body has gone so long without having something about which to feel that you do not know how to properly handle emotions when they arise. That's why you're always falling asleep on me."

"That is why I fall asleep? You do not believe it is from the sheer boredom instigated by the present company?"

Jack quirked an eyebrow, but she saw the corners of his mouth twitch in a grin.

"Yes, that is why. It is also why you do not cry."

This had her dropping her teacup back in its saucer. "I beg your pardon," she said more sharply than she meant to.

"Crying is an outlet, a channel through which people express how they feel about a current situation or occurrence. It is my belief that due to the young age at which you were forced to suffer through tragedy, you never properly developed healthy channels through which to express yourself."

Margaret's mind raced through his statement looking for holes in his theory that would allow her to continue to believe herself incapable of feeling, but she found nothing.

His statement was perfectly true, his arguments carefully crafted.

But--

"There are times, however, when I still feel nothing at all. Like sympathy, or - what was that word that you used?"

He looked up from his study of the sandwiches on the tray to say, "Empathy," before returning to his perusal of the food.

"Yes, empathy. How is it that I can be capable of feeling, but still have moments of nothing?"

Jack selected two sandwiches, placing one on a napkin and handing it to her. "That is a professional hazard."

She took the sandwich and placed it in her lap along with her forgotten teacup and saucer.

"Professional hazard?"

Jack nodded. "It is my personal opinion that what you need is distraction. Perhaps a hobby that does not involve international intrigue."

Jack took a bite of his sandwich.

She frowned at him. "I am in the domestic unit. I do not dally in situations involving international intrigue."

"Domestic intrigue, then," he said, setting down his sandwich and brushing his hands together as if to rid them of crumbs. "The point is, at a tender age in your development, you experienced a loss that would have had a fully developed adult lost as to how to comprehend what had occurred, and then you immediately entered service as a War Office agent. When you were child. I am no expert in the field of child development, but it seems to me that you missed a very important part of a person's emotional development by engaging in work that required the utmost level of objectivity."

Margaret sat perfectly still as she processed what he had just said, somewhere in her mind feeling the click of something that sent a pulse of warmth through her person.

"So what you are saying is that I am not abnormally wounded in my inability to feel, but rather that I don't know how to express the emotions that I might have and thus prevent myself from having them?"

Jack picked up his sandwich again.

"Yes, something like that," he said. "And through normal interaction with humans outside of a government agency, you'll likely develop the ability to process such emotions in due time. Now, eat your sandwich. You'll need your strength to listen to my story about our mystery man saving my life earlier today."

Margaret had just taken a sip of her tea, when Jack's words caused her to choke, spraying the liquid as she did so. "What?" she said, her chest heaving as she coughed to clear her throat from the dangerous drink.

Jack looked up, eyes wide in concern. "Easy, Maggie," he said, "It was rather shocking, I'll admit, but I did survive."

Margaret stared at him. "The mystery man?" she asked.

Jack nodded and then proceeded to tell her what happened at the meeting of the Gardening Society earlier that day. She listened carefully until he got to the part about the stone gargoyle.

"You're making that up," she said, but Jack shook his head.

"On my honor as a soldier, it was a stone gargoyle," he said.

Margaret wrinkled her brow. "Is our assassin reading gothic novels?"

Jack shrugged. "I questioned the same thing, but I didn't

have time to think on it with our mystery man grinning at me."

The events of the day raced through her mind, and she began talking, speaking the thoughts that lay jumbled in her mind. "The Duke of Lofton denied having any illegitimate offspring," she said, "So I went to the agent who holds the book myself to ensure the integrity of the item."

Jack looked at her. "You went to the book?" he asked. "I thought no one knows where it is."

Margaret shook her head. "No one does," she said. "I only know of the agent who guards it and where she is stationed. I often deliver missives to her for additions to the book."

Jack shook his head. "I still cannot believe these things exist," he said.

Margaret smiled at him. "There's more. I asked her if there were any unusual occurrences in the previous week, and she mentioned a man who had bumped into her at market and taken her for coffee."

Jack frowned at her mention of coffee, but she went on.

"While I was there, she received a lovely note from the man, apologizing again and thanking her for taking coffee with him."

"How is that unusual?" Jack asked.

"The agent seemed quite smitten with the man, and I asked her about him." She paused to ensure she had Jack's attention. "The man was American."

Jack's only reaction was to blink quietly at her.

Then he said, "American?"

Margaret nodded. "I think our American friend is poking around."

Jack picked up his teacup again. "Is he working for the Office then? Being married to Kate, it would not be a stretch."

Margaret shrugged. "I have never heard of an American

working for the Office, but it does not mean it has never happened."

Jack leaned back in his chair. "So let's review what we have learned today. Our assassin is getting bolder."

Margaret nodded. "An attempt on your life made in the presence of a swarm of gentlemen of the ton was quite daring, to say the least."

Jack agreed. "Indeed, and rather clumsy, too. How could he have ensured it was me that would be standing under that statue when it fell?"

Margaret pursed her lips. "But the mystery man, whom we had previously suspected of being the assassin, saved you."

Jack stepped in, "Saved me and made sure I saw it was him. I think that's important."

"I think so, too," Margaret said. "And more, someone sent word to the War Office, because the War Office alerted me of the situation."

"So who was it that alerted the War Office?" Jack asked.

Margaret shook her head. "The only thing I can imagine is if there was another agent there. Someone who you and I both do not know is an acting agent for the Office."

Jack shook his head but stopped the motion abruptly, his gaze traveling to hers.

"There was someone else," he said, his words sounding as if he had surprised even himself. "I'm not sure how I could have forgotten it."

Margaret waited, her sandwich and tea forgotten.

"The second butler, Fitzwilliam."

She sat up. "The strange man I encountered below stairs at the Harrison gala?"

"Yes, precisely him. He was there as well. I saw him just before I heard the statue begin to fall."

Margaret blinked at him. "So we have the dour second

butler from Lofton House and the mystery man in attendance at the second attempt on your life?"

Jack frowned. "It still doesn't sit well with me. Death by falling statue has too many variables."

"Unless the assassin was there to position you under the statue," Margaret said, and for a moment, she thought she saw something pass over Jack's face, but it was so quick, she couldn't be sure.

"It seems rather too obvious to be the man from Lofton House," he said and then looked at her, his brow wrinkling, "Doesn't it? And then there's Mr. Thatcher, going right for the source of this entire mess."

"The book," Margaret said, "But I'm beginning to believe the book is not part of this."

Jack looked at her, his gaze clear.

"Why not? Isn't that where you planted the information about me being an agent?"

Margaret nodded, but her lips pursed in consternation. "Yes, it was, but there was something that Richard said earlier today that has my curiosity piqued."

Jack sat up. "Go on," he said.

"Richard mentioned that there are too many obstacles between someone wanting the book and him actually obtaining it. That there are other ways of discovering the identities of agents."

Jack nodded but did not interrupt.

"He suggested I investigate families that the War Office has aided."

Now Jack said, "Because if the War Office helped these families, members of the family would have had the opportunity to get close to operatives."

"Precisely. And then this individual would have had opportunity and possibly motive."

"Motive?" Jack questioned.

Margaret felt some of her energy wane as she said, "Sometimes the War Office is not always successful in its missions."

Jack's face was expressionless in the candlelight, but she knew he would quietly react to such a statement. He had been a soldier in many campaigns and would likely know the reality of dangerous situations. Good intentions never guaranteed good outcomes.

"What is it we do from here?" Jack asked after several moments of silence.

"We do nothing," Margaret said, placing her untouched sandwich on the table and untucking her feet. "My assignment is to keep you safe, and that means you must stay out of sight."

She expected resistance from him, but Jack only sat there, leaning forward on elbows braced against his knees. After some moments, he stood, walking once more in the direction of the door.

"Then I suggest you get some sleep. I have a feeling you'll be doing some sleuthing when tomorrow comes, and you'll need your strength," he said.

Margaret raised an eyebrow at his retreating back but stood also, feeling the slightest tick of caution at her neck. Jack was a soldier after all and to acquiesce to her demands that he stay out of a situation that involved his attempted death did not sit well with him. However, he was right. She did need rest. Tomorrow she would go to the War Office and get a record of the families that had requested aid from the War Office, specifically involving the use of secret agents.

Jack reached the door in the corner of the room, setting his hand on the knob. But before turning it, he looked back at her.

"I hope you don't mind a sleeping buddy," he said and opened the door.

Captain Edwards came pounding into the room, ears flying out behind him, before defying the very laws of gravity as he leaped, gliding through the air as if he were a bird and not an over-large hound, landing softly on the bed, his rump falling sideways as he used his front paws to push himself the rest of the way over. The dog lay there, paws flung carelessly in the air, back arched in splendid relaxation.

"The captain likes to snuggle," Jack said as he walked past her, extinguishing candles as he went.

"Snuggle?" she asked.

Jack nodded, blowing out the remaining candle and getting into the bed as he shed his own dressing gown. The room was too dark to be certain, but Margaret thought he was likely naked. The thought sent a pleasant thrill through her.

"And he steals the covers," Jack said, sliding between the sheets and adjusting his legs in consideration of the sleeping dog.

Margaret went to the opposite side, carefully picking up the covers and getting in.

"You must be joking," she said, pulling the sheets up to her neck.

But no sooner were the words out of her mouth than Captain Edwards flipped over, crawling on his belly in her direction.

"Oh God," she said, just as the hound landed his front paws on her stomach, his head landing directly on her bosom.

She turned her head to look at Jack.

"Likes to snuggle," was all he said, then turned on his side, tucking his pillow beneath his head, and closing his eyes.

It was sometime later as Margaret listened to both Jack and Captain Edwards' soft snores that she thought about what Jack had said and wondered if one day she really would learn how to let herself feel. The dog moved then, his large head falling into the crook of her shoulder, his nose nestling under her chin, and in that position, he let out a great sigh that rippled along the length of her body. Lying there in the dark, Margaret felt an odd tug somewhere against her ribs and closed her eyes against it.

CHAPTER 16

"*A*t this juncture, I think it is necessary that I say I am completely against this plan."

Jack stood next to Margaret in the overheated and over-crowded drawing room of Admiral Esmund Bishop's townhouse.

"Your input is duly noted," Jack said, his eyes scanning the room for anything out of the ordinary.

He wasn't sure what would be considered out of the ordinary, as this was his first invitation to a musicale at the admiral's home. Jack had heard that the admiral hosted fellow members of His Majesty's Royal Navy on occasions at his home in Mayfair, whether it was in or out of season, for a chance to hear his accomplished daughters at their instruments. Upon arriving that evening, it was easily apparent that either the entire ton wished to be in attendance for the simple fact of impressing a Lord Commissioner of the Admiralty, or perhaps Admiral Bishop's daughters were, indeed, quite accomplished at their instruments.

Whichever the reason may be, the drawing room into

which the guests had gathered was brimming with the most fashionable people Jack had seen since his return to London.

And one of them most likely wanted him dead through no fault of his own.

"Using yourself as bait to lure the assassin out is neither wise nor prudent," Margaret continued.

"Prudent?" Jack asked, turning to look at her.

She wore a splendid ensemble of varying shades of blue, and it made her eyes spark in the chandeliers of the room. And once he was looking at her, he couldn't help but let his gaze travel the length of her. His body responded at just the sight, and in his mind, he imagined undressing her when he finally got her to his bedchamber that night. He pushed the thought away as they had very important matters to attend to. He could not allow himself to be distracted while someone was plotting his death.

Margaret nodded at him, but her eyes, too, scanned the room.

"It would be terribly inconvenient for me if you were to be killed," she said.

Jack smiled softly and returned his gaze to the buzzing room. "I shall keep that in mind, Lady Folton," he said.

As his eyes searched, he wondered momentarily what an assassin looked like, but he discarded the notion as he was fairly certain the assassin could look like anything or be anyone. For a moment, Jack wondered if the assassin were, in fact, a woman. He cast a glance at Margaret and thought the notion highly probable.

"I think this plan is one of absolute necessity," Jack said, and he heard Margaret give a rather unladylike snort beside him.

"And why is that?"

"When you requested the records from the War Office of

the families they had aided, how long was it they said it would take to gather those files?"

He felt more than saw Margaret's reaction to this statement. Her shoulders slumped beside him, and he turned in time to see her frown.

"Weeks at the earliest," she murmured and took a sip of her champagne.

"Precisely," he said. "I shall not be waiting weeks in the confines of my townhouse while a killer roams around London selecting targets at random."

Margaret pursed her lips. "The targets are very far from random, my lord," she said.

And Jack raised an eyebrow at her. "Well, except for you, of course," she added.

Jack looked about the room again, starting in the far corner where a set of doors opened onto what were presumably a terrace and the entrance to the townhouse's gardens. As the weather had finally turned, there were few people milling about the doors and terrace, preferring to stay away from the cool night air and in the throng of guests crowding the main part of the long room.

Jack imagined the second butler from Lofton House stepping in front of him to declare his guilt, as unlikely as that may seem, but staring at the terrace doors, Jack suddenly had an idea. And he knew Margaret would hate it.

"I think I will go for a stroll," he said.

Margaret snorted into her champagne, reaching out a hand to seize his elbow.

"You will do no such thing," she said, but Jack was already setting his own glass on a passing tray.

He turned, taking Margaret's glass and setting it on the same tray, before taking both of her hands in his.

"Maggie, do you trust me?" he asked, his voice so low he wasn't sure if she'd heard him.

But when her eyes darkened, turning the shimmering blues of a deep midnight, he knew that she had heard him.

"This cannot go on forever," he continued, "We must find the assassin now."

Margaret shook her head.

"He'll kill you," she said.

Jack frowned. "I'm a commodore in His Majesty's Royal Navy. Do you think me unable to take care of myself?" he asked.

And now Margaret frowned. "Arrogance does not suit you," she mumbled and pulled her hands from his. "I'll come with you."

"No, you won't," he said and turned, disappearing into the crowd before she could follow him.

WATCHING the place where Jack had disappeared, Margaret wondered if this was the first time in her life when her personal state resembled that of someone fuming. It was not a condition she had ever been struck with that she could recall, and the sensation felt odd. As if she wanted to cause bodily harm to the bloody man who so carelessly disregarded his life.

Without thinking, she snatched another glass of champagne from a passing servant and took a great gulp of the stuff. It fizzed down her throat and made her cough as bubbles made their way up the back of her nose. The entire thing was unbecoming for a lady and absolutely deplorable for an agent. She set down the glass of champagne on the next passing tray and wrapped her arms around her middle, physically demanding herself to get a hold of not only her person but her mind.

Jack was a commodore, a military man trained in all

aspects of battle. He could take care of himself. Surely, he would not do anything rash that would put him in peril. Surely, he would not be that stupid.

This time when a servant passed her, Margaret selected a glass of lemonade and turned herself about the room, cataloging the guests as she did so. There were earls and marquesses, dukes and ladies, and mere misses. There was even a baron and a baronet. There was no one to cause Margaret suspicion, but as the room was filled with titled gentlemen and women, her suspicions were raised for other reasons.

The assassin could be targeting any of these persons in this room.

The thought was weighty and threatened to suffocate her. But it was valid, as Margaret did not know many other agents actively working for the Office. There could be any number of them in this room tonight. And somehow, the assassin had figured out how to identify them.

For a moment, Margaret's thoughts drifted to Miss Beaupre and the book ensconced at Kensington Palace. But just as soon as she thought of it, she discarded it. The book was safe. Miss Beaupre had confirmed it.

But then why did their American friend ask such questions about it? What was he trying to discover and for whom? Was he aiding the Duchess of Lofton? Did he, too, know that the Duke of Lofton was still alive?

Amidst these rambling thoughts, Margaret became aware of something else. A conversation being held directly behind her by two women she had not had a chance to glimpse.

"It was him, was it not?" one woman said, her voice harshly nasal and pinched.

"I believe it was, but he is hardly seen at such functions. Not since, well, you know," came a second voice, this one crisp and cultured.

"And why would he be here? At the home of a Lord Commissioner of the Admiralty?" this from the nasal voice.

"It seems rather upsetting, doesn't it?" came the cultured voice again.

Margaret shifted on her feet, her heart racing, hoping the nasal voice would explain what was so upsetting about someone or other being at the admiral's home and preferably, a name of this someone. Perhaps Fitzwilliam. That would tie everything together nicely.

"I remember his dear sister, the poor lass," came the nasal voice, and Margaret frowned.

This conversation that had sounded so promising was very likely to go completely off course, and Margaret would learn nothing useful about this gentleman whose appearance was so odd. A flicker of apprehension passed through her, though, at the women's words, and Margaret's mind settled on Jack. She looked at the spot where he had disappeared and wondered where he had gone and if he was safe.

She swallowed and forced herself to believe that he was, for she would be useless to him if she thought anything else.

"Why, hello, Lady Folton, what a pleasure to see you again!"

Margaret startled herself out of her own thoughts and looked up, hoping to find the source of the masculine voice, but when her eyes met only air, she looked directly about her, her gaze settling on Sir Toby Hall, his large ears and round spectacles shining in the light of the chandeliers.

"Sir Hall," Margaret said, curtsying, "So good to see you again."

Sir Hall bowed, almost bouncing on the heels of his feet in some unknown source of amusement.

"Have you seen the gardens, my dear?" he asked, his eyes bright and wide. "The Bishops have a splendid assortment of day lilies. They're almost finished for the season, but you can still see them. I would be happy to--"

He moved as if to escort her toward the terrace doors along one side of the room, but Margaret carefully extracted herself.

"Oh, I would love to, but perhaps some other time. I'm just waiting for someone, you see," she said, smiling until her face hurt.

She thought she saw disappointment cloud Sir Hall's overly exuberant face, but then like a snap it was gone, and his expression hung brightly between them like it had its very own sun.

"I will surely take you up on that offer of viewing them another time, Lady Folton," Sir Hall said with a twisted grin of amusement.

Margaret smiled again, but she feared it resembled more of a smirk than anything.

"That would be splendid, Sir Hall," she said, and with a jaunty salute, the bouncy man took off into the crowd.

Margaret trained her ears, hoping the women behind her were still speaking, but when she centered on the sound of their voices, all she heard was a delicate explanation of embroidered leaves. She sighed and drank the rest of her champagne in a single swallow. Setting the empty glass on a table, Margaret pressed into the crowd in search of Jack.

* * *

JACK STOOD with his hands on his hips, eyeing the display of day lilies that made up one side of the terrace garden bed. This particular bed wrapped around the entire length of the stone terrace and overflowed with various species of day lilies.

He stood at the base of the steps, the night air swirling

about him in a confusing mass of wind and captured conversations. There were a few couples strolling along the terrace, and parts of their speech reached him as he paced back and forth along the edge of the steps. But otherwise, the night remained quiet, the gardens silent about him and around him, and no one had approached him since he'd left the confines of the townhouse.

Making his circuit, he turned back, pacing once more along the ridge until he turned with the curve of the terrace, his footsteps carrying him into the place where day lilies gave way to delphiniums and phlox. He didn't stay overlong at this end of the terrace, for the lights from the drawing room did not reach it, leaving it in shadows that welcomed assassins, he was sure. Turning back he made his way toward the steps once more and, just as he made the curve, he caught sight of a very familiar figure in blues disappearing into the hedges of the gardens. He frowned but picked up his pace, following her into the heart of the gardens.

Did she really think him mad enough to disappear into the darkness when someone was trying to kill him? He wanted to lure the assassin out of hiding, so he could get a look at the man or ascertain some other clue as to his identity. He did not want to give the man the perfect opportunity with which to complete his mission.

He entered the hedges and spotted the scrap of blue disappearing around a corner, and he followed, picking up his feet until he was almost running after her. When he found her, he would be sure to tell her he did not support her plan in the slightest. What was she thinking going out into the dark with an assassin on the loose?

Rounding the corner, he slowed, spotting Margaret only yards in front of him, her eyes searching the opening in the hedges, likely searching for him. He opened his mouth to call out to her, but he never got the chance. He saw her attacker seconds before she did as the man stepped from a row of hedges, his hands going up as a string of wire fell perfectly around Margaret's throat.

She didn't have time to scream. He knew that. One moment everything was sound and calm, and the next, there was a wire about her throat, strangling her. He saw her hands go up in reaction, her knees buckle with the realization that her air was being cut off.

And then his body moved.

He couldn't recall having made a conscious decision, of having had any sort of plan. It was as if one moment he was standing there, watching the woman he loved have her very life threatened, and the next his body connected with the attacker.

They went down in a heap, their bodies striking dirt and grass, pitching them up against the hedges of the garden. Aromas swamped him. It was an odd thing to realize in the heat of battle, but there it was. The sensation stunned him, and his mind raced ahead, keeping his body moving to fend off the assassin, while at the same time a part of him struggled to identify the scents that assailed him the moment he had made contact with the attacker.

Jack knew he was deep within carefully cultivated gardens, and he shoved at his persistent mind, quieting the urge to identify the smells that engulfed him. He gained his feet, crouching low to keep his assailant off balance as to his intended target. In the darkness, Jack caught a glimpse of Margaret, collapsed on the ground, hands at her throat, but in that glimpse, he saw her chest heaving and knew she was all right. Hurt and confused, but all right.

And in taking that glimpse, Jack had left himself exposed, a powerful right hook connecting with his jaw, sending him backwards before he had known he was even hit. Once more on the ground, he rolled, surging to his feet several paces away from the last attack. Swirling and crouching, he caught sight of the assailant and for the first time, Jack realized how short the man was.

Something in his brain suddenly settled, its urgency over identifying the smells that had come with the attack, quieting with this new piece of evidence. And with the quieting of his mind, Jack stilled, his body frozen as he looked at the assailant standing feet away, a black blur in the darkness, arms ready in a boxer's stance. And the attacker had frozen, too, as if somehow knowing that Jack had made a connection that the attacker had never wanted made.

Out of the blankness that had cloaked Jack came the sound of Margaret's strangled breathing. He dropped his hands and reached behind him, finding Margaret's shoulders. Swinging about, he lifted her, pulling her bodily into his arms and then he ran. His long, powerful legs carrying him back the way they had come, but instead of turning in the direction of the terrace, he swung around, going deeper to the other end of the gardens.

When he knew he had put enough distance between them and the attacker, Jack eased Margaret back in his arms.

"Is there a back way out of here?" he asked.

Margaret still held a hand to her throat, her mouth gasping for breath. She held up the other hand, pointing in the direction they were moving. Jack put on speed, running once more in the direction she pointed. It was only moments later when they burst from the walls of the garden and stumbled onto the alley that ran between the homes in this area.

Margaret coughed suddenly and tugged at his arm.

"Let me walk," she said, but it came out hoarse and garbled.

He shook his head, turning in the direction that would lead them to the street and their carriage. They emerged moments later, and Jack found the Folton colors amid the sea of carriages at the street. Making his way to the conveyance, he called up to Margaret's driver with instructions to head toward Number 13 Claremont before climbing in, settling Margaret on his lap.

He cupped her face in his hands, his fingers trailing down to the angry red welt at her throat. In the dim light of the carriage, the redness stood in stark contrast to the paleness of her neck. He trembled at the sight of it, his body responding in a way his mind could not fathom just then.

"Are you all right?" he asked and was surprised to find his voice had gone weak.

Margaret nodded. "I think he's trying to kill me now, too," she croaked, and Jack smiled at her in the darkness before placing a tender kiss against her lips.

"God, I love you, Maggie," he said, the words falling effortlessly from his lips.

He felt her still against him, and he laid a finger against her opened mouth.

"I do not need to hear you say the same, darling. I just needed you to hear it from me," he said before she could speak. "Besides, we have more important things to discuss."

Margaret closed her mouth and watched him.

"I know who the assassin is," he said.

CHAPTER 17

*M*argaret's throat burned, and several reasons sallied forth to give her opportunity to burst into tears at any moment, should she be capable of such a feat. But instead she sat, numb and mute beside Jack as her carriage bounced its way through London.

"Sir Toby Hall," she finally said, her voice strained against the bruises that she was sure bloomed around her throat.

Jack nodded, his face resigned in the dim light of the carriage. "And I believe you will find Sir Toby Hall in those files you requested from the War Office," Jack said, his gaze focused on the floor of the carriage.

Margaret watched Jack, watched the way his shoulders slumped as he named his friend an assassin of British operatives. Without really knowing why, she slipped her hand into his, bringing it to rest in her lap as her fingers threaded through his. Somewhere he had lost his gloves, and the heat of his skin burned through the silk of her own glove. She unlaced their fingers long enough to pull the glove from her hand, and then rethreaded their fingers. The entire time Jack stared at the floor.

"I would?" she said when he did not say more about why Sir Toby Hall would be in War Office files.

Jack's hand was firm in her own, but his other worried the weave of his breeches. It was the first time she had seen him make any such unnecessary gesture, and her eyes fixated on it, her stomach roiling.

Sir Toby Hall.

In her own mind, she thought of the little man with his odd ears and his rounded head that matched the shape of his spectacles and came to only one conclusion. That the man was perfectly harmless, if a little over eager to share on the subject of flora.

But an assassin?

And then Margaret recalled their first meeting. The sadness that came to his eyes when he spoke of his sister, and she said without feeling, "Martha."

"I don't know the details of it," Jack said. "Or rather, I don't know the version that the War Office would know, now that I understand they have a hand in these things."

He spoke at the floor, and Margaret picked up a hand, massaging the place where the wire had pulled into her skin.

"But Sir Toby's father had a post in India. He was a man at the British East India Company. Diplomatic post or some such thing. It must have been around the time Toby was an adolescent. Perhaps fifteen or sixteen."

Margaret thought about the man she knew now with his gray ring of hair and skin gone soft around taut muscles made strong by Jackson's Saloon. Her fingers pressed into the abused line of skin at her throat.

"That would have been around 1780 then," she said, calculating his age in her head.

He turned his head to cast a small grin at her. "It was 1778 actually," he said. "Or at least that was the year his family left India."

His gaze returned to the floor of the carriage as he continued. "His sister, Martha, the one for whom the roses are named. She was taken hostage during the conflict there between the East India Company and the Kingdom of Maratha."

Margaret swam back in her memory, pouring through her history lessons her governess pounded into her as a young girl, and then more during her training to enter the War Office as a domestic agent. If she recalled correctly there were several conflicts between the East India Company and the Kingdom of Maratha on the Indian sub-continent. It had something to do with the British supporting one of the parties laying claim to power in the region, or the right to be called Peshwa. The British had provided troops in the conflict at the time in question.

"What happened to Martha?" Margaret asked.

Jack shook his head. "Sir Toby's father pleaded with the East India Company for help, but none came," Jack said. "Like I said, there is probably more detail in the files at the War Office. But--"

He stopped and turned his head toward her again, his eyes searching hers but for what she could not say.

"She was raped," he said, the words toneless in the dark, "Repeatedly. She was raped and beaten until finally she succumbed. No help ever reached Sir Toby's family, and they left India then."

Margaret felt her abused throat close for reasons other than physical hurt. Her heart slowed, and she feared it would stop completely at Jack's words. But then with a thunderous bump, it started again, and she felt within her a surge of something she could not name. It passed over her limbs in a quiet rush of sensation that left her fingers tingling and her legs restless. In a breath, she remembered what Jack had said. About letting herself feel, giving herself permission to allow the emotions to come, and having come, evaporate from her as they should. But as the wave passed over her, it was followed by nothing but the familiar empty void.

She gripped Jack's hand more tightly.

"And now he wants to hurt all of those who were not there to save his sister," Margaret said.

And Jack nodded. "What is it that they say about revenge? It's best to wait?"

Margaret nodded, in her mind feeling a tug of sympathy. "Something like that," she said, and then she turned her gaze to the window, watching as carriages passed in between the flicker of lamplight and passing townhouses.

"What do we do now?" Jack asked.

"The War Office will intervene likely. Apprehend Sir Hall and bring him in for treason."

Thinking on this, she turned back to Jack suddenly. "How is it that you knew it was him?" she asked, suddenly realizing she had accepted Jack's statement for fact without questioning him.

Jack turned that small grin in her direction. "He smelled like Martha roses," Jack said, "And it's rather ironic as he never would let anyone have a sprout of those flowers. Now it will be his undoing."

"Martha roses," Margaret said, and then something else came into her mind. "Jack, do you realize you've unmasked a traitorous assassin using your hard earned knowledge of cultivating flowers?"

Jack blinked at her, his eyes flashing in the dark. "Yes, I believe that's true. What of it?"

She smiled at him in the dark, the movement hurting as it pulled at the skin along her jaw and throat, but she kept smiling. "Don't you see?" she said. "That's quite a feat to accomplish, and you did it without any shred of luck whatsoever."

Jack only blinked at her still, and she felt her euphoria at her realization ebb. But then Jack's face melted into a smile, his mouth moving wide and the flash of his teeth coming through the dark.

"I suppose I did," he said and leaned forward to kiss her.

Margaret moved into him, welcoming his heat, his desire, his love. She wished for a moment that she had returned his declaration of love, but just then, she had been unable to do more than breathe. And now as he kissed her, she felt the words pooling inside of her, willing her to speak them.

She broke the kiss, easing him away from her. "Jack," she said, and then said nothing more as the carriage lurched to an unexpected halt.

She grabbed at Jack's broad shoulders to keep from spilling onto the floor of the carriage as their conveyance came to a sudden stop. Once more her heart ceased beating in her chest and her stomach flipped with anticipation.

"Jack, what's happened?" she whispered, knowing that he could not possibly have any more information than her but needing to know he was there.

He only shook his head as a shouted command rang through the night.

"Stand and deliver."

* * *

MARGARET RAISED an eyebrow that almost made Jack laugh.

"Highwaymen?" Margaret whispered. "Doesn't one need be on a highway to have highwaymen accost them?"

Jack raised his own eyebrow. "I am not sure, my lady, but it does seem rather suspicious. Does it not?"

Jack let go of her long enough to turn toward the window of the carriage. He took in the sight of three mounted men, shadowed in the darkest pitch of black. Their faces were shrouded, and even in the lamplight along the street, he could not make out their features. Suddenly, the door opened, and Jack found himself staring down the barrel of a gun. He put up his hands out of reflex and moved back, spreading his arms to shield Margaret sitting behind him.

This fourth man was slighter than the other three and moved with a rather unusual degree of grace, as he mounted the steps into the carriage, pistol held steady in one hand. Gaining purchase within the carriage, the fourth man had them pressed nearly to the opposite door. Margaret sat pinched at his back, her small hands pressing into him as if holding him steady.

And then the man spoke with the most refined feminine voice Jack had ever heard. "Terribly sorry about this," it said, right before the gun struck the side of his head and everything went black.

* * *

WHEN NEXT HE opened his eyes, the room swam in front of him. Images colliding with one another as colors and shapes defined themselves and became objects and persons.

Multiple persons.

Jack pushed back, his arms tightening to fight the bindings on his arms and legs. And as he pulled tightly, he found his arms and legs flying free, his entire person coming up off the chair in which he had found himself.

"Easy, mate," came a voice from behind him, easing him back into his chair with a soft hand at his shoulder. "I apologize for the behavior of my wife," the voice continued. "She's quite a spirited one when the mood strikes her."

Jack blinked rapidly as everything suddenly swung into focus, and the room stood before him in perfect clarity. But before he had time to take in the appearance of anyone standing before him, he heard Margaret's crisp voice from beside him.

"Lady Lofton," she said, her tone perfectly even and without surprise.

Jack swung his head in the direction of her voice and found not only Margaret seated perfectly at ease beside him but the Duchess of Lofton standing just in front of her, her hands calmly folded before her, the absolute picture of quiet domesticity.

Seeing Margaret unharmed, Jack sagged in relief, his feet sliding along the floor as his muscles gave out. He leaned back in his own chair, finding it plush and firm, and rather finely crafted. Looking about the room, he realized they were in some sort of library. The room was well appointed with heavy, masculine furniture and deep, inviting colors.

And there was an entire contingent of soldiers standing all about them. At least they appeared to be soldiers, if Jack was to tell anything by their alert stances. His eyes traveled from one to the other. There was the Duchess of Lofton, the pregnant maid from their visit that afternoon to Lofton House, the stoic butler who would not give up his guard, and then--

"Kate," Jack said, his eyes riveted on his childhood friend.

She pointed at her own head. "Very sorry about clubbing you, Jack," she said. "We had to make it appear that we were really kidnapping the lot of you should your carriage have been followed."

"Oh, that's quite all right," Jack found himself saying as he moved his gaze to her American husband.

And then he paused once more in his scan of the room. "You," he said, as their mysterious man lounged on the arm of a sofa set before them.

"It's Nathan Black, actually," the man said. "And I would

apologize for the blow to your head, but I did save your life earlier this week. I think that makes us even."

Jack only blinked at him as the Earl of Stryden stepped up next to the man. And then Jack blinked harder.

"He does have another son," Margaret said from beside him, her tone having turned indignant.

The Duchess of Lofton laughed. "Did he tell you he didn't?" the duchess asked, her face alight with a smile.

Margaret frowned. "I suppose he never did say that," she mumbled.

Lady Lofton tilted her head. "Did you ask the wrong question then?" the duchess asked. "Richard is always terribly truthful when asked a question."

Margaret fixed her gaze on their mystery man, now identified as Nathan Black, and only frowned. "I suppose I did," she said.

And then a small, pretty woman with blonde hair wrapped tight at the nape of her neck, sporting what looked to be a man's black jacket and breeches, sat down on the sofa directly in front of them. It wasn't until she was fully seated that Jack realized it was the Countess of Stryden.

"It was me who gave you the blow, and my husband who apologized for it. But I won't apologize for it," she said, her face so stern, Jack sat back.

And then she burst into a laugh. "I'm just joshing you, my lord," she said. "I just hope it looked authentic enough to throw off any pursuers."

She smiled at them, a noticeable overbite forming lines around her mouth. Jack could only stare.

"I think it would save us time if you just tell us what you already know," Margaret said from beside him.

The Duchess of Lofton took a seat next to her daughter-in-law, smoothing her lavender skirts over her knees.

"Richard is alive," she said, "But someone made an attempt on his life, and he is now in hiding."

Jack looked at Margaret, but she made no outward sign of having heard what the duchess had just said.

"As we are all agents for the War Office in some capacity or another, we had all heard of the existence of the book of names," she went on, and Jack raised his eyebrows at this. "Its existence is rather famed for its value, and our first inclination was to believe that someone had taken possession of it and managed to decipher it."

"But that couldn't have been," Kate picked up the story. "Because my husband made contact with the agent guarding the book and ascertained that it had not been disturbed."

Now Margaret pursed her lips, and Jack imagined what she was thinking.

"We tasked Nathan here with following Viscount Pemberly in the chance that his life should be threatened again."

Margaret held up a hand. "Again?" she asked.

And now the pregnant maid stepped forward. "Mr. Thatcher was in the park the day you both were nearly run over by that curricle. That was when we first suspected the two of you were involved in something."

Margaret lowered her hand.

So Jack asked, "And who are you?"

The young woman smiled, lifting some of the weariness from her eyes. "I'm Mrs. Nora Black, Nathan's wife," she said.

Jack nodded. "This is quite the family you have," he said, directing this comment to the Duchess of Lofton who only smiled at him.

"So when we determined the integrity of the book, we knew the assassin must be coming at agents through another means of detection."

"And that was when we intercepted your request for files

containing information on families aided by the War Office," the Earl of Stryden said.

Jack thought Margaret would explode out of her chair, as her body straightened, her hands clenching the arms of her own chair. "You intercepted my request?"

Her question was carefully spoken for the tension that he could see in her body, and Jack wanted to smile. Lady Margaret Folton was channeling her emotions even if she did not realize it.

The Countess of Stryden stood and walked to a heavy desk set off to the side. "Indeed, and we have the files you requested."

The woman bent and picked up a large parcel wrapped in brown paper and tied with string. It looked like any package a lady may have acquired in her afternoon shopping. Jack marveled at its inconspicuous state. No one would suspect important documents lay within it.

The countess walked to Margaret and handed her the bundle. "You will need to tell us what you are looking for, however," she said. "We only made it this far when it became apparent that we would need to abduct the both of you for your own safety."

Margaret looked up sharply at that, but the countess only tapped two fingers against her own throat. Margaret mimicked the gesture, one hand moving to the vibrant red line along her throat.

"Although," Mrs. Nora Black came around the sofa then, "We were not expecting the assassin to target you now after so many attempts on Viscount Pemberly."

The woman pulled a footstool in front of Margaret and lowered herself on it. "May I?" she said, and bent to inspect the line along Margaret's throat before Margaret could grant permission.

In a few moments, Mrs. Black called over her shoulder,

"Hathaway, will you have them send up my medicine box with the tea cart?" she asked.

Margaret waved a hand. "Oh, that's truly not necessary," she said, "It's but a small pain, and--"

"Nonsense," the Duchess of Lofton said. "Now then, who is it that you are looking for and where is my husband?"

Jack would expect nothing if not complete focus from the Duchess of Lofton, and so he said, "Sir Toby Hall. At least, in answer to the first part of your question."

"White Chapel," Margaret said from beside him. "In answer to the second."

And then her head tilted, and Jack knew something bothered her. "Are you truly all agents for the Office?" And then turning to Jack as if he may hold the answers she sought, "How does everyone not know this?"

"I am not technically an agent and neither is Mr. Thatcher. We sort of married into the situation," Mrs. Black said from her footstool beside Margaret.

Margaret only shook her head.

Jack blinked. "You asked for a ship of the fleet during a war for a man who is not even in allegiance with the Crown?" Jack asked, his eyes wide in amazement as he looked at Kate.

Kate shrugged. "What would you have done?"

Jack's head turned toward Margaret before he could stop it, and he sat back, letting the scene continue without comment from him.

"Sir Toby Hall," Mr. Nathan Black said. "Is this revelation in connection with that mark on your neck?"

Margaret nodded. "It would appear Sir Toby Hall tried to kill me this evening. Jack intervened to save my life, and in doing so, he recognized a unique scent on Sir Hall."

Mr. Black looked at Jack. "Unique scent?"

"Sir Toby grows a special hybrid strand of roses that he

named after his deceased sister, Martha. Martha roses contain an original mixture of heritage and plum roses. Both species of roses used to create the hybrid are extremely powerful in scent. The combination gave them an unmistakable aroma. An aroma I smelled on the attacker tonight."

Lady Stryden shook her head. "But couldn't anyone have that scent on them if they had these roses?"

Jack shook his head. "Sir Toby has never allowed anyone to have a sampling of these roses. He would be the only one to have the scent on his person, because he is the only one to have the roses."

Mr. Black scratched at his chin. "So Sir Toby Hall it is then," he said.

Beside him, Margaret had opened the parcel and was leafing through it when she suddenly stopped, extracting a single ream of parchment. "Here it is," she said, "Family Name: Hall. Person of Interest: Martha Hall," Margaret read from the parchment.

But she stopped and handed the ream to the Duchess of Lofton. "Viscount Pemberly has already told me the story. I do not need to read the details," she said, and without question, the duchess accepted the ream as Margaret settled into her seat.

Leafing through the papers, the Duchess of Lofton gave no notion that she was reading anything untoward. But when she finished, she quietly passed them on to her son, Nathan.

"That is awful," was all she said. "It appears Sir Hall's sister was taken hostage during the conflict in India between the East India Company and the Maratha kingdom. When seeking aid from the War Office, no aid was found."

Jack shook his head. "I've heard that, at that point in the fighting, the Crown's resources were spread so thinly between the colonies and the sub-continent, there were not men to spare."

"Or women," Lady Stryden added.

And Jack nodded in her direction.

"And now he's seeking vengeance against the War Office?" Mrs. Black asked.

"It would seem so," Margaret said.

Mr. Black had finished reading the papers and grimly handed them to his brother.

"Do you think Sir Hall knows you've marked him now?" Mr. Black asked Jack.

Jack remembered that moment in Admiral Bishop's gardens when his body tensed and his opponent seemed to freeze.

"Yes, I think he does know," he answered.

"This will change things," Kate said.

And her husband nodded. "He'll be both desperate to finish the game he's started and panicked at being discovered. When a hare is panicked it goes to ground," Thatcher said.

Margaret sat up. "We will not be using Viscount Pemberly as bait," she said before anyone could say anything else.

The room in general stared at her, but Jack was fairly certain he saw a knowing smile on Lady Lofton's lips.

"I suggest we employ our most useful spy," Lady Lofton said.

Margaret asked, "Your most useful spy? You mean there are more of you?"

Lady Lofton only laughed. "No, he's not a spy. At least not yet. He's just terribly useful at learning what happens within a house of the ton."

With this, the duchess turned in her seat and, looking to the stoic butler standing guard behind her, she said, "Hathaway, will you rouse Samuel?"

CHAPTER 18

*M*argaret stared at the boy as he shoved several chocolate biscuits from the teacart into his mouth, washing them all down with a drink of warm chocolate.

"You just want to know what's happening in the house?" he asked when his mouth was empty.

The lad could be no more than ten, his limbs still gangly, mostly elbows and knees, and his thick shock of dark hair sticking up where it had wedged into his pillow. The boy had been awakened with some haste, and his mother, Mrs. Black, had dressed him in clothes that contained more patches than whole pieces of fabric. It was anyone's guess if he were just a lad or a street urchin.

"Yes, Samuel, and we especially need to know what Sir Toby Hall is about," Mr. Black said to him.

Samuel nodded. "I think I can manage that. I'll be back in due haste," Samuel said, and before Margaret could realize what he was about, he took two of the chocolate biscuits and crumbled them in his hands, smashing them against his palms until chocolate smeared his their entirety.

Taking his now dirtied hands, he reached up and smeared his messy palms along his face. At this gesture, Margaret's mouth fell open without care. When his hands came away, it appeared as if the boy had spent days without a bath, covered in street filth, mud, and grime, when in fact he only just smeared chocolate all over his face. And then he leaned over and kissed his mother on the cheek.

"Do not worry, Mother. Grandfather taught me what to do," he said and ran from the library while Margaret continued to stare, seeing not a gangly boy but a young girl, standing too straight and walking with too great a care in a white pinafore and shiny black boots.

Margaret felt within her that strange vibration, and without thinking, she pushed it away, turning to the remaining people in the room.

"You're sending a child to discover the whereabouts of Sir Hall?"

The Duchess of Lofton looked at her. "He is no child, of that I can assure you. It is only luck that he happened to return in time to be of use. Otherwise, he would be all the way in York with Great Aunt Lydia and completely useless to us."

The woman stood.

"I suggest we take our rest as we may. It will be a long night, and a longer day tomorrow. Lady Folton, might I have a word with you before I retire?" Lady Lofton asked, turning just in the doorway of the library.

Margaret hesitated a moment and then, looking once at Jack, stood and followed the duchess from the room.

Margaret had never been in the bowels of Lofton House and found the furnishings in the corridor to be conservative but tasteful. Lamps lit along the way provided plenty of light for any person venturing in the corridors at night, and it made Margaret wonder as to the activities of Lofton House.

"You're in love with Viscount Pemberly," Lady Lofton said when they had traveled but only a few paces in the hall.

Margaret stopped short, the duchess' words ringing in her ears. Lady Lofton turned toward her when she must have realized she was walking alone, and giving Margaret a small smile, took her elbow gently and pulled her along the corridor.

"It is rather obvious to everyone," the duchess continued. "Although, I do not think it so obvious to you."

Margaret felt her throat closing, and she wanted to reach up, stroke the bandage Mrs. Black had placed across her neck earlier. But she wasn't one to make such a gesture of vulnerability, so she kept her hands where they were. But then Lady Lofton paused, drawing Margaret around so that they faced each other.

In the light of the lamps along the corridor, Margaret saw with clarity the lines framing the older woman's eyes and mouth. The lines were gentle, and Margaret wondered if that was what a lifetime of memories did to a person and, with this thought, she wondered if she would have that with Jack.

"I do love him," Margaret finally said without any further words from Lady Lofton.

And the duchess only smiled softly, before picking up Margaret's hands in her own.

"Margaret," she said, "I remember when Richard first met you, and he told me all about you. I was sad, Margaret."

Here the duchess paused, and Margaret felt it difficult to meet the woman's gaze. She, too, recalled that day in late November long ago when she had first met the Duke of Lofton. He had been kind to her and at a time when the scars of her parents' deaths were fresh and painful. She had always remembered that. But hearing about it from another person cast a dubious haze over the memory, and Margaret suddenly wondered what else she had perceived incorrectly.

"But I am not sad any longer," Lady Lofton said, and Margaret's eyes snapped to hers. "Viscount Pemberly is a noble man and a kind one. He will help heal the wounds you have not let come to light."

Here the duchess released one of her hands to pat the top of the other ever so gently. The woman's touch was soft and somewhere about her the smell of roses lingered, and for but a moment, Margaret wondered if this is what it would have felt like to have her mother touch her today. Would her mother's skin be so soft? Would she still wear the scent of lilacs?

But then Lady Lofton squeezed her hand.

"But be warned. It will not be easy. You will need to be braver than you ever have been before this," she said. "And if anyone makes the suggestion of acquiring a goat, you say no."

And with that the duchess let go of her hands and walked away, disappearing around a bend in the corridor.

Margaret stood where she had been left, the heat of the older woman's touch dissipating from her hands.

CHAPTER 19

*J*ack looked up when Margaret returned to the library and stood when she approached the furniture grouping the remaining members of their party still occupied.

"Is everything all right then?" Jack asked, and while Margaret smiled at him reassuringly, he saw the ghost of something pass over her face.

"Quite all right," she said and took a seat on the sofa he had adjourned to when their unexpected interrogation had broken up.

He resumed his seat and slipped his hand into Margaret's. The gesture was so normal for him that he did not realize the impropriety involved until he saw the quick glimpse from the Earl of Stryden. But the earl only smiled, an expression full of knowing, and Jack felt himself relax into the sofa cushions.

"Has the countess retired as well?" Margaret asked as she looked between the Misters Black.

Nathan Black stood in front of the dormant fireplace, staring absently at the empty hearth while the other Mr.

Black lounged rather comfortably in a chair across from them.

"The little wife has gone to sit with Nora, who is having a lie down until Samuel returns," the earl answered.

"And apparently Kate has gone in search of a kitchen, and Mr. Thatcher has followed her," Jack said.

Margaret looked at him, her face a mask of confusion. "A kitchen?" she asked.

Jack nodded. "She said she needed to expel some energy. Mr. Thatcher looked quite excited at the prospect."

Margaret nodded. Jack saw the weariness about her. The sagging slant of her shoulders, the stiffness in her back as she tried to keep herself upright.

"I think it's best if you also rested," Jack said, and then before she could utter the protest he had already seen coming, he added, "Your body needs to recover from the near strangulation. You'll want to be in prime shape when Master Samuel returns, and we must make our next move."

He saw her hesitate, but finally, she nodded in agreement. And then as if more confused, she looked about her person and then at the Misters Black.

As if reading her mind, the earl stood and yawned outrageously, before saying to his brother, "Do you fancy a game of chess, brother?"

Nathan Black turned from his spot at the fireplace, and Jack knew the man was questioning his brother's statement. But Jack knew Nathan Black was too skilled to show such an emotion.

So instead the other man said, "I believe I do."

Together the brothers walked to the far side of the room, taking up places across from one another at a small table set with a chessboard.

Jack was fairly certain he heard Nathan Black ask if his brother even knew how to play chess, but the earl just waved off the question. When he looked back, he saw Margaret already dozing, and very carefully, he pulled her toward him. She started once, her eyes fluttering, but he eased her tension with softly spoken words.

"Trust me, Maggie," he said, and then she slept, curled into his arm, her hand pressed to his chest.

* * *

JACK LOVED HER. She had almost died. They had almost died. And somewhere in her, something vibrated against a restraint so long in place she thought it natural.

Margaret thought of little boys and young girls, running about doing state business, and she thought of pirates and dogs. But her thoughts must have been dreams, for Jack suddenly shook her arm, and her eyes flew up to see the young boy come through the door at a run.

His face was still marked with chocolate and his hair rumpled, and he smiled as if he had just been told he now owned a sweets shop. She wasn't sure if she had slept long or how it was that she had even slept, but she sat up, running her hands over her hair and dress as if to straighten them.

"Sir Hall is most definitely moving. To where I am not sure, but the servants are in an uproar," Samuel said, plucking a biscuit from the teacart and settling onto the sofa next to the Earl of Stryden.

He downed the biscuit in two bites as Mr. Black walked into the room with a waddling Nora. The boy stood awkwardly and ran to his mother, wrapping his arms around her extended stomach, as he was careful not to get his chocolate-covered face on her. Lady Lofton appeared behind them all, still wearing her lavender dress and looking as though she had not had a lie down at all. Turning about and snatching another chocolate biscuit, Samuel resumed his seat on the sofa.

"Like I was saying, the house is preparing for its master to leave. Trunks are being packed and boxes filled. It looks as if the man is going for an extended journey or perhaps he's moving house."

"The hare goes to ground," Mr. Thatcher said.

Margaret looked at the young boy. "You learned all this by going round the house?" she asked.

Samuel shook his head and accepted a glass of milk from his mother. Margaret had not seen the woman leave and wondered from where the glass of milk had come.

"I don't just go round the house. I go in," he said, taking a giant gulp of his milk.

Margaret blinked at him. "But isn't that suspicious? Didn't you attract notice?"

Samuel shook his head and wiped his mouth with the napkin Mr. Black handed him.

"No one ever notices the servants. I go in through the kitchen. Mrs. Mallory, the cook at the Hall residence, gave me a delicious strawberry tart. She makes the best strawberry tarts."

"You go right in?" Jack asked.

"Of course," Samuel said with a smile. "And Sir Hall is definitely going somewhere. Of that, I'm certain."

"Samuel, you've completed excellent spying work once more," Lady Lofton said. "Now we must formulate a plan."

Margaret looked at the woman. "What sort of plan?" she asked.

Lady Lofton smiled. "The sort where the hunter becomes the hunted."

It was just at that moment that the stoic butler and apparent house guard charged into the library.

"Your Grace, it appears Master Samuel was followed,"

Hathaway said, and Margaret straightened in her seat, her senses coming alive, striving for the alertness she knew she would need.

But when Hathaway's words settled over her, it was with a stuttered realization that it was not her own safety she was concerned with, but rather it was Jack's. She cast a glance in his direction and found he, too, was at the ready.

"Splendid," Lady Lofton said and turned to Samuel. "You've brought him right to us. Well done, boy."

Samuel raised his eyebrows over the rim of his chocolate biscuit and then shrugged his shoulders. "It was the least I could do," he said.

But then Nathan Black was stepping in to take command. "Hathaway, do we have confirmation on how many have followed?"

Hathaway said, "There are reports of four persons in the alleyway. All men judging by their stature."

"Does that mean they are rather tall, then? Broad-shouldered or stocky perhaps?" Margaret asked, while in her mind she pictured the diminutive Sir Toby Hall.

"Yes, that is precisely what I mean," Hathaway answered.

Margaret frowned while Jack said, "But Sir Toby is a small man. Well-muscled from his days at Jackson's Saloon, but still small."

"It doesn't mean he's not out there. It only means he has sent the brawn of his army ahead of him to take the first assault," Lady Stryden said.

Nathan Black nodded. "Jane, Nora, take Samuel and go to the nursery. Lock yourself in and use the nanny's entrance to leave if needed."

"No," Nora said, using all her strength to pull herself up from the sofa. "The servants' quarters," she said at her husband's stern look. "No one ever thinks to look in the servants' quarters."

Margaret thought she saw Nathan Black smile, but the moment was brief, and soon Nathan was helping Nora and Samuel from the room. But Lady Lofton stopped him.

"Will you be so kind as to give that woman a gun?" she asked.

Margaret wanted to raise an eyebrow, but Hathaway stepped forward, extending a pistol to Mrs. Black.

"Mistress," he said, bowing ever so politely.

The entire scene was unusual, to say the least, and Margaret could only stare. Mrs. Black took the gun as if it were only a dusting rag and drew her son from the room with a hand to his shoulder. Lady Lofton disappeared behind them.

"Kate and Thatcher, we'll need defenses on the ground level."

"I would prefer to be stationed in the kitchen. What say you, Mr. Thatcher?" Kate said.

Mr. Thatcher grinned. "I reckon I can handle that," he said, and with that, the two of them departed, each receiving more armament from Hathaway as they passed the butler on the way out the door. The hair on the back of Margaret's neck rose as she watched the quiet butler hand out a near arsenal of weaponry and wondered if that was a skill his references often spoke of.

"Alec and Sarah, we'll man the corridors. We need to know who is where and at what point the persons are in the house."

The earl and countess both nodded as they armed themselves.

"I'll take the third floor," the countess said as she left the room.

She was followed by her husband who called, "I'll be on the second."

Finally, Mr. Black turned to them. "I trust you both to be

capable of defending yourselves, but just to be safe, I ask that you remain within the library." He paused here to look at Hathaway. "Hathaway has many years of experience with making this house secure, and I assure you that when the walls are breached, the intruders will be forced to go a certain way. Do you understand my meaning?"

"You'll send Sir Hall directly to us," Margaret said.

And Mr. Black nodded. "Will you be ready for him?" he asked.

Jack stood beside her, walking over to the butler to accept another pistol. Margaret watched him assess the feel of the gun in his hand until he turned back and said, "We'll be ready."

Mr. Black nodded to the butler. "Hathaway, please let our unexpected guests know that we will be receiving visitors tonight."

CHAPTER 20

*K*ate worked the dough until its elasticity pulled against her knuckles. Flour coated her arms, working its way into the folds of her pushed-up sleeves. When the door to the kitchen opened, she did not make any outward appearance that she had heard it, nor that she heard the footsteps that followed as their guests entered.

Somewhere from deep within the house, the sound of a clock chimed through the still air, and dimly she counted the strikes of the bell as she listened to their guests slowly approach her. She heard their footsteps move along the floorboards, heard them as they separated at the servants' stairs, three sets of footfalls climbing while one continued in her direction. She smiled, kneading the dough with greater care, caressing it with every fold.

"I rather enjoy an egg in pasta, don't you?" she said, turning to pin her gaze on the target.

He was as Hathaway had suggested, a tall, meaty bloke with dark clothing and a typically plain face. There was nothing about him that suggested anything unusual to her, except for the fact that he was likely a hired thug.

271

"It's a pity you won't be around to try it," she said just as Thatcher swung the iron pan against the man's head.

The light evaporated from the man's eyes, his pupils rolling back as his eyes closed, and his body gave way. He slumped to the ground in a harmless heap.

"Well done, Mr. Thatcher," Kate said, smiling at her husband.

"And I should say well acted, Mrs. Thatcher," he said in return.

Quickly, Kate dusted the flour from her arms, wiping them vigorously on a rag. Bending, she pulled various armaments from the man: pistol, knife, and a long heavy weight of wood, likely used as a club. She nodded to Thatcher and watched as he pulled the prone body of the hired thug to the pantry, closing the door and jamming the handle with a chair before returning to Kate.

Moving as silently as possible, Kate followed Thatcher down the hall in the direction Hathaway had suggested. Not very far into the corridor they came across the door to the housekeeper's room, a small space that had gone unused in the many years that a butler alone had run Lofton House.

Earlier, Thatcher had placed a lit lamp in the room, so that they would at least see their way for a short time. Entering through the main hall door, Kate closed it softly behind them until only a crack was left, just enough to see the kitchen door in the rooms beyond. Meanwhile, Thatcher had found the panel of bells that made their mechanical journey up through the floors to the various rooms above. Selecting a single cord, Thatcher reached above the bell that it was connected to and pulled in the opposite direction. The bell remained silent, but Kate saw the cord move within the wall.

Having signaled those above stairs that their guests had arrived, Thatcher extinguished the lamp, freezing in the place where he stood below the bells. He had another signal to give that night, and he wouldn't want to lose his place in the dark, Kate thought. And so she turned and watched the kitchen door.

* * *

THE MAN WAS A BIG BLOKE. His shoulders went at least as wide as the servants' stairs. Alec contemplated this for a moment and how he would not enjoy getting into an altercation with this man, but as it was currently his assignment to do just that, he waited patiently for the man to make it up a few more steps. Alec wanted the man in the perfect position, so that when he made his move, it would result in the most debilitating conclusion possible. And so it was a couple of more huffs before the bulky man finally looked up, registered that Alec stood there on the landing above him.

"Good evening, mate," Alec said, smiling brightly at the man's blank stare. "Would you be so kind as to hold this for me?"

With that, Alec pushed the loaded teacart from the library down the stairs. The heavy cart crashed onto the stairs, cutlery and china flying in all directions. The man ducked, covering his head to protect himself from the flying implements and in doing so, prevented himself from seeing the oncoming furniture that sailed into him. The man fell backwards with the weight of the cart, his body striking the stairs as he tumbled down the way he had come. Reaching the first floor landing, Alec watched as the man's body landed awkwardly around the newel post, heard the crack as bone gave way, and cart splintered.

When the chaos had settled, Alec sauntered down the steps, pistol in hand, and stopped before the incapacitated thug. One leg was bent awkwardly underneath the man, and his arms held the heavy cart pinned to his chest.

When the man blinked up at him with the same blank stare, Alec smiled and said, "Would you be so kind as to unload yourself of any weaponry? In this house, we only allow women to remain armed."

* * *

NATHAN WAITED in the recesses of the second floor landing. The lamps cast light out and away from him, concealing him in a pool of shadow. When the tremendous crash came from the area of the servants' stairs, he did not move. He kept his breathing steady and his hand sure as it gripped the butt of the pistol in his hand. He would need to get close to any intruder should he want to be effective with the weapon, but his hope was only that the very presence of the gun would suffice.

Footsteps sounded suddenly out of the echoes of the crash from somewhere behind him, deep within the house. Whoever it was, they were running without care to their steps, as if the crash had spooked them into plunging ahead. Nathan swore under his breath. There was nothing worse than a man whose only interest in a case was the payout in the end getting his cackles up mid-assignment.

And it was at that moment that the two thugs Nathan had suspected were coming up the front staircase rounded the landing and kept climbing. Nathan swore again, pushing himself from his hiding spot in pursuit of the intruders. It had been unwisely hopeful of him to think the thugs would all separate, but if the crash at the back of the house was anything to go by, at least one of the intruders was no longer an issue. However, these two goons were likely to give Nathan a headache.

By the time he reached the third floor, his chest heaved with the exertion, but his muscles remained tight and ready. What he was not ready for was the scene before him.

"You gentlemen are trying to convince me that you're here to apprehend a lady and her beau," Sarah crooned, looking up at the gentlemen through her eyelashes.

At some point, Sarah had shed her black attire and now sported an incredibly frilly dressing gown, its lapels not quite closed along her throat, leaving a gaping expanse that invited the gaze of any gentleman onlooker. Nathan blinked at her, settling back to watch what she would do next.

The first thug walked directly up to her, taking her by the shoulders and appearing to bend her over in a kiss. And Nathan would have believed it if he hadn't been at a slightly greater angle than the second thug. From his perspective, he clearly saw Sarah's hand go up, gripping the man's throat with just thumb and finger. Before the man could make any sound at all, Sarah's grip tightened, restricting the air to his lungs. Sarah made a moaning noise as the man may have made some gurgling noise as the air stopped moving within him, but again, from this distance, Nathan would not have suspected that the small blonde woman in front of them was choking the air from the much larger hired thug.

That is until the man dropped completely to the floor in a useless mound of mercenary. The second thug started at this.

"What the--" he said.

But Nathan had already brought the butt of his gun down on the man's head, rendering him unconscious before he could finish his sentence.

Nathan looked at Sarah just as she turned in the direction of the sound coming from the servants' stairs. Alec emerged, carrying one more gun than what he had left the library with earlier that night.

"Did you meet with success then?" Nathan asked, and Alec smiled brightly.

"Indeed, I did," he said, and as if seeing Sarah for the first time. "And it appears my lady wife has met with equal success, but has done so in much more daring attire."

Sarah blinked at him, clearly confused, until she looked down at her person. "Oh," she said, before shedding the dressing gown to show her black breeches and lawn shirt were still in place. The only difference being her bare feet and the open collar of the shirt.

"I'm afraid it was not so daring, my lord," she said.

Nathan removed the guns from the hired mercenaries on the floor before going to stand next to Sarah and Alec.

"Did that seem too easy to anyone?" he asked quietly, his eyes traveling about the walls and floors as if to see through the very substance of the house to the enemies they could not see lurking within.

Alec said, "I'm not sure. Do we believe this Sir Toby Hall capable of a mass assault?"

Sarah added, "I'm not entirely certain a member of the ton, especially one with Sir Hall's description, would be capable of much more. It's not as if he plans these things on a regular basis."

"And in his nearly forty years of planning his revenge, he hasn't made a single mark," Alec said.

Nathan frowned, absorbing both Alec and Sarah's arguments, but still not liking the feel of the conclusions.

"Something is not right," he said, just as a piercing scream rent the air.

Before Nathan had time to realize that the scream sounded very much like Nora, a gunshot split the night, its blast echoing through the eerily still halls. Without thought, Nathan took off at a run, his feet taking the stairs two and three at a time. He heard Alec behind him, but his thoughts were only on his wife, their child growing inside of her.

Finally reaching the fourth floor, Nathan burst through the servants' quarters, ducking into one room and then the next, searching for his wife as his heart pounded in his chest.

And then suddenly he stopped when he heard, "Bloody hell, woman, did your husband teach you to shoot like that?"

Alec collided with him as he had stopped so abruptly in the corridor, but he heard his brother's whispered, "Bullocks."

And then both brothers were running down the hall, throwing themselves into the room from which the voice had emerged only to find Richard Black, the Duke of Lofton, sitting on the sill of an open window, one leg in the room while one was still without, clutching his arm as blood oozed from between his fingers.

"An assassin bent on exacting his revenge on spies can't kill me, and my own daughter-in-law draws blood. That, I believe, is the very definition of irony."

Richard turned, a smile coming to his face as he saw Alec and Nathan standing there. Nathan's heart thudded in a relief he could not fathom as he had longed for his father to return. But then Richard said, "I understand we're under attack." And there was no more time for relief.

"We've disarmed three intruders and a probable fourth below stairs by Kate and Thatcher," Nathan said. "But it all seems rather too easy."

Richard nodded and climbed the rest of the way through the window. "I was worried about as much," he said. "That was why I chanced coming here."

Richard straightened, and Nathan saw for the first time his father's unkempt state, the shadow of beard along his jaw. He looked to Jane to find her standing, absolutely frozen as she shielded Samuel behind her and Nora stood next to them both, the gun still smoking in her hand.

"Richard," Jane finally said, a choked whisper more than a word, and Nathan felt that thud of relief in him once more. "You bloody bastard," Jane said more firmly, and Nathan felt everything fall right back into place.

"What is it that has raised your suspicions?" Sarah asked, and Nathan realized suddenly that she was in the room.

"Lady Folton came to me asking questions about Nathan, and I knew that she was following the wrong lead. But that also let me know that you all were on to something."

Alec nodded and said, "We've identified the assassin with the help of Viscount Pemberly. It is the assassin who has sent this attack on the house. We believe the assassin is aware that Viscount Pemberly can name him and has turned to desperate measures to stop the only man who can identify him."

Richard nodded as he worked his soiled cravat loose. When he went to tie it around the clotting wound on this arm, Jane finally stepped forward as if released from her trance, taking the cravat from him as she tied it securely around his arm.

"And the assassin would be?" Richard asked.

"Sir Toby Hall," Samuel said brightly from the other side of the room.

Richard frowned and looked at Jane. "Did you have the boy spying again?"

Jane only smiled softly at him and kissed his whiskered cheek. "We're glad to have you home as well," she said.

"Sir Toby Hall," Richard said. "That name sounds familiar."

Sarah nodded. "His family requested help from the War Office during one of the conflicts with the Maratha Kingdom in India."

Richard nodded, "Yes, that's it. His father was positioned

with the East India Company. Something about a sister, I believe."

"Yes, his sister, Martha," Nathan said and then looked to Samuel as if to indicate the matter should be left at that.

Richard only frowned harder. "I suppose I can understand Sir Hall's need for vengeance, if the War Office was unsuccessful in helping with the family's request."

"Indeed," Jane said, "But it does not warrant the attempts on the lives of those who had nothing to do with the War Office at the time of such happenings."

"No," Richard said. "But it would explain how he identified agents without getting his hands on the book held at Kensington Palace."

"He likely worked with agents at the time of the incident with his sister and made the connections from there."

"It would be easy enough to do," Alec said. "But why in the end would he select Viscount Pemberly?"

"Because Lady Folton paid him a call," Richard said. "Undoubtedly, he had marked Lady Folton as an agent and when she began to pay too much attention to Viscount Pemberly, he made the connection that he, too, was an agent."

"But he was not an agent," Nora said.

Richard nodded. "No, he wasn't, but the War Office just managed to fall into its own trap."

"And now Sir Hall will kill Viscount Pemberly because he is the only man who can identify him."

"Or so he thinks," Nathan interjected. "Pemberly has relayed to all of us the connection, and we can identify him from here."

"And now he's trying to flush out the bastard by sending a siege of paid thugs. This man really is an amateur."

Nathan nodded.

"And amateurs are always the dangerous ones."

Richard nodded and looked at Jane. "Well, my darling,

this whole story started in this house. It would only be fitting should it end here."

Nathan felt a stab of curiosity at his father's words, but Jane only smiled.

"I agree, your grace," she said, "What say you we go find ourselves an aspiring assassin?"

Richard moved toward the door. "Where are we keeping Folton and Pemberly?" Richard asked.

"In the library," Alec responded.

Richard stopped, the movement so startling, Jane collided with him.

"The library?" he asked.

Nathan nodded. "You have always said it's the most secure room in the house."

"Dear God," Richard said and ran from the room.

CHAPTER 21

*M*argaret waited in the dimmed light of the library. Jack had extinguished all but one lamp that stood in the opposite corner of the room. Their eyes had grown accustomed to the near dark, and she knew they were at an advantage should anyone enter the room. But Margaret did not like lying in wait. There was something vulnerable about their position that did not sit well with her.

"Jack," she whispered, and he made a noise as if he'd heard her, but he did not turn, his eyes remaining fixed on the bell pull in the corner, waiting for the signal from below that Sir Toby had arrived. "Jack, I'm not sure I like this situation."

Jack looked at her then, his gaze searching her face. "What is it?" he asked.

"I feel like we're just waiting for him to come kill us," she said plainly.

"That is mostly what we are doing, yes," he said and returned his gaze to the bell pull.

The pull did not show the slightest sign of having moved, and Margaret felt her uneasiness grow. Hathaway had assured them that all entrances to the house would remain locked and barred. The only way in would be through the kitchen, and Kate and Thatcher would be there to send the signal up from the bowels of the house. But no signal came and the night went on, the darkness swallowing them until Margaret felt the uneasiness reach her hands, the slightest tremor working its way through her fingers.

"Something's wrong," she said.

But Jack only shook his head. "Steady, Maggie, you only need to be steady now."

Margaret ignored him and looked behind her.

They had taken up a position behind the large desk set to one end of the room, their backs to the shelves of books that lined the walls. Jack faced the bell pull as she eyed the only door into the room. But her gaze wondered involuntarily, recalling once more the rumors she had heard about Lady Lofton and a chestnut roaster. She wondered if this were the room, the room where the duke had had a secret exit installed should his family ever have need to escape again.

The stories were just rumors, and she had never heard anything to verify the validity of them, she reminded herself. But now, sitting with her back to the shelves, she wondered about it. And more, she wondered who all knew of the second entrance's existence, should it, in fact, exist. Margaret thought it unlikely that the Duke of Lofton would tell everyone of its existence, if the secret passage were meant to be just that, secret. But then wouldn't some servant find it out? Wouldn't Lady Lofton or even the Black brothers know if it?

"Jack," she tried once more, "I have a feeling our position is not secure."

Jack kept his eyes on the bell pull.

"I think you're--" But he stopped whatever he was saying, turning his entire body toward her. "No, that's not right," he said. "You never have a feeling unless it's necessary. What is it?"

Margaret felt a measure of relief that she finally had his attention but it was brief.

"There were rumors that the Duke of Lofton had--"

"Put in a second entrance to his library?" came a voice from directly behind them.

Margaret jumped, sending her into Jack, which sent them both spilling across the desk. The candlestick she had been holding as a weapon skittered to the floor along with the pistol Jack had taken from Hathaway. Scrambling to her feet, Margaret righted herself in time to see Sir Toby Hall extend his own pistol at Jack's head, as Jack remained crouched on the floor where they had fallen. Sir Hall stood framed in a panel of the shelved wall that had swung outward. A light flickered from the blackness beyond the panel, and Margaret thought it likely there lay a passage beyond that led to another room in the house.

"Sir Toby," Jack said then. "What a lovely surprise."

While the words were cordial, the tone was not.

"I am certain it is, Jack," Sir Toby responded. "It is only fortunate enough that some servants can be bribed to obtain such information as to allow for this intimate meeting."

Margaret felt the muscles along the back of her neck stiffen, and she looked to the bell pull in the corner, still and silent as it lay untouched, a signal gone unsounded.

"Servants can be bribed?" Jack asked. "This is not revolutionary, Sir Toby."

Sir Toby laughed, his head tilting so as to cast the light of the single lamp over the lenses of his spectacles.

"Especially butlers who have their roles usurped by old men," Sir Toby added, and Margaret's mind flicked to Hathaway, the butler guard who had seemed too old to hold such a post, and the watery young man who had appeared in places he should not have.

And as if reading her mind, Fitzwilliam stepped from the passageway behind Sir Toby, his features melting like wax in the candlelight. He looked to Margaret and then Jack, tugging on the sleeves of his coat as if he were uncomfortable.

And then he muttered, "I won't have my post taken by some old man. I worked too hard to get where I am."

Sir Toby smiled at Fitzwilliam's words.

"It was fortunate that I bumped into Mr. Fitzwilliam when my attempt with the gargoyles failed. It was good to have an alternate plan in place should the worst happen."

Jack looked briefly at Margaret before refocusing on Sir Toby.

"But I'm afraid our acquaintance must come to a rather abrupt end this evening," Sir Toby said.

"It doesn't have to be that way, Sir Toby," Jack said. "In fact, if you knew the truth of it, you would feel remorse in killing me."

"How's that?" Sir Toby asked, stepping away from the hidden passage.

"I'm not an agent at all, Toby," Jack said, his tone going soft. "I am only here out of a terrible case of bad luck."

Margaret heard something in Jack's voice when he spoke, and she wondered briefly if he no longer believed his own sentiments concerning luck. It was an odd time to think on it, but for a strange moment, it became the thing that mattered most. If Jack were to die that night, she needed him to know that it was not luck that made him the man he was, the man he had become. It was his own self-worth that had brought him there, his own intelligence and strength. Luck was but a fickle creation, brought about when someone felt the need for advantage in life. But Jack didn't need such a thing.

Sir Hall laughed at Jack's words, his small round head going back as he let the laugh radiate from his open mouth. The weak light from the single lamp glinted grotesquely off his round spectacles.

"Then I must say, I'm very sorry that it was you, Jack. As you would be the only one who could recognize the scent of the Martha rose on me."

Sir Hall seemed to dim himself then, his gaze reflecting on something within him.

"It's a pity that my dear Martha's roses should be the thing to end my plan for vengeance. For she deserved more, Jack." And again like a lamp receiving more fuel, Sir Hall sparked, his eyes rounding behind his glasses. "She deserved more than this damned country gave her."

Margaret took a step slightly backward, the heel of her shoe connecting with the gun that Jack had lost in their fall. The contact made a soft thud, and she daren't move another step for fear that Sir Toby would hear her, suspect something, and out of reaction shoot Jack. She kept her breathing steady, kept her gaze focused on the barrel of the gun.

"I have only the comforting thought that I managed to eliminate one agent for the War Office before you ruined my scheme. And what a great one that was. The Duke of Lofton. There was talk back then of him coming to the Office. It was only when we returned to London that I learned he had, in fact, joined their ranks. And what agonizing pleasure it was to wait and watch as he became so respected in society. It was a pleasure to put a bullet in him."

"Then I regret to disappoint you."

Margaret swung her gaze to the door where Richard Black stood, his clothes filthy and rumpled, his arm bandaged, a deep red stain coloring the fabric. A thought passed through her mind of the muffled noises they had heard earlier, and she wondered once more if one were a gunshot.

"Lofton," Sir Hall said, and then in a sickening movement, he swung the gun in the direction of the door.

Margaret dove for the pistol at her feet as a shot went through the air. Moving just as quickly, she straightened in time to see Lofton dive for cover as the paneling directly behind his head splintered with the impact of the bullet and Jack surge forward, his hands connecting with Sir Hall in such a way as to knock the gun loose, pulling them both to the floor.

Margaret's hands shook, the emotions within her roiling in an uncontrollable wave of sensation. Jack struggled on the floor with Sir Hall, the men rolling until Jack was pinned to the carpet and that was when Margaret saw it. The flash of blade as Sir Hall pulled a long knife from his boot, its lethal edge glinting in the light.

Margaret's hand released its grip on the gun, her body losing its strength as she saw the knife positioned over Jack's throat, the small, muscular man driving the knife closer and closer to ending the life of the man she loved. Catching the gun at the last moment with her other hand, she held it awkwardly in her grip, pressed it to her stomach as her body raged with emotions she could not understand.

She closed her eyes, welcoming the darkness to stop whatever it was that thundered through her. And there in the darkness, she saw her mother, smiling at her in the reflection of her dressing mirror as she dabbed lilac water at her ears and throat. She saw her father, his feet propped up as he read the papers in his study, a clay pipe pressed between his lips. She saw their faces as life left them, as their very existence was extinguished. Somewhere in the darkness her mother's cries of pain reverberated through her, echoing into the silence until there was nothing but the sound of her own rage, boiling within her.

And then there was Jack's voice. Jack telling her to feel, Jack telling her to trust him, Jack telling her to let her emotions out.

Margaret took a breath, her hand sliding into the grip of the pistol as she raised her arm.

And then, finally, Margaret let herself feel, and when she opened her eyes, she pulled the trigger.

By the time Jack reached Margaret, the gun she had used to shoot Sir Toby Hall in the head lay at her feet, her arms clenched about her middle as if her arms themselves held her together, kept her from falling into pieces right there on the carpet. Gently, he folded her into his arms, bringing her head to lie against his chest. He cupped the back of her head with one hand, massaging the tight muscles at the base of her neck.

"You trusted me, Maggie, didn't you?" he said softly, as her arms finally released their grip, and her hands came to rest against his back.

"I did," she whispered, but her voice lacked strength.

"It will get better," he said, "I told you this takes time."

She nodded, her head rustling against the fabric of his jacket. He looked over her head to see Nathan Black and the Earl of Stryden carefully moving Sir Toby's body out of the direct line of vision of anyone who should walk into the room, while Lady Stryden draped a sheet over the body, and it was then that Jack noticed Thatcher standing just inside the passageway, holding Fitzwilliam in custody. Lady Lofton stood near the door with the duke, her hands curiously exploring a bandage on his arm. The duchess looked to be scolding the man about making architectural improvements without her knowledge, and Jack smiled into Margaret's hair.

"We'll need to send for Agent Crawley," Mr. Black said, and Margaret picked up her head from Jack's chest.

"Yes," she said, "He'll know what to do from here."

"But not you," Jack said, keeping his grip on her firm. "You will be needing rest."

When she began to protest, Jack laid a hand against the bandage still at her throat, and the protest vanished from her eyes.

"I suppose you are right, my lord," she said, but her conviction was noticeably lacking.

Jack took Margaret's elbow, and he was only slightly surprised when he was met with no resistance.

But when they passed by the Duke of Lofton at the door, the older man stopped them.

"Viscount Pemberly, I don't believe we've had the opportunity to be properly introduced."

The duke extended a hand to him, and Jack took it, releasing Margaret's elbow for the moment.

"Pleased to finally meet you," Jack said, noticing how young the duke looked even though he must have been nearing sixty-five years of age.

"I know this is a rather awkward moment to mention this, but I've been rather impressed by your work on this assignment."

Jack raised an eyebrow. "My work?"

The duke nodded. "I think you would make a rather fine agent for the War Office. A man of your talents and knowledge would be a boon to have among our ranks."

Jack knew the duke would want some sort of response from him, but at that moment, he could not think of anything. His mind floated back along the past, the many times luck had seen him through a tight spot only to push him higher up in life. Never before had someone mentioned his talents or knowledge being anything at all. It had always been that Jack was just there, was just the last man standing to take up the fleet, to fill a post, to do a job. And so Jack only stared at the Duke of Lofton.

"I think that is a splendid idea," Margaret said from beside him, and he realized he had taken too long to respond.

So he nodded. "Yes, I think that would be a splendid idea," he said, mimicking Margaret's words.

He looked at her then to see a small knowing smile on her lips.

"Splendid," the duke said, his own smile on his face.

"Richard, you really must let them go. They're young, and they want to be alone," Lady Lofton said from behind her husband. "You may not remember feeling as they do, as it has been so long for us."

Richard barked out a laugh and put an arm around his wife, pulling her closer. "Not that long," the duke said and bid them goodnight.

But once more he stopped Jack, leaning in close so that only Jack could hear. "I know you'll be good for her, lad," he said.

And Jack looked at him, the question he wanted to ask plain on his face.

Lofton whispered, "I've never seen her with a hair pin out of place until she met you."

He winked once at them, and then turned back to his wife, who pulled him in the direction of a chair to sit down, and as they left through the library doors, Jack heard the duchess mutter something about Richard and retirement, but they had moved into the corridor before he heard any more on the matter.

As Jack descended the stairs beside Margaret, he said, "I believe this is the part where you tell me you told me so."

Margaret shook her head. "I would never do anything so crass, my lord. However, I would tell you that I love you."

He stopped on the landing, touching her arm to stop her as well. "You would then?" he said, when she turned to face him.

The events of the night showed in the weary shadows under her eyes, but her hair fell about her shoulders in disarray, and Jack remembered what the Duke of Lofton had just told him.

"Yes, I would," Margaret said, "I love you, Jack."

Her face radiated even as her eyes told him she was exhausted.

"I love you, too, Maggie," he said and kissed her.

umber 13 Claremont
December 1815

"WHY DO you have two volumes of Mr. Higsworth's History of Horticulture?" Margaret asked from where she sat on the floor, piles of partially unpacked crates strewn about her like victims of a terrible explosion.

"Because I ran out of room in the first one to put notes in the margin," Jack replied from his position across the room where he carefully shelved several volumes onto the book-cases that now lined the room.

What with the wedding and all, they had not had much time for unpacking until now, and when Margaret's things had been delivered to Number 13 Claremont, it had made matters that much worse. But even as she was covered in a thin layer of dust and surrounded by more mess than they had begun with, she felt an odd sense of calm sweep over her. It was calm like none other she had ever felt. For that was the very thing.

She felt it.

She felt the sweep of anticipation every morning she awoke. Although she wished such exhilaration came from waking in Jack's arms, more often than not, she awoke with Captain Edwards on her chest, his drool making a wet spot on her nightdress. And from there, her days were filled with adventure and wonder with Jack, in making their home and their lives together. With not a little bit of time spent on Jack's tutelage as a new agent for the War Office. In the domestic sector, of course.

A knock sounded at the door, and Reynolds' head emerged, as there was only enough room just inside the door for him to do that.

"My lady," he said to Margaret, "Your package has arrived."

Margaret's face split into a smile so bright it actually hurt. She reached up to her face to make sure she was all right.

"Please bring it here, Reynolds," she said and began the arduous task of unearthing herself from the boxes.

"Package?" Jack asked, making his way toward her.

Reynolds returned quickly, the cushioned crate in his arms. Margaret walked as swiftly as the boxes would allow her over to Reynolds, reaching into the crate to pull the precious delivery from its spot, nestled deep within a cocoon of blankets. She cradled the small treasure to her chest, and turned to Jack, watching as his face melted into apprehensive wonder, and Captain Edwards sprang from his spot on the sofa to bay furiously at her and the bundle in her arms.

"I've decided to call her Lady Josephine," Margaret said to the squirming bundle of puppy in her arms. "Isn't she gorgeous?"

She looked up at Jack to find his face still cast in an expression of disbelief.

"It's another one of him," Jack said, pointing indelicately

to Captain Edwards, who was wagging his tail so hard, he was in danger of wagging it clean off.

Margaret nodded. "I know," she said, "Lady Josephine came by special delivery from a breeder in Burgundy."

Jack raised an eyebrow. "You do realize it's another Basset type hound. Surely, one is enough."

Margaret frowned at her husband. "You did advise me to acquire more hobbies, my lord," she said and, finally, Jack's expression turned into something resembling dubious pleasure.

And then he laughed, throwing back his head as he let it out, Captain Edwards imitating his master in his own baying call.

When he was finished, he held out his arms, and Margaret passed him the wiggling puppy.

"Hello, Lady Josephine. Welcome to our family," he said.

And Margaret felt the pulse of happiness come from deep within her.

* * *

LOFTON HOUSE
December 1815

JANE WANTED TO LAUGH. "It is really not all that bad," she said, but she knew they didn't believe her.

Sarah sat on the sofa directly across from Jane, her hands gripping her softly rounded stomach as Alec sat on the floor near her, leaning back against the sofa as he helped Samuel with the chestnut roaster at the open flames in the hearth.

"You've never had children," Alec said, and this did make Jane laugh.

From deep within the house, another cry split the air, this

one so loud and piercing that even Richard looked up from the ledger he was reviewing at his desk.

"Good God, she's going to kill him for doing that to her," he mumbled.

Nora had gone into labor nearly eight hours before, and although the doctor assured them the delivery would be quick as this was Nora's second child, at that moment Jane was fairly certain Nora was discussing the definition of quick with the good man.

"Your experience will be entirely different from Nora's," Jane said, her statement punctuated by another teeth-rattling scream.

Samuel looked up at the ceiling. "Are you really certain Mama is all right?" he asked.

Richard stood up from the desk, making his way over to the lad to squat next to him on the floor. "Your mother is doing exactly what her body was made to do, Sammy. So let's make sure we have some nicely roasted chestnuts ready for her when your little brother gets here."

Samuel scrunched up his face at Richard. "Little sister," he said, "I'm hoping for a little sister."

Richard smiled then, and Jane saw in his face utter relaxation for the first time in years. As he had promised, he had cut back on his assignments, spending less and less time at the War Office. It had been as if they were newly married once more. That is, without the goat. Jane felt the warmth of contentment as it flooded the room.

"I think Nora would like a bowl of Kate's pasta when she's through having that baby."

Jane sat up a little in her chair. "That reminds me," she said. "We received a wonderful letter from Kate just last week."

Sarah looked up from where she had been massaging the growing baby in her stomach. "You did?" she asked.

Jane nodded. "It's apparently beautiful this time of year in South Carolina," she said, "and Thatcher's family is utterly delightful. Thatcher's mother is teaching her how to make buttermilk biscuits with grits and okra."

Richard said, "Okra? Grits? Are these foods you are speaking of?"

Jane smiled. "I believe they are. Kate was most excited about it, so I assumed it had something to do with a kitchen."

"That does sound like her. But what of Thatcher?" Sarah asked, a haze of concern clouding her pretty face.

"Kate says he's been in the fields with his father nearly every day since they returned."

The concern left Sarah's face to be replaced with a small smile as she absently rubbed her belly.

Only when the door to the library opened did the group within realize that the house had been silent for some time. Jane turned to see Nathan standing in the doorway, his hair rumpled, his shirtsleeves rolled to his elbows, and a proud smile spread brilliantly across his face.

"Would you like to come meet your granddaughter?" he said to her.

At his words, a surge of tears sprang to her eyes, and Jane struggled to keep them down.

"It's a little sister!" Samuel yelped, leaping to his feet.

Nathan laughed. "It is, Sammy," he said, "And in just a bit, we'd like you to come meet her, too."

Jane stood slowly, smoothing down her skirts as an old wound opened within her. But there was something different about it this time. This time when she thought on it, she felt an odd sense of connection, a pull toward the little baby girl she had not yet met. Something that told her the little girl was a part of her, and she a part of the little girl. It was silly and ridiculous, and yet, Jane felt it.

Richard came up beside her and, taking her hand,

followed Nathan from the room. When they entered the chamber where Nora had given birth, Jane was not certain what she would find as Alec had been right. She had never given birth to a child, and she had never been privy to another's birthing room.

But when she saw Nora sitting up against a bank of pillows, a tight bundle in her arms, Jane felt her heart thump madly in her chest, her hands shaking as she looked at the pair.

Nora glanced up and, finding Jane's face, she smiled, her eyes tired as her body radiated the love she felt then for her newest child.

With an urging hand from Richard at her back, Jane walked up to the bed, peering down at the wiggling bundle. And before she could say anything, Nora held up the baby to Jane. She hesitated, but only for a moment as her eyes settled on the perfectly formed nose, the rosebud mouth, and soft eyelids closed in slumber.

And when the weight of the baby girl settled into her arms, Jane could not stop the tears. She let them flood her eyes and run silently down her cheeks.

"Her name is Jane," Nora said.

Jane looked up, the trail of tears drying against her skin, and her mouth opened, but nothing emerged.

Richard said from behind her, "Oh God, not another one."

But his tone was good-natured, and Jane felt a laugh brewing within her. She looked back down at the baby in her arms to find she had opened her eyes. The tiny gray eyes watched her, inquisitive even at her birth.

So Jane finally spoke.

"It's nice to meet you little Jane," she said, "I'm your grandmother and also named Jane, but you can just call me Grandma."

Taking a step back, Jane settled into the chair at Nora's

bedside, holding the baby cradled in the crook of her elbow as she continued.

"Now, little Jane," she said, "before you know it, you will be off into the world, and I have only so much time to teach you everything you must know."

Baby Jane made a gurgling noise as if she understood everything Jane said to her. Nathan came to perch on the side of the bed, taking his wife's hand in his own as they watched the new grandmother hold her first grandchild. Richard stepped up beside her, a hand coming to rest on her shoulder. And sitting there surrounded by her family, she felt the weight and warmth of little Jane put the last seal on a wound that had run so deep for so long.

And with her little eyes watching Jane in a way that only innocent children had, the intrinsic gaze of wonder and delight and love, Jane smiled at her granddaughter and said, "Let me tell you about a little thing called spying."

ABOUT THE AUTHOR

Jessie decided to be a writer because the job of Indiana Jones was already filled.

Taking her history degree dangerously, Jessie tells the stories of courageous heroines, the men who dared to love them, and the world that tried to defeat them.

Jessie makes her home in the great state of New Hampshire where she lives with her husband and two very opinionated Basset hounds. For more, visit her website at jessieclever.com.